I sat in the guest's chair and watched. The whole show was pretty dull. Until it was almost over. It was ten to three when *the* call came. By that time I'd moved my chair round behind Day so that I could read what was coming up on the computer. I was also wearing a pair of lightweight Koss headphones plugged into one of the sockets on the desk in front of his. I saw the name come up in light green print on the darker green screen. 'John from Stockwell,' it read. 'Paranoid.' Day looked through the glass partition at Stretch and smiled to himself. It was his choice. Play or pass. He played.

'And now John from Stockwell,' he said. 'Talk to me, John.'

'Hello, Peter,' said a voice in my ears. It was a strange voice. Cold, with no trace of an accent, like a robot's.

'Share your pearls of wisdom with a waiting world,' said Day. 'Or at least the part reached by our transmitters.'

'I enjoy killing people, Peter,' said the voice. I looked at Day who shrugged.

'Of course you do, John,' he said. 'So do I when there's an R in the month.'

'You don't believe me, do you? Then I'll show you,' said the voice, and there was a note of triumph in his tone . . .

Also by Mark Timlin

Hearts of Stone
Zip Gun Boogie
The Turnaround
Take the A-Train
Gun Street Girl
Romeo's Tune
A Good Year for the Roses

Falls the Shadow

Mark Timlin

HEADLINE

Copyright © 1993 Mark Timlin

The right of Mark Timlin to be identified as the Author of
the Work has been asserted by him in accordance with the
Copyright, Designs and Patents Act 1988.

First published in 1993
by HEADLINE BOOK PUBLISHING PLC

10 9 8 7 6 5 4 3 2 1

All rights reserved. No part of this publication may be
reproduced, stored in a retrieval system, or transmitted,
in any form or by any means without the prior written
permission of the publisher, nor be otherwise circulated
in any form of binding or cover other than that in which
it is published and without a similar condition being
imposed on the subsequent purchaser.

All characters in this publication are fictitious
and any resemblance to real persons, living or dead,
is purely coincidental.

ISBN 0 7472 4142 2

Phototypeset by Intype, London
Printed and bound in Great Britain by
HarperCollins Manufacturing, Glasgow

HEADLINE BOOK PUBLISHING PLC
Headline House
79 Great Titchfield Street
London W1P 7FN

For all the friends I've lost beneath the power lines.

ACKNOWLEDGEMENTS

Thanks to all the following:

The staff of Greater London Radio for allowing me access to their studios.

Peter Lavery, aka The Savage Pencil, for editing *Hearts of Stone*.

Nanci Griffith, for *Late Night Grande Hotel* which got played constantly while I wrote this book.

Vanessa, for being a real good friend and putting up with listening to all my shit.

Robin Cook, for all his kindness and encouragement. And the occasional swift half.

The Sweetheart Of The Rodeo.

'Legs' Lexton.

Graham Greene and T S Eliot, for the title.

Nigelle de Bar, at Armes de la Chasse, London.

Anthea J. – Baby, you're the ginchiest.

Maxim and Dolores Jakubowski.

The Big Ripper.

Hazel. Four years on, and still standing, just about.

Plus anyone else who took time to give a damn. And there's plenty.

If there is a hell, we're in it

1

Sometime in the latter part of that year I decided to go back into the private investigation game. Working in a bar had turned out to be too dangerous.

I was lucky. I even got my old office back. When I'd let it go, a *very* optimistic firm of surveyors and valuers had opened a branch office there. I think the business lasted about nine months before the recession claimed another victim. Bullseye.

I saw it was for rent one Thursday morning and went straight round to the agents. Business was so bad that I got the place for the same rent as I'd paid previously. One year in advance. No deposit, no premium. I must say the surveyors had done the place up nicely. I told you they were optimistic. Hessian-covered walls, new false ceiling with concealed lighting, hot water and central heating from a gas-fired boiler, and new wiring throughout. How bad?

In fact the firm had gone down the pan so fast they'd even left behind a smart desk and swivel armchair upholstered in oatmeal-coloured material. I got to keep the furniture as a bonus. I collected my client's chair, law books, electric kettle and mugs out of storage, had the phone re-connected, invested in an answerphone, shoved an ad in the *South London*, and I was back in business.

The Monday morning, a week after the ad appeared, I opened up at ten sharp and there was a letter waiting for me on the chocolate brown carpet the surveyors had donated. I picked up the letter and dropped it on the desk. Then I put on the kettle, made tea, and sat down and examined the envelope. It was high grade, grey stationery, typed on an electric with an italic typeface, and franked first class post. The franking machine had printed a message in red on the grey paper: '93.7 Sound of the City'.

I ripped open the envelope with my thumbnail. No respecter of high grade stationery, me.

The letterhead screamed 'Sunset Radio' in capital letters an inch high, with an address in Brixton. I knew the station. I listened to it all the time. It was one of the new, low-power local radio stations that the government had franchised a few years previously to combat the pirates. Commercial, locally orientated, broadcasting twenty-four hours a day a mixture of music and chat. Being based deep in south London it pumped out a high proportion of jazz, soul, blues, dance music and reggae. To stop the natives getting restless, I imagine. It was a bit patronising, but the mix suited me fine.

The letter was dated the previous Friday and read:

Dear Mr Sharman,

Regarding your advertisement in last Tuesday's edition of the *South London Press*, a situation had arisen within our organisation that requires the attention of a discreet and professional private investigator. I wonder if you could ring me at the above number at your earliest convenience?

Anthony Hillerman
Director of Programming

Discreet and professional. I'd never been accused of being either of those before. As I reached for the phone to call Hillerman, it rang. I picked it up and answered: 'Nick Sharman.'

'Are you the detective?' asked a female voice.

'That's me.'

'I saw your ad in the paper. I need your help.'

'Yes?' I said, and pulled over a pad and picked up a pen.

'It's my dog. It's gone missing.'

I was silent for a moment. I didn't know if it was a joke or what. 'Your dog?' I said.

'That's right.'

'Have you tried Battersea?'

'Of course I have. I think my husband's got him.'

'Oh, yeah?'

'Yes. He's gone too.'

'Have you been to the police?'

'What good would they do? They never got my video back that was stolen last year.'

'They might have more luck with your husband,' I said.

'I don't care about *him*. Good riddance. It's the dog I'm worried about.'

Fair enough, I thought. 'Were they together?'

'When?'

'When they disappeared.'

'No. My husband went months ago. Prince vanished two weeks ago.'

'He liked the dog?'

'No, he hated it. That's why I'm so worried. Please help me, he's all I've got.' She sounded close to tears.

I'd been going to give her a blank, but she was so obviously genuinely distressed that I didn't. 'OK, Mrs . . . ?' I said.

'Cochran.'

'OK, Mrs Cochran. I don't usually do lost dogs, but I'll make an exception. Where do you live?'

She gave me an address in Herne Hill.

'Are you there now?' I asked.

'No, I'm at work, but I'll be in this evening.'

'About seven?'

'Yes.'

'I'll call round, if that's all right?'

'Of course.'

'Do you have a photo?'

'Of the dog?'

'I was thinking more of your husband.'

'Yes. And of Prince.'

'I'll need to borrow them.'

'Fine. I'd like the one of Prince back. You can do what you like with Eddie's.'

'Eddie?'

'My husband.'

'Eddie Cochran?' I said. I still wasn't sure if it was a joke or not.

She sighed. She must have heard it a million times. 'His dad was a rock and roll fan. His surname was Cochran. He never got over losing Buddy Holly, Ritchie Valens and The Big Bopper in that plane crash. When Eddie Cochran got killed it was the last straw. My husband was born a year later, so naturally he was christened Edward. Edward Vincent Cochran, because Gene Vincent was injured in the same crash.'

Better than The Big Bopper, I thought. 'Of course,' I said. 'See you at seven then.'

'See you,' she said. 'Goodbye.' And hung up.

I broke the connection, got the dialling tone, and

tapped out the number for Sunset Radio. It was answered on the second ring. 'Sunset Radio, the sound of the city, good morning,' said a woman's voice. I asked for Tony Hillerman. 'I'll put you through to his secretary,' said the voice. Which wasn't exactly what I'd asked for, but would have to do.

There was a click and two more rings and another woman's voice said, 'Tony Hillerman's office.' She had a lovely voice, deep and sexy, so I didn't mind too much.

'Is he there?' I asked.

'Who's calling?'

'Nick Sharman.'

'Regarding?'

'Regarding a letter I had from him this morning.'

'Oh, Mr Sharman, of course. I'm so sorry. I'll put you straight through.'

There was another click, one more ring, a pause, and a man's voice said, 'Tony Hillerman.'

'Nick Sharman,' I said. 'You wrote to me.'

'I did. Thank you for being so prompt in your reply.'

'The letter arrived this morning,' I said. I wanted to give the impression of someone on top of the job. Discreet and professional was what I was aiming at. 'You said you had a problem.'

'We do. But I don't want to speak about it on the phone. Could you come in?'

'Sure. When?'

'Today. Lunchtime. I'll get Sophia, my secretary, to go out for some food. We can talk whilst we eat.'

Sophia. I liked the sound of her more and more. 'What time?' I asked.

'Twelve-thirty, quarter to one.'

'I'll be there.'

'I look forward to it,' he said as he rang off.

I looked at the letter again and then at the phone. Two jobs in one morning. Things were looking up.

2

I arrived at Sunset Radio at twelve-thirty precisely. The building that housed the station was located close to the market and the railway. It was a newish place, four storeys high, with a giant transmitting aerial on top. The outside was painted the same shade of grey as the envelope I'd received that morning, broken only by the smoked glass windows of the ground-floor reception. I parked my Jaguar round the back by a loading bay and left it in the safe hands of an elderly party with no teeth and a mop of dirty grey hair, wearing at least three overcoats and half a dozen scarves that seemed welded to his neck with filth. He appeared to have packed his whole life into a BR hand cart, and threatened to clean the motor's windscreen with an unsavoury-looking dishcloth until I gave him a nicker not to.

The back walls of the place had suffered a little from graffiti, mostly advertising hopeful bands, but the rest of the building was spick and span. I pushed through the glass doors of the reception area, and walked across a carpeted floor towards a large grey desk containing two video screens and a bank of telephones. Hidden speakers were pumping out Michael Jackson's latest single at a modest volume. Behind the desk was a slender young black woman in a navy blue suit and cream blouse. She smiled at my approach, exposing an impressive set of brilliant white teeth. I smiled back.

'I'm here to see Tony Hillerman.'

'You are?'

'Nick Sharman.' I refrained from adding, 'Private eye to the stars.'

She referred to a sheet on a clip board in front of her. 'You're expected, Mr Sharman. I'll get someone to show you up.' She picked up a phone and whispered something.

Within ten seconds a black teenage boy with a high top fade, baggy jeans and an NWA T-shirt stuck his head around a door behind the desk. 'Yes, Josie?' he said.

'Show Mr Sharman up to Tony's office, will you, Clyde?'

'Sure.' Then to me, 'Follow me, please.'

I smiled again at Josie, which was no hardship at all, and followed the boy. He took me along a carpeted corridor where every wall and door seemed to be decorated with a 'No Smoking' sticker to a small lift which also featured the voice of Michael Jackson, hit the button marked '3', and we were whisked upwards. He smiled too but said nothing. I was finding Sunset Radio a most agreeable place.

When the lift stopped, the boy led me down another corridor to an office door. He knocked and opened it, gestured for me to go in, smiled again and went back down the corridor. I pushed the door further open and crossed the threshold. Inside was a fair to middling-sized office containing a desk, three chairs, filing cabinets, copier, fax, shredder, and all the other accoutrements of modern commercial life. There was also a TV and video hookup and an expensive Sony mini system playing the same old song. In the wall on my left was another door.

Behind the desk sat a woman. Sophia, I imagined. When I entered she stood up to greet me.

She was tall, with olive skin and a great mass of dark brown hair that fell below her shoulders. She was wearing a red woollen dress that clung to every curve like it couldn't bear to let go, and I for one didn't blame it. With the dress she was wearing black tights and black low-heeled shoes. 'Mr Sharman,' she said, 'Josie called to say you were on your way up. Welcome.' Off the phone her voice was just as deep and sexy as it had been on it.

'Nick,' I said. 'You must be Sophia.'

She dimpled up nicely at that. 'That's right,' she said. 'Tony's in his office. I'll show you in.'

She came round the desk and opened the connecting door and ushered me in. The office inside was bigger, furnished with an executive-sized desk, two chairs, one each side, and an L-shaped sofa with the long arm of the 'L' against one wall. In front of the sofa was a low table covered with plates of cold food, bottles of mineral water and a fruit bowl. There were huge speakers on each side of the window which were also playing Sunset at a low volume. Jacko's record had finished and had been replaced with a commercial for a local courier service. Behind the desk in there sat a dark-haired man in a grey suit, blue button down shirt and an extravagantly patterned tie. When he stood to greet me I saw that he was under average height. Smaller than Sophia, in fact. Hence, I guessed, her choice of low heels. Big rule of office politics – the staff should never tower over the boss. Mind you, she could have towered over me anytime. 'Mr Sharman,' he said, advancing towards me, hand outstretched. 'Welcome to Sunset Radio.'

These really were the most welcoming people I'd

met for years. Much more and I'd begin to feel nauseous. 'Mr Hillerman,' I said, gripping his mitten in mine and getting a fierce pump of the hand for my troubles.

'Tony,' he insisted.

'Nick,' I parried.

'Sit down.' He indicated the sofa against the wall. 'Sophia's laid on some sandwiches and salad and fruit. There's Evian water or else you can have a Coke or 7-UP from the machine. Or coffee,' he added.

Evian water! I thought. I'd've preferred a beer, but obviously that was a zero option. 'Coffee,' I said. 'If it's no trouble.'

'Sophia,' said Hillerman.

'No trouble at all,' she said with a smile. I hoped she was staying for lunch. 'It won't be a moment.' And she turned and left in a small cloud of a perfume which I couldn't identify but which smelt like forty nicker an ounce.

'Sit down,' said Hillerman again. 'Sophia will be lunching with us in case we need notes to be taken.' I felt an improvement in the atmosphere even as he spoke.

'That'll be nice.' I sat down.

'There's chicken or smoked salmon sandwiches, a bean sprout salad and kiwi fruit,' he said proudly. 'I believe in healthy living.'

'Good,' I said. I knew I wasn't going to get on with Hillerman. Healthy living indeed.

As I was making myself comfortable, Sophia returned carrying a big silver tray with a giant coffee pot, cream jug, sugar bowl and three cups. 'Here we are,' she said, and bent gracefully at the knees to put it on the table in front of me. I caught the briefest glimpse of the tops of her breasts and the white lace of her bra. Too brief.

'Pull up a chair,' said Hillerman to his secretary.

'Pull up a sofa,' I said and patted the cushion next to me. Hillerman gave me a slitty-eyed look. I wondered how long it was going to be before I wore out his effusive welcome. Sophia smiled at me and joined me on the couch.

As she sat, her dress slid up her long thighs, and as she tugged it down, I noticed that on the third finger of her right hand she was wearing a distinctive ring, featuring a black stone set in a gold surround. I checked the same finger of her left hand. Nothing. That was promising, if not definite in these liberated times.

'What about calls, Sophia?' asked Hillerman, rather nastily, I thought.

'I've told the switchboard to hold all calls until further notice.'

'Good. Come on then, dig in. There's plenty here for everyone.'

I picked up a dainty sandwich and bit off half of it. Sophia poured coffee and the aroma filled the office. I had a vision of her pouring my breakfast coffee. It was almost too much to bear. 'Black or white?' she asked.

'White,' I said. 'One sugar.'

Hillerman frowned like I'd said a rude word, then his face cleared. It wasn't his body after all. 'So what do you know about Sunset, Nick?'

'I listen to it,' I replied. 'I live in Tulse Hill.'

'Good reception?'

'Crystal clear.'

'That's what I like to hear. What shows do you like best?'

'Music. The blues and soul programmes mostly.'

'We're very proud of our coverage of that demography of music.'

Demography. What a fucking plank!

'What about the talk shows?' he asked.

'I listen to the breakfast show,' I said, and smiled at Sophia as if she might get my drift. 'And the late night phone-in, when I can.'

'Good,' beamed Hillerman. 'Do you like Peter Day?'

Peter Day was the presenter of the midnight to three in the morning slot. *Day At Night* it was called, but wasn't as bad as that sounds. Day started off with a few personal viewpoints on the news, both national and local, then opened up the phone lines. His gimmick was that he slagged off every caller. It didn't matter what angle they came from. Day would always find some way to insult them. He was an irascible, miserable, sarcastic sod. I quite liked him. He played the occasional record too. His taste and mine were almost identical so I caught his show as often as I could.

'Yes,' I said. 'But I don't think I'd want to give him a call.'

Hillerman wasn't amused. 'That's the problem,' he said.

'How?'

'Day has been a bit of a thorn in our collective sides since he joined the station,' explained Hillerman. 'I'll be perfectly honest with you, Nick.' I hate it when people say that. It always means exactly the opposite. 'Sunset Radio is just a stepping stone. Part of a master plan. The institutions and individuals who finance the business are looking at a wider horizon. A bigger picture.'

'Yes?' I said, trying to look more interested in what he was saying than in Sophia's thighs. Her thighs won.

'A nationwide commercial top forty stroke rock station, in competition with Radio One,' said Hillerman triumphantly. He actually said 'stroke'.

Can you imagine the type of person who does that? 'The frequencies are there, the demand is there, and so is the advertising money. Even in these straitened times.' Mentally I put up my fees by fifty per cent. 'But Day is a bit of a maverick,' he went on. 'And any real trouble could lose us the franchise we need so badly.'

'Why don't you just sack him?' I asked. 'Or is that a silly question?'

'Not at all. We can't sack him, and I don't know that we want to. Day has a contract, of course, but then contracts are made to be broken. But he also brings in an audience. A little controversy keeps radios switched on. And radios switched on bring in advertisers. Ultimately that's the name of the game. Oh, and he's related to the MD.'

So that was why they, or rather Hillerman, couldn't sack him. And it rankled. And it showed.

'It's never just what you know,' I said.

He nodded. 'But understand this, I have no argument with Peter. He's a pro. Unfortunately he seems to have upset a rather unpleasant splinter group that operates in the area.'

'Pick a number,' I said.

'I know what you mean, but this group is *particularly* odious.'

'And they are?'

'They call themselves Sector 88.'

If that was supposed to strike fear into my heart, it didn't. I was none the wiser. 'What's their specific point of view?'

'Neo-Nazism. White supremacy. They're anti-black, Asian, Jewish, homosexual, feminist. You name it, they're anti-it.'

'So they've got plenty of targets round here. It must be a full-time job.'

'Precisely. Some time ago they sent some of their

literature to the station. Peter got hold of it, gave it rather cavalier treatment.'

'I remember,' I said. 'Of course. About a month ago. It was very funny.'

'Sector 88 didn't think so.'

'And he had some of the loony tunes call him up. He gave them pretty short shrift too.'

'That was the beginning of it.'

'Of what?' I asked.

'They made some rather public threats, followed by hate mail and then a few parcels through the post.'

'What kind of parcels?'

'The usual.' He looked over at Sophia. 'Dog excrement. Human faeces. Offal.'

'Nice,' I said. 'But nothing explosive?'

'No. Not yet. But there's always the possibility.'

'Have you told the police?'

'Of course.'

'And?'

'What do you expect? There's been nothing dangerous. Just unpleasant. The police have taken details, but they're very busy.'

'And what do you want me to do?'

'Find out who's sending the stuff. If you can get names, the police will take further action.'

'Why me?'

'You're a local man. You know the territory. Besides, we encourage local businesses. It's part of our brief.'

'Fair enough. Why don't you just get Peter Day to tone down his act?'

'Impossible. He's a man of integrity.'

'There's very few of us left,' I said. 'What's he like? In the flesh, that is.'

'He's OK,' replied Hillerman. 'Except when he's

had too much to drink. Do you drink?'

Warning signs flashed in front of my eyes. 'Lips that touch liquor will never touch mine,' I said, and winked at Sophia. She smiled in return. I was going to put my hand on my heart but thought maybe that was pushing it a little too far.

'Good,' said Hillerman. 'Peter can be a very bad influence.'

I shook my head sadly.

'So, are you interested in the job?' he asked.

'Yes.'

'Good. How much are your fees?'

'Three hundred a day,' I said, without turning a hair. 'Plus expenses.'

'No problem. Let's give it a week to see how things go. Does that suit you?'

I nodded. It suited me fine.

'Sophia,' he went on, 'will you go to Accounts and get a cheque made out to Mr Sharman for twenty-one hundred pounds? I'll clear it with Simon. And get two hundred and fifty in cash for expenses.'

'And I'm not very good at expense sheets,' I said. 'I tend to lose receipts.'

'Better make that five hundred,' said Hillerman dryly. 'I'll sign the slip.'

Sophia got to her feet and left the room. 'I'd like to meet Peter Day,' I said.

'Of course. I'll speak to him later, arrange a time and place and let you know. Can I have your number?'

I took out one of my business cards and wrote my home number on the back. 'Anytime,' I said.

'So is there anything else you want to know?' asked Hillerman.

'Just one thing,' I said. 'Who opens the parcels that arrive here?'

'Whoever they're addressed to. Clyde in the post room opens any that are addressed just to the station and finds a home for them. Anything addressed to a particular presenter or department gets shoved in their cubbyhole. You see, we get hundreds a week . . . records, CDs, tapes from hopeful bands and DJs, videos, books, scripts. It's a deluge. Almost impossible to vet.'

'I hope you've warned your staff.'

'Of course. Anything vaguely suspicious gets sent to Security.'

'Right,' I said. 'I'll speak to Day and have a general nose round. Then I'll speak to some acquaintances of mine into agit-prop politics, and a friend who works for the local press. See what I can dig up on Sector 88. I suppose there's no proof that they're actually sending the stuff?'

'No, but it's pretty obvious.'

'Not good enough, I'm afraid. That's why the police can't do much. They can hassle the group, but they're on a hiding to nothing without anything solid to go on. Give me a few days and I might come up with something.'

Just then Sophia came back into the room carrying two envelopes and a pad. One of the envelopes was white and thin, the other brown and thick. She gave them to Hillerman who signed on the pad twice then passed the envelopes to me. 'You're on the firm as of now,' he said. 'Welcome aboard.'

3

I went back to the office via my bank where I deposited the cheque. As I got in, Hillerman called me. He'd arranged for me to meet Peter Day later that evening in a wine bar in Brixton. He actually apologised for the choice of venue but explained that Day always went in there for a livener before his show. He didn't actually *say* 'livener' but I knew what he meant. I told him not to worry.

I sat down and made a few calls, with little result. I tried the local paper, but my pet journalist was out on a story. Then I phoned a couple of people I thought might shed a light on Sector 88, but all I got were ringing tones or answering machines. I left messages where I could, then hung around until it was time to visit Mrs Cochran.

I got to the address she'd given me just before seven. It was in the middle of a row of terraced houses in a street opposite the park. The tiny front garden was neatly tended, and there was a light behind the frosted glass in the front door. I rang the bell. Through the glass I saw a vague shape coming towards me. A woman opened it. 'Mrs Cochran?' I asked.

'Mr Sharman?' she replied.

'That's right.'

'Come in.'

She led me down a short hall that smelled of furniture polish and into a tiny living room. 'Sit down,' she said.

I chose the sofa.

She was a washed-out blonde, late twenty-something. Or maybe younger, and just looked older. 'Would you like some tea?' she asked.

'Yes, please.'

'Sugar?'

'One.'

She left the room and went into the back where I heard her clinking crockery. Whilst she was gone, I took a look round. It was a cosy room with a two-piece suite, a coffee table, TV, video, old-fashioned stack stereo, a pile of vinyl albums and tapes, and a bookcase without books. The carpet was dark brown and matched the curtains drawn across the window. The light source was two table lamps, one on the bookcase, one on top of the TV set.

She was back quickly. She must have had the kettle on the boil. It was the second time that day I'd had refreshments served on a tray. I could get used to it.

She put the tray on the coffee table and sat on the armchair opposite me. 'Either one,' she said, and I helped myself to a cup.

'Do you smoke?' she asked.

'Yes.'

She took a packet of Silk Cut from the pocket of the cardigan she was wearing over a shirt and dark trousers.

I put my cup down on the floor beside me and accepted one. She lit them both with a disposable lighter. As she did so I noticed that her fingernails were bitten down to the quick. She fetched two ashtrays from on top of the bookcase and gave me one. I put it down next to my cup and saucer.

When we were settled she said, 'Do you think you can help?'

'I'll be honest, Mrs Cochran,' I replied, 'I don't know. But I'll try. Tell me what happened.'

'Simple. My dog's gone missing.'

'Not lost?'

'What, Prince? Not a chance. He's a big softy. He wouldn't stray. He knows where he's well off.'

'What about your husband?'

'Does he know where he's well off, you mean?' she asked, and smiled. The smile transformed her face and she looked years younger.

'I didn't mean it quite like that.'

She stopped smiling. It was like a light being switched off. 'No, I don't suppose you did. He buggered off four – no, five – months ago. Good riddance.'

'Do you know where he is?'

'He's been seen.'

'Where?'

'The Elephant.'

'With the dog?'

'No, it was a bit ago, before Prince went.'

'You say he didn't like the dog?'

'He hated him, the poor little devil.'

'But you think he might have taken him?'

'I wouldn't put anything past him.'

'Why? If he hated him so much.'

'To spite me, of course. That's why I'm so worried.'

'Why didn't he like Prince?'

'Well, first of all he was the wrong sort.'

'Of what?'

'Dog. Breed, I mean. Eddie wanted a Pit Bull or a Doberman or a Rottweiler. Something like that.

19

A real *man's* dog.' She put a bitterly mocking edge
on the last sentence. 'As if *he* was a real man. But
I knew I'd have to look after the creature so I got
one *I* wanted. Here, I've got a photo of him.' She
took two photographs out of her other cardigan
pocket and passed one to me. It was a Polaroid snap
of a little West Highland White Terrier sitting
on the living-room carpet, begging. He was a cute-
looking little fellow with his head cocked to one side
and his tongue sticking out.

'Nice,' I said.

'Yes, he is. I named him Prince. Of course, that
was wrong.'

I didn't ask why. Perhaps I should've.

'And this is *him*.' She passed me the other photo-
graph, also a Polaroid but taken outside, maybe in
the back garden of the house. It was a head,
shoulders and chest shot of a tough-looking character with receding blond hair cut very short, squinting
into the sunshine. He was wearing a white shirt
stretched too tight over his frame, with the sleeves
rolled up to show big, tattooed arms. He didn't look
like Mrs Cochran's type at all. Obviously she agreed.
'I'm bloody glad he's gone,' she said. 'We never got
on.' Once again I didn't ask why.

'What happened to Prince?' I asked.

She looked puzzled.

'Exactly how did he disappear?'

'I don't know. I was in the front doing a bit of
gardening. He was with me. The gate was closed.
The phone rang and I went to answer it. I was
talking for maybe three or four minutes, that's all.
When I got back he was gone.'

'Was the gate still shut?'

'Yes.'

'Did he have a collar on?'

'Of course. A red tartan one. He looks ever so sweet in it. There was a silver tag with his name and address on it, attached. You know.'

I knew.

'And you've been to Battersea Dog's home?'

She nodded.

'But not the police?'

'No. What do they care about a poor little lost dog?'

I had to agree with her sentiment. Finding lost dogs hardly fitted in with the new high-tech police presence. 'Did anyone see anything?'

'What, round here? No. It's a ghost town in the afternoon. Most people are out earning their mortgages. I don't know the neighbours anyway. They keep themselves to themselves. So do I.'

'Can I keep these?' I asked, tapping the photos on my knee.

'Of course.'

'I'll get them back to you.'

'Thank you. How much do you charge?'

'Let's see how I get on first.'

'No,' she said firmly, and went back into her cardigan again. She pulled out some bank notes, folded over tight. 'There's a hundred pounds here. I know it's not much, but I want you to take it.'

'Mrs Cochran,' I said, 'I'm not really a lost dog finder. I may very well come up empty-handed. In fact, it's more than likely. I don't want your money. I mean it.'

'And I don't want your charity,' she said. 'If you don't take the money, I don't want you looking for Prince. I pay my way.'

I thought about it for a moment. How easily Hillerman had doled out over two and a half grand that afternoon, and what sacrifice a ton must mean

21

to her. 'Fair enough,' I said. 'You're the boss.'

'Good.' She smiled, and again her face changed. She reached over and handed me the cash. I put it in my pocket.

We finished our tea and cigarettes and I left, taking her phone number and giving her mine at home, and promising to keep in close touch. By that time it was past eight. I drove straight to Brixton, parked and went to the wine bar where I was due to meet Peter Day.

4

I pushed open the door about eight-thirty and took a squint around. I'd never seen Peter Day in the flesh, but I'd seen plenty of photographs in the papers and reckoned I'd know him if I saw him. The place was quiet, and as far as I could see there were no media stars in situ. But I was early so I went to the bar and ordered a bottle of Perrier. As far as Sunset Radio was concerned I was TT and I didn't want to spoil the illusion. Christ knows why. Sometimes a wind-up takes on a life of its own. I paid for the drink and took the bottle and glass over to an empty table with a good view of the door. I poured an inch of mineral water into the glass and lit a cigarette. The bar was early-in-the-week quiet with just a couple of tables occupied and one or two lonely-looking punters sitting at the bar.

I sat there and smoked three cigarettes and watched the Perrier go flat as a couple more customers came in, but none who looked anything like Peter Day.

Eventually, as nine o'clock struck on the Town Hall clock, the door banged open and he arrived. He looked exactly like the photographs I'd seen in the press, except for the fact that he was ten years older in the flesh, and tiny. He stood only five four or five in the smallest pair of cuban-heeled boots I'd ever seen. He posed in the doorway like a little bantam cock checking out the farmyard. Oh good, I thought. Colonel Tom Thumb. He was in his mid-forties, with grey, collar-length hair, wearing a navy blue double-breasted suit over a blue denim shirt. I caught his eye and nodded and he headed over in my direction. He stood in front of the table as tall as he could. 'Sharman?' he said.

'That's me.' I replied, and stood up. Not a good idea, but fuck him. The cheque was in the bank with a jockey on it, and I had five, no, six hundred nicker in cash in a warm pocket close to my heart. He looked up at me and we shook hands. He had a grip like a vice. I'd've bet that six ton that he worked on it with one of those little exercise machines you can buy in sports shops. 'You're big, aren't you?' he said.

I'm not particularly, just bigger than he was. In fact, almost everyone in the world was bigger than he was, children included. No wonder he was so bad-tempered on the radio. 'Want a drink?' he asked. 'Oh, no,' he said with a mean little look at the Perrier bottle. 'I forgot. You don't, do you? Can I get you the same again, or an orange juice or something?'

I smiled a non-committal smile. 'Sure,' I said. 'An orange juice would be fine. Stick a vodka in it. A large one.'

'But Hillerman said . . .'

'Vodka's not drinking,' I said. 'Odourless, colour-less. You've seen the ads.'

'So you . . .'

'That's right,' I said. 'I lied.'

'Why?'

'Showbiz. I just love it. I'd do anything to get close to you entertainment folk. Just to touch the hem of your garments is to fulfil my existence.'

'You're taking the piss, aren't you?'

'My, but you're quick,' I said. 'I bet you've got A levels.'

He laughed and shook his head. 'And old Tony Hillerman thinks you're as pure as the driven.'

'I can do the job,' I said.

'Good. A large one, is it?'

I nodded, and he went to the bar and stood on tip-toe and peered over the top to order. I sat down again and lit another cigarette.

He came back and put my drink in front of me, and what looked like a large scotch on his side of the table, and sat down. I added a little flattened Perrier to the glass to kill the kick. I was supposed to be working after all, it was still a long time to the midnight hour, and Hillerman had warned me about Day's drinking. Heavens, sometimes I'm so responsible, I frighten myself. 'Tell me about Sector 88,' I said, after he'd taken a swallow of his drink.

'There's not much to tell. Bunch of brainless, gutless shits. They think they're in Germany, 1933. Black shirts, swastikas, *Juden raus*. You know the deal.'

'You've been doing your homework.'

'Know thine enemy.'

'Fill me in.'

He sat back and took a hit on his drink. 'They were founded four or five years back. An offshoot of the NF. No *Führer* as such, just a loose committee.'

'Any names?'

'They use pseudonyms – except they couldn't spell the word.'

'Like?'

'Great White Master. Grand Wizard.' He saw my look. 'I know, I know, more like the Klan. They don't know what the fuck they are.'

'Any sheets and pointy hats?'

'No. Para-military gear mostly.'

'And no burning crosses?'

'Not yet. It's just an excuse to dress up, get a hard-on and come in their riding breeches.'

'You don't take them seriously?'

'Fuck 'em. Course I don't.'

'They didn't take Hitler seriously, and look what happened there.'

'I don't see these idiots building concentration camps in Hyde Park and gassing Indian shop keepers.'

'But they've got under Hillerman's skin.'

'He's just scared of bad publicity.'

'Or someone burning the station down.'

'Oh, yeah, that too. Pompous little shit.'

He was, I had to agree. I was thinking of 'demography' in particular.

'But he's loyal,' said Day. 'I'll say that for him. Another Programme Director might have given me the rocket.'

'He might have given it to *you*, if you weren't related to the managing director.'

'You've been doing your homework too.'

'That's what I'm paid to do.'

'They wouldn't fire me, brother-in-law or no brother-in-law. That's who he is – Vincent. Vincent Crane, MD of Sunset Radio. My brother-in-law. Or maybe they *would*. Who knows in this business any more? But that's another story. I'll tell you about it sometime. When we get to know each other a little better. If we do.'

'Is he your sister's husband or your wife's brother?' It wasn't really important but I asked anyway.

'My sister's husband. That way he can't get rid of me unless he gets rid of her first. And there's no way he's getting rid of Joanie. She wears the pants in that house. *And* the boxer shorts, probably.' He grinned suddenly. 'Old Joanie's got it well sorted.'

'Do you get on with him?'

'If I don't see him.'

'That's families.'

'You got one?'

I held up my thumb and forefinger, a quarter of an inch apart. 'A small one,' I said. 'A daughter. Lives in Scotland with my ex-wife and her new hubby.'

'How old?'

'Twelve.'

'Mine too,' he said. 'She lives in Newcastle with my ex-wife and her new hubby.'

'Snap,' I said. 'Want another drink?'

'On with the motley,' he said. 'A large Bell's with enough water to quench a mouse's thirst, but barely.'

I went up to the bar and got the drinks. We sat and drank for the next two hours and it didn't seem to affect him at all. We talked about nothing much, just getting to know each other like he'd said. He was entertaining company. Eventually, just after eleven, he invited me to come over to the station and sit in on his show. I agreed, so we drank up and left the bar.

5

We walked the short distance to the radio station. When we got to the front door, Day pressed a button by the side and a security man sitting at the reception desk looked up. He recognised Day and buzzed us straight through. As we walked across the carpet towards him, he turned down the volume on the loudspeakers which were playing *Ride On Time* by *Black Box*. 'Stan,' said Day, 'this is Nick Sharman. He's a private detective, looking for the Nazi tossers who're sending us all that shit and stuff in boxes. He's to be allowed to come and go as he wants.'

The security man looked me over. 'I hope you find them bastards,' he said. 'It's disgusting what people do.'

I agreed, and Day led me past the desk and through the door that Clyde had taken me through earlier that day. 'Did you get a look around this morning?' he asked.

I shook my head.

'I'll give you the tour then.' He took me across the corridor into what he called the production office, which contained a coffee machine and a block of paper-strewn desks in the middle. He explained that that was where the jocks and presenters hung out when they weren't on the air, and nattered to each other or any of the staff that they could hijack.

At one end of the office were two cubicles. One housed the telex machines loaded with huge rolls of paper that stuttered out messages from AP, Reuters and IRN twenty-four hours a day, the other a pair of adapted VCRs that recorded every moment of the station's transmission for the station log. 'Very important, that,' said Day. 'In case of legal action.'

The production office was a tip. There were records, books, tapes, CDs, newspapers, magazines, piles of paper, and all sorts of other junk strewn about everywhere. Every inch of wall space that wasn't lined with shelves was covered with photographs, cartoons cut from magazines, and the kind of in-joke messages that apparently the people who work at radio stations love. Day showed me his cubby hole where his mail and messages were left for him. There were a pile of envelopes and three parcels waiting for him. One was what looked like a book wrapped in brown paper. The other two were Jiffy bags: one about eight inches by five, the other slightly larger and thicker. Day riffled through the envelopes and stuck them in his pocket, then began opening the parcels. 'Are those all right?' I asked.

'Sure,' he said. 'The shit comes in boxes, just a bit bigger than the ones you get wedding cake in. They're all hand addressed in capitals with black marker. And they're all posted letter rate from Brixton or the Elephant or Waterloo main post offices. You can spot them a mile off. Look at these.'

A book was addressed to him on a white label with the publisher's name and address printed across the top. He tore open the parcel to show me a copy of the latest shopping and fucking epic from an expatriate actress living in Los Angeles on her film rights and alimony. The smaller of the Jiffy bags had been franked with a little message proclaiming the attractions of *Roxette*.

30

'EMI,' said Day. 'They've been pushing that lot for months.'

He opened the bag and took out a CD reissue of a Coleman Hawkins Blue Note album. The other Jiffy was also franked. This time it simply read '*Love Thang*'. 'A&M,' explained Day. 'That's a new single they're punting about.' He opened that bag also and showed me two more CDs. One was by Sting, the other by *The Carpenters*. 'No surprises there,' he said, and stuck the discs back into the envelopes, took out a small bunch of keys, unlocked a desk drawer and dropped them in.

After locking it again, he took me through a door in the far wall that led out on to a small loading bay, opening in turn on to the narrow service road at the back of the building where I'd parked my car earlier. The loading bay was accessed by an aluminium shutter that rolled up into the ceiling, and a single, small metal door next to it.

We went back into the production office and Day got two cups of coffee from the machine and gave me one. 'Come upstairs,' he said, 'where the real work gets done, and meet my engineer.' We went out into the corridor again.

Next to the production office were two executive offices and the men's and women's washrooms. At either end of the corridor was a fire door and stairs to the first floor. Another corridor led from the top of the stairs. Off this were four doors, two on either side. On the left were the doors to Studio One, and the engineer's booth adjacent to it. On the right the doors to Studio Two and its engineer's booth. Studio Two was where Day did his show. Leaning against the door stood a six foot six inch black man chewing on a sandwich. 'Yo, Stretch,' said Day, and went to give him a high five.

The black man popped the last of his sandwich

into his mouth, chewed on it and gave Day a disgusted look. 'Cut that "Yo" crap, man,' he said. 'I've told you before, I get that shit all day from people think they my brothers. I tell 'em I got no brothers. I got three sisters and enough nephews and nieces to start a school. And you *know* I hate white men who try to do soul shakes. You can *never* do it without looking stupid.'

'Nick,' said Day, 'this is my man Stretch. The best engineer on the station.'

'I ain't your man, man,' said Stretch, and made a disgusted sound with his tongue against his teeth. 'But you're right about the other.' He looked at me with a hint of amusement in his eyes.

Day ignored his comments. 'Stretch, this is Nick Sharman. He's a private investigator looking into that Sector 88 bullshit.'

'It's about time someone did,' said Stretch, and stuck out his hand. I shook it. It was big enough to hide a football, and I made sure there was no suggestion of a funny hand shake as I did so.

'How are you doing?' I said.

'So you're lumbered with this fool,' said Stretch. 'I thought I was the only one crazy enough to put up with him.'

'It's a living,' I said.

'Barely,' said Stretch dryly.

'Stretch is the only one in the place who dares say things like that about me,' said Day.

'To your face,' said Stretch, and pushed himself away from the door and went to his booth. 'Twenty minutes to showtime,' he said to Day. 'Better get your ass in gear.'

Day grinned and pushed open the studio door. 'He's only kidding,' he said. 'Come in and have a quick look round.' He ushered me inside. The studio was small and windowless. Compact, he called it. I would have said claustrophobic, but what did I know? According to him it was fitted out with the latest state-of-the-art equipment. It was lined with sound-deadening insulation material painted pale grey. The carpet was pale grey also. In the centre of the studio was a large console. On one side of the console was a mixing desk where the presenter sat. Day told me that it was possible to run a whole show single-handed from that desk. Using the faders for volume and the VU meters for balance, it was quite simple.

Mounted on a floating boom in the centre of the console was a microphone shrouded in a foam pop hood. Directly in front of the presenter's chair, coloured red, was the button that operated the ten-second delay that was supposed to be used to cut off swear words and slander from callers. Day told me he never used it. He said that if he couldn't divorce the station from legal action he shouldn't be doing the job he was doing.

'Besides,' he said, 'it adds a little spice to the proceedings.'

On the right were six slots for the looped cartridges, or carts as he called them, that carry the station ID, and DJ jingles, and ads, and announcements that have to be repeated throughout the day. Also on the desk were the headphone sockets that allow the presenter to hear the incoming telephone calls and messages from the engineer.

On the presenter's left was a twin turntable set-up, and above that a pair of the latest CD players. On top of the console was a computer terminal and keyboard. The terminal was wired into an identical one on the engineer's desk so that information could be relayed to the presenter. On the wall above the door was the red light that operated when the microphone was open and the studio was live and on the air. On the other side of the console was another microphone boom in front of a chair for guests or interviewees. Mounted on the wall was a pair of big Lintone professional speakers to relay the broadcast back into the studio.

Behind the console were half a dozen shelves loaded with cartridges, and a phone for outside calls. Day explained that the phone had no bell, just a flashing light to show that it was ringing. The studio was separated from the engineer's booth by a half-glass, soundproofed partition. The engineer's booth, which was the same size as the studio proper, was decorated with the same grey insulation and grey carpet. There was a desk facing the glass partition. Behind this was a wheeled office chair for the engineer's use. On top of the desk were a pair of six-line switchboard's to take in-coming calls for phone-in shows, a separate telephone which was an extension of the station's main switchboard, the computer terminal with keyboard that was the twin of the one on the presenter's console in the studio, and a fixed mike that fed straight into the presenter's headphones when a toggle next to the mike was pressed down. Next to the desk was another twin turntable, pair of CD players, and cartridge deck which could be used for transmission.

So that was the studio set-up. The nuts and bolts. Then Day told me how the actual show ran. As well as engineering, Stretch's job was to suss out the callers before they got on the air. That was where the computer helped. He'd punch up the name of the caller and the area he or she was calling from. Next to that he'd put in his own summary of the situation. 'Loony', or 'pissed up', or whatever. Day could take the chance on letting the caller on air, or cut him or her off. Ultimately it was his decision.

Sometimes, of course, a real psycho got on the line with no warning. That was how the spokesman for Sector 88 had done it. He'd pretended to be calling about something innocuous and when he'd got through, he'd started his rant. Of course Day had loved it. He'd given him a right hard time. I knew, I'd heard the show. I told him I'd enjoyed it.

'That's the point, dear boy,' said Day. 'Really, nothing else matters. Now you are going to stay, aren't you?'

I'd've liked to see him get rid of me.

I sat in the guest's chair and watched as Day and Stretch got ready for the show to start. Day obviously forgot all about me as he got into his presenter's mode. I didn't mind. It was an interesting experience watching him, and I wondered if we'd get a call from Sector 88 during the next three hours. As it happens, we didn't. In fact, the whole show was pretty dull that night. Later on he told me that it happened that way sometimes.

Pretty dull, that is, until it was almost over. It was ten to three when *the* call came. By that time I'd moved my chair round behind Day, so that I could read what was coming up on the computer. I was also wearing a pair of lightweight Koss headphones plugged into one of the sockets on the desk in front of him. I saw the name come up in light green print on the darker green screen. 'John from Stockwell', it read. 'Paranoid.' Day looked through the glass partition at Stretch and smiled to himself. It was his choice. Play or pass. He played.

'And now John from Stockwell,' he said. 'Talk to me, John.'

'Hello, Peter,' said a voice in my ears. It was a strange voice. Cold, with no trace of an accent, like a robot's. But I put that down to the telephone line.

'Hello, John,' Day replied. 'What words of wisdom have you found down Stockwell way on this Monday night?'

'Tuesday morning,' said the voice.

'My apologies there, John. Let's be accurate in all things.' Day turned his head and winked at me. 'So what's up?'

'I just wanted to talk.'

'Are you lonely, John?'

'Everyone's lonely, Peter. We're born lonely and we die lonely.'

'A philosopher,' said Day. 'Just what we need at this late hour. Thank God I can get out of here soon and go home to bed.'

'Don't mock me, Peter,' said the voice. 'You mock everything and everyone, don't you?'

'That's my life, John,' said Day. 'Not an easy one, but mine nevertheless.'

'Why *do* you mock?'

I saw Day glance at the clock on the studio wall. It was just coming up to eight minutes to three. 'Because it's what I do best, John,' he said. 'It's what I enjoy.'

'I enjoy doing some things too, Peter,' said the voice.

'Like what? Share your pearls of wisdom with a waiting world. Or at least the part reached by our transmitters.'

'I enjoy killing people, Peter,' said the voice. I looked at Day who shrugged, then through at Stretch who also shrugged. Day motioned for the call to go on. Seven to three.

'Of course you do, John,' he said. 'So do I when there's an R in the month.'

'You don't believe me, do you?' said the voice.

'Like I believe in Santa Claus,' said Day.

'Then I'll have to show you,' said the voice, and there was a note of triumph in his tone, as if that was exactly what he'd wanted Day to say.

'Do it then, John,' said Day, and cut him off in mid-gloat, going into a short station break. 'Paranoid was right,' he said to me. 'Where do these insects come from? Oh, well, just one more.' I looked at the next name on the screen. 'Marge from Clapham', it read. 'She's an old friend of mine who claims that an angel lives in her roof and flies out to do good at three every night,' said Day as the break ended. 'Marge, what's the flight plan tonight? Do tell.'

Five minutes later he wrapped up the show and handed over to Jack Kelly who jocked the *Early Bird* show from three to six from Studio One. Day flipped the toggle of the intercom. 'Whaddya say, Stretch?'

'Another night, another nicker,' he replied. Pragmatic man, our Stretch. And not a bad judge.

'Drinking?' said Day.

Stretch pulled a face. 'I need food.'

'Ben's is open.'

Stretch pulled another face.

'I'm buying,' said Day.

'Double chilli?'

'It's your stomach.'

'You're on.'

'What about you, Nick?' said Day. 'You coming too?'

'Might as well make a night of it,' I replied.

'Good man. Do you know Ben's?'

'Who doesn't?'

Ben's is an all night licensed café, take-away and pool hall on the borders of Brixton and Loughborough Junction. I think everyone in the area knows it. It's a hang-out for cabbies, nurses and doctors from King's College Hospital, off duty coppers, crooks, clubbers returning home, and obviously the night staff at Sunset Radio. The speciality of the house is enchiladas. Hot and cheesy. At three in the morning they are a guarantee of no sleep. I usually stick to the Mexican beer that Ben serves straight from the deep freeze with a rime of ice on the bottom of the bottle. With double chilli, you not only get a sleepless night, but also breath so fiery you can empty a bus. I marvelled at the strength of Stretch's stomach lining.

'Come on then,' he said. 'Let's go.'

We went in his car, a top of the range Audi with four-wheel drive and an in-car stereo system that could wake up a cemetery. He put on some Bunny Wailer and jacked up the volume. It was only a short drive and I thought my ears could stand it. We left three months' supply of rubber on the road as we peeled away. Stretch's driving made double chilli look attractive. We walked into Ben's at three-twenty precisely.

Ben was behind the counter chewing glumly on a piece of Mozzarella. Next to him was his son, who did most of the cooking whilst Ben did most of the moaning. Ben pushed himself to the front when we came in. The radio was tuned to Sunset, and George Jones was giving it plenty of lachrymose country ballad with a steel guitar backing.

Ben gave the three of us a morose look then said to me, 'Hey, Nick Sharman. You ain't been in here for yonks. Where you been? I thought you was dead, or inside.'

'Hello, Ben,' I said in reply. 'It's good to see you, too.'

'Yeah,' he said, examining the cheese. 'Now why

you hangin' out with these bums?' He gave Day and Stretch a beady look. 'You get yourself into trouble.'

'I can do that well enough for myself.'

'Yeah, I know,' he said. Then to Day: 'Who that geezer?'

'Who?' said Day.

'That last geezer – John. Say he like to kill people. You shouldn't allow that, Peter. He taking the piss. You got that thingummybob that cut the nutters off. Use it.'

'Ben knows almost as much about running a radio station as we do,' said Day.

'More,' said Ben.

'I thought I was the one taking the piss,' said Day. I could tell he wasn't pleased.

'Don't you believe it,' said Ben, pulling from the fridge three beers so cold that your hand stuck to the bottle. 'I know better.'

'Yeah, Ben.'

'Yeah,' he said. 'You wanna eat?'

Stretch chimed in. 'Give me a full cheese with double chilli.'

'You?' said Ben to me as his son ambled over to the stove.

'Egg and bacon sandwich.'

'You want chilli sauce on the egg?' said Ben.

'No, Ben, I don't.'

'You, Peter?' asked Ben.

'How's the chip fat?' asked Day innocently.

'Hot,' said Ben. 'How you think it is?'

'Is it clean?' Day winked at me.

'What the fuck you saying? This is a clean place.'

'Immaculate,' said Day. 'The cockroaches always wash their hands after they've been to the toilet.'

Ben went so red I thought he was going to have a seizure. 'What you mean?' he demanded, and glared at the other customers who were beginning to look a little uncomfortable. 'You saying my place got bugs? You shit.'

'Only joking, Ben,' said Day. 'Give me a chip butty.'

'I ain't gonna serve you. Get out of here, you bum.'

'Come on, Ben,' said Day. 'Give me a chip butty and I'll give you a free plug on the air tomorrow night.'

'Two.'

'OK, two.'

'One chip butty coming up. Chilli?'

'No, thanks.'

Whilst Ben threw a handful of already half-cooked potatoes into the sizzling fat, I said, 'What *did* you think of that call?'

'Crazy man,' said Stretch. 'We get 'em all the time.'

Day nodded. 'He's right. If we worried about freaks like that, we'd never get a show on air. Forget about him. He was probably wanking himself whilst he was talking. A fucking pervert.'

Stretch laughed and said, 'Pool, gentlemen? Who fancies paying my car tax for the year?'

'Watch him,' said Day. 'A perfect example of a misspent youth.'

Day and I waited for the food whilst Stretch went into the back to rack up the pool balls. Ben and his son joined us later, and Ben brought a litre bottle of Tequila with him. Why a Bubble loved Mexican food and drink so much I'll never know. I ended up losing fifty nicker to Stretch, and getting so pissed I had to get a cab home.

6

After all that I didn't wake up until noon, feeling like something the cat would turn up its nose at, much less drag in, out, or anywhere else. When will I ever learn?

I drank several cups of tea and managed to force down a slice of toast and strawberry conserve, then phoned an old friend of mine who worked at Lambeth Town Hall. I got several wrong connections and spent a spell in switchboard limbo before I got put through to the poll tax division. The land that time forgot. 'Community Charge,' said a voice I recognised at the other end of the line.

'Andy?'

'Yes.'

'Nick. Nick Sharman.'

'Hello, Nick, long time. How are you?'

'Not bad. You?'

'Terrible. It's this bloody job. It's doing me in.'

'I can imagine.'

'You remember what I used to be like,' he went on as if I hadn't spoken. 'I used to swim, play squash, cricket, football. I was in good shape. Didn't smoke or drink.' I knew I'd have to let him get it out of his system before he'd listen to me. 'Christ! Now I smoke sixty a day and drink like a fish. I swear I've got an ulcer, chronic dandruff, and piles.'

'It's a tough life,' I said.

'I'm sure I'd beat my wife and kids if I had any. But who'd have me? I've put on two stone and my hair's falling out. I'll be glad when we get shot of this lot. Have you paid yours?'

'What?'

'Your Community Charge, of course.'

'Most of it.'

'Most of it! See what I mean? Have you had a summons?'

'One or two,' I said. 'Every time I get one I send a few quid and they go away.'

'Charming. You're just the sort of person I need.' He paused for a beat. 'Christ, but you're a bloody liar, Nick.'

'Do what?'

'I've just brought your file up on the screen. You've paid fifty quid.'

'Well, that's most of it, isn't it?'

'That's bollocks and you know it.'

'Sorry, mate, it sort of slipped my mind.'

'It's people like you who're driving me to drink.'

'Sorry,' I said again.

'So what are you after, a rebate?' he asked. I was glad to hear he hadn't totally lost his sense of humour.

'A body.'

'Dead or alive?'

'Alive. At least he was a couple of months ago.'

'Makes a change.'

'Doesn't it?'

'Whereabouts?'

'He was seen at the Elephant and Castle.'

'It's a long shot.'

'But worth a try.'

'Why should I do you any favours?'

'Old times.'

'Bollocks. I tell you what, send me a cheque for the balance of your charge and I'll see what I can do.'

'It's urgent,' I said.

'When is it anything else with you? Send me a cheque.'

'I'm doing it now,' I lied.

He sighed. 'You know this is highly illegal, don't you, Nick? These files and the information included in them are supposed to be confidential.'

'I'm not any old Tom, Dick or Harry,' I said. 'This is a matter of life and death.'

'Don't tell me. I don't want to know.'

The silence stretched along the line. 'Andy?' I said eventually.

He sighed. 'What name?'

'Eddie Cochran.'

'Are you fucking serious? Is this a wind-up?'

'No.'

'Eddie Cochran! I don't know. Whatever will they come up with next? How about Mick Jagger? We've got hundreds of them. Or Mickey Mouse? Frank N. Stein? Bloody Arnold Schwarzenegger if you want.'

'Eddie Cochran,' I repeated.

'Are you sure this isn't a wind-up?'

'Perfectly sure. Try Edward Vincent Cochran.'

He didn't answer for a moment then said, 'Blimey, he's here.'

'Where?'

'Kennington. A recent change of address.'

'That sounds like it might be him. Where was he before?'

He read out Mrs Cochran's address in Herne Hill. 'That's my boy,' I said. 'Where's he moved to?'

'The Walpole Estate. Heavy duty, Nick. The

43

locals call it "Rancho Notorious". Bad hombres hang out there, pardner. Even the burglars go about in twos.'

'Amusing, Andy,' I said. 'I know the place. It's no better or worse than any other estate round there.'

'Which isn't saying much.'

'So give me the exact address.'

'Thirty-nine, Maxwell House.'

'Like the coffee?'

'No, like Robert Maxwell. They named half the estate after prominent socialists from the sixties. Wilson, Benn. You know Lambeth.'

'Bad mistake with Maxwell after what happened.'

'That's life.'

'Too right. Has Edward Vincent paid, by the way?'

'He's bang up to date. An honest citizen, and an unusual one in that neck of the woods.'

'Wonders will never cease.'

'There's got to be *one*.'

'Yeah,' I said. 'Listen, I owe you for this. How about a drink one night?'

'With you? Christ, aren't I in enough trouble?'

'It'll take your mind off work.'

'OK, Nick. You can buy me a couple. I'll give you a ring. Still at the same number?'

'That's right.'

'I'll be in touch. And, Nick?'

'Yeah?'

'Don't forget the cheque, will you?'

'It's in the post.'

7

I went to the address Andy had given me for Cochran right away, hangover and all. I took a cab to where I'd left my car. Luckily it was in a side road, not on a yellow line, so it hadn't been towed away. It was the best time to visit the estate. The kids who bothered to go were at school. Anybody with a job was busy earning a crust, and most of the rest were still tucked up safely in bed. There were a few signs of urban unrest littered about. Shards of glass from about a million broken bottles, a few burnt-out shells of cars, and boarded-up flats with smoke-blackened bricks above the windows. The usual.

I parked my car on a street on the edge of the estate, out of harm's way, and walked through the flats until I found Maxwell House. It was a grey, water-stained tower block with a pile of old furniture where the dustbins used to be. A big black rat poked his head out from between the cushions of a G-plan sofa, decided I wasn't edible and scampered away to find something that was.

Cochran's flat was on the tenth floor. Of course the lift was out. I caught up with an old lady struggling between the second and third floors, and carried her shopping as far as the fifth. By then I was knackered. I think she'd bought every tin in the supermarket. I refused her offer of a cup of tea and soldiered on. By the time I reached ten I was wishing I'd never got into the Tequila the night before, and had persevered with the nicotine-flavoured chewing gum and cut out the fags.

The door of Cochran's flat was covered with a steel shutter. Not exactly my idea of a warm welcome. I rang the doorbell next to it. A minute went by and I rang again. After another minute I heard signs of life from the other side of the metal. Eventually it was opened, and the subject of one of the Polaroids I had in my pocket stood in the doorway.

'What?' he said.

'Eddie Cochran?' I asked, although I knew it was and saying the name made me feel foolish.

'What if it is?'

'My name's Nick Sharman. I'm a private detective.' I gave him one of my cards which he glanced at and handed back to me.

'Oh, yeah?'

'Yes,' I said. 'Your wife's dog's gone missing. She's asked me to look into its disappearance.' Saying that made me feel even more foolish.

He grinned an evil grin. 'Is that right?'

'Yes.'

'What do you want me to do about it?'

'I'd like to talk to you.'

'You'd better come through,' he said. 'I'm in the kitchen.'

I followed him down the hall. The door to the kitchen in front of us was open, and was the only light source. The other four doors off the hall were closed.

We went into a room which had a view of the War Museum and over to the river beyond. 'Sit down,' he said. 'Cup of tea?'

'Thanks.'

'So the little bastard's gone,' he said as he plugged in the kettle. 'Too bad.'

'Your wife thinks you might have taken him.'

'Does she, the bitch? She would. As if I've got nothing better to do.'

'So you didn't?'

'What, take that mutt? Not me. I was glad to see the back of it. And her.'

I didn't mention that the feeling was mutual. 'It was just an idea,' I said.

'She gets lots of funny ideas, does Sheila. Maybe I'll go round and tell her some of *my* ideas.'

'I wouldn't bother,' I said. I was getting tired and talking to Cochran seemed to be making my hangover worse.

'But I'm not you, am I?' he said back.

Thank Christ, I thought. It would be wrist-slitting time if he was.

'So she's hired a poncey private detective to find old Prince. What a laugh!' he continued.

'She doesn't seem to think that it's funny.'

'I do.'

You would, I thought. 'So you haven't seen the dog?'

'No.'

'And he's not here?'

'I already told you that. I wouldn't have that rug rat round here.' He grinned 'So you've wasted your journey. Anyway, how's she paying you? She's got no money. Are you taking it in kind?'

I felt like putting his head into the waste disposal. 'Why did you dislike the dog so much?' I asked, ignoring his question.

'Because it looked stupid. Like a mop head on legs. And she had to go and name it after that nigger poof. Why couldn't she have given it a proper name?'

'Like what?'

He thought for a minute. It looked like it hurt.

'Like Elvis. That's a proper name.' I swear he said that, straight-faced.

'Elvis the West Highland White,' I said. 'It does have a certain ring to it.'

He looked at me and his eyes narrowed. 'Are you taking the piss?' he said.

'No,' I said. 'Not at all.'

'Well, the fucking thing's not here. I don't know where it is.'

'Mind if I take a look round?'

'Yes, I fucking do! I'm telling you. Now get out before I lose my temper and throw you out.'

'I don't think you could.'

He puffed out his chest and clenched his fists until his biceps stretched the material of his shirt. 'I wouldn't bet your life on it.'

'I'm not.'

'Course you're not. You're scared, like the rest of them.'

'The rest of who?'

'That's for me to know and you to find out.'

That sort of conversation was a waste of breath, and I'd already wasted enough climbing ten flights of stairs to his flat. 'Thanks for your time, Mr Cochran,' I said, got up and went back down the hall.

He crowded me as far as the front door. He thought he was tough and I couldn't be bothered to show him different. Besides, the state I was in he might have punched the shit out of me. I left without having my tea. I was tempted to stop on the fifth floor to ask the old lady if her offer of a cup was still open.

8

I went back to my car and drove to the office. The digital display on the new answerphone was flashing that I had four messages waiting. I made a cup of tea, sat down, lit a cigarette and pressed the re-wind and play button. The first message was from my tame journalist. He said he'd be in his office all afternoon slaving over a hot word processor, and I should give him a call. The second was from one of the people I'd tried the previous day, who was well into local fringe politics. Please call back, was the message again. Pretty soon our answerphones would be well acquainted. Who knows? They might even meet, fall in love and produce a family of portable fax machines. The third message was from Tony Hillerman. Another nasty package had arrived at Sunset. What he didn't say was, what was I doing about it? But the unstated message was there nevertheless. He wanted me to get in touch as soon as I got back. The final message was from Peter Day. He asked if I'd heard. I imagined he meant about the parcel. He seemed to lose a lot of his communication skills on the machine. He also said that if I was doing nothing to meet him same time, same place as last night for a chat, and left his home number for me to get back to him.

I returned the calls in the order that they had

come in. First I got through to the local paper. My man was there.

'What's cooking?' I asked when I got through.

'Maybe I should ask you that,' he replied. 'You don't usually get in touch unless there's something nasty brewing.'

'Sector 88,' I said.

He was suddenly *very* interested. 'What about them?' he demanded.

'That's what I'm asking you.'

'Very nasty people,' he said. 'Neo-Nazis. The organisation's based on the Fascists of the thirties. They've been tied in with some fire bombings of Asian shops and houses, painting swastikas and graffiti on synagogues, busting up a gay rally or two. You know the type of thing. But no proof. Nobody seems to know who the top man is. We actually tried to infiltrate them last year. One of the young boys in the office got a number one crop, a pair of DMs and a Harrington jacket and went to one of their meetings.'

'What happened?' I asked.

'The usual. A lot of slogans and shouting, but nothing worse than you get at the local Conservative Club, really. He tried to get closer to the committee but they blanked him. It seems you've got to pay a lot of dues before you get into the inner sanctum.'

'So?'

'So we dropped the story. Is something happening?'

'Could be.'

'Give me a clue.'

'I can't right now, but . . .'

'Don't tell me. I'll be the first to know when the story breaks. I'll get the scoop. You've been watching those afternoon films again, Nick. I've warned you about that before.'

'Look, Chas,' I said, 'dig me out anything you can on these creeps. No bullshit, if a story does happen – and I'm not saying that it will, but it might – you'll get the hot poop, I promise.'

'Why do I always believe it when people tell me that?'

'You're an eternal optimist. When have I ever lied to you?'

'Hold on, I'll run the list off the computer.'

'Amusing. Will you do it?'

'OK, Nick, I'll bell you tomorrow. Next day latest. But don't mug me off. If I read anything about this in the *Standard* first, I'll be well pissed off.'

'It's what living in London's all about, Chas.'

'Funny man, see ya.' And he hung up.

Next I got on to my agit-prop pal. 'Sector 88,' he said. 'Christ! Don't you ever learn?'

'What?' I said.

'Bad news, Nick. The politics of the steel toe cap.'

'So I've heard, but what do they do exactly?'

'They fire-bombed a left-wing book shop in Catford last Christmas.'

'Proof?'

'None.'

'Then how do you know?'

'That's my business.'

'That's what everybody says. These goons are bad news underneath, but on top they're as harmless as a vicarage tea party.'

'That's about it.'

'Who's the gaffer?'

I could almost hear him shrug over the phone. 'If anybody knew that they might be able to break them up. Get some evidence.'

'But evidence of what?' I asked.

He went through the depressing list again. Minority baiting by the dispossessed was the name of the game. What it boiled down to was that if you weren't young, white, male and unemployed, or in a dead end job, you might end up on Sector 88's hit list. It was a pretty depressing thought. I asked him to try and get me more details, but he didn't sound hopeful. I promised to get back to him within a few days.

Next I telephoned Hillerman. He wasn't a happy man. 'Have you made any progress?' he demanded when I got through to him.

'Not a lot,' I said. 'I do know that this crew exist, and their aims and ambitions. I also know that they can be pretty heavy, but no one seems able to get any proof of the things they've been accused of. And no one knows who gives the orders. I sat in on the show last night, but they didn't call.'

'So I heard,' he said. 'Get on the case, Sharman. That's what we're paying you for.'

'What was in the parcel?' I asked.

'Shit. It's not very nice.'

Understatement of the year I'd say, but then he didn't have to open it. 'Who found it?' I asked.

'Clyde. He recognised the style and passed it to Security.'

'And the packaging was the same as the others?'

'That's about it.'

'I'm coming up again tonight,' I said 'Perhaps they'll call then.'

'How will that help?'

'I don't know. Don't worry, I'm making enquiries of my own.'

He grunted as if he wasn't impressed.

'Have you kept the parcel that came in today?' I asked.

'No. We've passed the whole thing over to the police.'

'And?'

'The usual. Nothing.'

'Next time, call me. I want to see what one looks like.'

'It's not a very edifying sight, believe me.'

I was getting tired of talking to him, and my head was beginning to hurt again. 'Let me worry about that,' I said. 'I'm working on it. You've got to give me some time. I can't perform miracles.'

He sighed, as if paying me a couple of grand guaranteed it.

'Don't worry,' I said. 'As soon as I get a break, you'll be the first to know.'

'I hope it's soon.'

'So do I,' I said. 'I'll keep in touch.' And we said our goodbyes and hung up.

Finally I called Day at home. His answerphone was on. I left a message saying that I'd see him in the wine bar at nine.

After that I didn't know what to do.

9

So I did nothing. Just sat and pondered until it was time to meet Peter Day, with only a break for cod, chips and a gherkin from the local chippie. I ate them out of the paper with salt, vinegar, and one of those little packets of tomato ketchup that is impossible to get into without spraying it all over the place. The plastic fork broke the first time I tried to cut the batter. But that's life in the white heat of a technological society.

I called Mrs Cochran to tell her that I'd located her husband, but there was no answer. I made a note to try again the next day, and maybe go and see her, but that was really the extent of any constructive undertaking until I locked up the office and left.

I arrived at the wine bar at nine and Day was already waiting for me. He'd got in a couple of drinks and was sitting at the same table that we'd shared the previous night. 'How's tricks?' he asked when I sat down.

'Not so good. Hillerman's right on my case. That parcel that came for you today's got him at it. He wants results, like yesterday.'

'That's showbiz,' he said, and grinned. 'You wanted in. If you can't stand the heat . . .'

'Yeah,' I said. 'Same as usual, was it?'

'That's right. A nice little tribute. Shit. Human. Fresh. It gives me a warm feeling right here.' He touched his chest.

'God, you are popular.'

'I'll survive. I expect I'll get a call tonight about it.'

'Good. Maybe whoever calls will give something away.'

'They already did. A box of shit.'

'Yeah,' I said.

We sat and chatted and had a few drinks. The more I got to know Peter Day, the better I liked him. He was good company, with lots of funny stories. But when I tried to find out about his past, he clammed up. I let it go. When and if he was ready to open up, he'd do it. So we kept the conversation light and the drinks few and far between. But I did get the impression he was a lot more concerned about Sector 88 than he was letting on.

At a quarter to eleven we went to the station. Once again he checked his cubby hole and found a few more freebies. When I remarked on them, he invited me round to his flat soon to go through his record and CD collection. I told him I'd look forward to it. We got coffee and went upstairs. Stretch was in his cubicle chatting on the phone.

Around 11.45 they started to get the show on the road and I was forgotten again. As the second hand on the studio clock hit midnight, the newsreader who worked from a tiny cubicle on the floor above gave out the news, sport and weather, and at four minutes past precisely Peter Day took over. The first hour went smoothly, the topics covered ranging from the state of road sweeping in the area to the political situation in the new Russian Republics. Day was in fine form. He argued with just about everyone, cutting some off in mid-sentence with a sarky comment. Business as usual. Then at five past one, just after the next news bulletin, Stretch typed up 'Bill from Streatham' on the screen.

'OK, Bill what's it all about? And for God's sake make it interesting,' said Day. 'I'm about ready to give up on you lot tonight and make a break for home.'

'Did you get our gift through the post, Mr Day?' said a voice in my headphones. Day looked over at me.

'What particular gift was that, Bill?' he asked.

'You know. Something to remember us by.'

'Us?' said Day. 'Who's us? Spit it out, Bill, if that really is your name.'

'Friends of Freedom,' said Bill proudly.

Day went almost as red as Ben had the previous night. He pulled down a fader so the voice in my earphones which was still ranting on almost disappeared. 'Friends of Freedom, ladies and gentlemen,' he almost spat. 'So speaks the voice of the Friends of Freedom. Also known as Sector 88, if I'm not much mistaken. In other words, and let's not be afraid to say the word, Nazis. The kind who fifty years ago were gassing and burning Jews and gypsies and homosexuals in the greatest holocaust the world has ever seen. The Nazis who send rotten meat and human and animal waste to radio stations who dare to broadcast any criticism. These are your so-called Friends of Freedom. The Friends of Freedom who burn down the homes and businesses of any minority they see fit to persecute. Who fire-bomb shops that dare sell literature that disagrees with their point of view. Nazis. Fascists. Scum. Dirt. And as far as I'm concerned, they can go straight to hell. Now what do you say about that, Billy, old boy?'

Now it was Bill's turn to throw a wobbler. 'You dare call *us* scum, you cu—' And that was the end of Bill. Day's hand shot out as quickly as a snake striking, and cut him off.

'And that just about sums up that particular Friend of Freedom,' he said. 'Now we go to a commercial. Back soon.' And he slid a cart into its slot and cut the volume. 'Wanker!' he said. 'Does he really think he can hijack my show? Tossing little shit!'

'I think he was a little miffed,' I said.

'Bloody good job.'

'But I'm afraid I'm none the wiser.'

'Don't worry about it. The listening figures are good. Hillerman's just being a pain in the arse. Do what you can. Don't forget, I'm a man of influence round here. The whole thing will probably blow over in a few days anyway. It usually does.'

I nodded, the commercial ended, and a woman came on who was convinced that her child was the spawn of Satan. Day agreed that it probably was, which was the last thing she wanted to hear but brought a smile back to his face, and the show rolled on.

Shortly after two we got the second call. 'John from Stockwell' came up on the screen, and Stretch gave a thumbs-up sign and a big grin from behind the soundproof glass. Day looked over at me and raised his eyebrows. He took the call and said, 'Hello, John, how's every little thing with you tonight?'

'Hello, Peter, how are you?'

'Surviving. But barely. It's having to talk to the dregs of humanity that does it.'

'Would you be referring to me by any chance, Peter?'

'If the cap fits . . .'

'I don't know that I like that kind of remark.'

'I don't know that I care *what* you like, John. If what I say offends you, then change stations. It's your choice. It was still a free country when I came into the studio tonight, even if there are some factions of society who would like to change that.'

'But I like listening to you, Peter.'

'I'm touched.'

'In fact I like you so much that I sent you a little present.'

Day's face suffused with blood again. 'So you're one of them, are you, John? I thought you were just a pathetic, harmless little creep, but obviously I was wrong. We've been all through this once tonight, and I'll tell you exactly what I told your friend. Take your present and go straight to hell.' And he cut John off before he could reply. 'They're really coming out of the woodwork tonight,' he said to me over a station break. 'I'll be glad when this is over.'

Which it was before long. I declined the offer of another visit to Ben's. Many more of them, especially if they ended with a session on the pool table with Stretch, and I'd not only end up with ulcers but be broke too. I made my farewells and went back to my car and drove home. I was inside the flat and in bed by four.

10

When I got up the next morning I went straight down to the office. It was just after ten when I unlocked the door. The answering machine showed that there were two messages waiting. I sat at my desk and ran them through. The first was from Chas.

'Nick,' he said, 'I caught the late show on Sunset Radio last night. It was very interesting. Especially the calls from Sector 88. What's happening down there? Has this got something to do with what you were talking about? I'm in the office all morning. Give me a ring.'

The second call was from Sheila Cochran. 'I've been trying to get you, Mr Sharman,' she said. 'To find out if you've got any news on Prince. I'm at work now and can't take calls but I'll be in this evening. Will you phone me or call round, please?'

I phoned the paper right away. 'Nick,' said Chas when I got through to his extension, 'what's going on? Is this Sunset thing anything to do with you?'

'It is.'

'Why didn't you tell me?'

'I've nothing to tell.'

'Don't give me that. Day almost had a fit on air last night. I've called the station, but they're saying nothing.'

'Maybe they've got nothing *to* say.'

'Don't try and kid a kidder, Nick. I know when I'm being brushed off. I'm used to it. Tell me what's going on.'

'I don't know.'

'What would you say if I told you that I had something on Sector 88?'

'What?'

'Oh no, mate. A favour for a favour. You show me yours, and I'll show you mine.'

I thought for a moment. 'OK,' I said. 'But not on the phone.'

'When?'

'Lunchtime?'

'Yeah, I'm free.'

'Your tab.'

'Do what?'

'You're on expenses.' So was I, but I'd already lost fifty of it to Stretch at pool.

'I'll toss you.'

The way my luck was running, I'd lose. 'Fair enough. Where?'

'I'm feeling lucky, so as you'll be paying let's make it the Italian down by Streatham station?'

'Good enough. One o'clock?'

'I'll be there.'

'See you then,' I said and hung up.

I kicked my heels round the office for the rest of the morning, then drove up to the restaurant and parked at the back of the station. When I got inside, Chas was already waiting for me. He was sitting at a table in the back, a martini cocktail in front of him with a green olive in it. 'You're ambitious,' I said.

He picked up a ten-pence piece from the table in front of him. 'Call,' he said, and flipped it into the air.

'Heads,' I said. He caught the coin and slapped it on to the back of his hand, then showed it to me. Tails it was. I'd been right about my luck. I shrugged and turned to the waiter who was hovering behind me. 'Two more of those,' I said. 'Very dry.'

'Good man,' said Chas. 'I'm going to enjoy this lunch.'

We chatted inconsequentially until the drinks arrived. After my first mouthful of the smoky brew, Chas said, 'Come on then, Nick, let's have it.'

'Off the record?'

'Naturally. I'm surprised you have to ask. Come on, spit it out.'

So I did. I told him everything I knew. What the hell? I was getting nowhere fast on my own, and I could trust Chas as far as I could trust any journalist. About the distance I could kick him uphill.

As I was talking, the waiter came over to take our orders. Chas chose veal marsala, I had spaghetti with meat balls and a green salad. Chas ordered a bottle of the most expensive red wine on the list. Typical journalistic behaviour. He still had a touching faith in the concept of a free lunch. And in this case his faith was vindicated.

'Interesting,' he said, when I'd finished and he was halfway through his second martini. 'A nice little page three lead for Friday's paper.'

'Off the record,' I reminded him. 'Besides, it's nothing, and you know it, mate. So what have you got for me?'

'I've got a name, and the time and place for Sector 88's next meeting.'

'Go on then.'

'The name is Smith.' He saw the look on my face. 'OK, Nick,' he said. 'It's probably a fake. But the meeting's planned for Sunday night, eight o'clock, at the Masonic Hall in Norbury.'

'Masonic Hall,' I said. 'That's a laugh. How do you know?'

'I have my sources. It's kosher, believe me.'

The waiter interrupted us by bringing the food and wine. When he was satisfied we had everything, and had done the usual boogie around the table with a three-foot-high pepper mill then split, I asked: 'What about the story?'

'What about it?' Nick said innocently.

'You know.'

'Am I going to use it, do you mean?'

'Right.'

'If it was anybody else but you, probably. But you have this knack of blowing everything up, literally. No, I think I'll wait 'till Monday. You will be going on Sunday, won't you?'

'I might.'

'Don't be coy, Nick. It doesn't suit you.'

'OK,' I said. 'I'll be going. Satisfied?' He was right. Being coy didn't suit me.

'I think I might join you. Do you mind?'

'The more the merrier.'

'I might even bring a photographer. Who knows what he might capture for posterity?'

'Who knows?'

'Shall we meet up first?'

I nodded.

'Seven o'clock in The Bull in Norbury,' he said.

'And I'll expect you to put your hand in your pocket,' I told him. 'If I'm giving you copy, you can bloody well pay for it.'

'It'll be a pleasure.'

'I have got one story you can use on Friday.'

'What?'

I took the picture of Prince out of my pocket and

gave it to him. 'Help out a lady in distress,' I said. 'Find her dog.'

He looked up at the ceiling. 'Jesus!'

'Come on, Chas. Let's see the soft heart under the hard bitten exterior. Put a bit in the paper about it at the weekend. You know people love a sob story.'

'And you'll tell me any developments on the Sector 88 front?'

'Of course I will.'

'You're twisting my arm, but I'll do a human interest story. Give me her number and I'll give her a ring. Can I keep the photo?'

'Sure you can.' I wrote down Sheila Cochran's number on a paper napkin, and he put it and the photo into his pocket. 'I knew you wouldn't be able to resist,' I said.

He pulled a face, called over the waiter and ordered chocolate gâteau, coffee and brandy for dessert.

We finished the meal without mentioning business again, just chatting about old times. When I'd paid the bill, I dropped Chas back at his office and drove to mine. The telephone began to ring when I got inside. I caught the call before the answering machine cut in. 'Sharman,' I said.

'Hello, Nick. Peter Day.'

'Hello, Peter,' I said. 'What's new?'

'Not a lot. You?'

'I might have something. Any more parcels today?'

'No. I've just spoken to Hillerman. Everything's fine. What have you got?'

'A meeting of Sector 88, at the weekend. I'm going to go along.'

'Will you be all right?'

'Why not? They don't know me.'

'What are you going to do?'

'Don't know yet. I'll busk it.'

'Are you coming up tonight?'

'Might as well, but we've got to stop meeting like this. People will talk.'

'Very funny. Usual place?'

'Yeah. I'll catch you about nine.'

'I'll be there. Well done, by the way.' And he rang off.

I spent the rest of the afternoon trawling around for more information on Sector 88, but information on that particular nasty little cadre was as rare as hen's teeth. I was glad I'd spoken to Chas, otherwise I'd've begun to feel that my detecting talents were pretty rare also.

At seven I got into the car and drove to Herne Hill. There was a light on behind the front door of Sheila Cochran's house again. I rang and she answered and invited me in and offered me tea. I accepted. The house was warm and cosy. It was pleasant to take time out there. She brought in the tray and gave me a cup, and offered me a cigarette. I accepted and said, 'I'm glad you called. I tried to get you yesterday. I've found your husband.'

'Well, that's the bad news,' she said. 'Is there any good?'

I shook my head. 'He says he hasn't seen Prince since he left here. There were no signs of a dog in his flat. I didn't see the whole place, in fact he threw me out, but I was in the kitchen and if there was an animal in the place I'd've expected to see feeding bowls there. There was nothing.'

'Where is he?' she asked.

'At a flat in a tower block in Kennington.' I told her the address, but she didn't make a note of it. I guessed he was off her Christmas card list. 'He struck me as a not particularly pleasant man,' I said.

'You don't have to mince words with me,' she said. 'I told you he was a bastard.'

'Why did you marry him? I'm sorry, that's none of my business.'

'Don't worry about it. I married him because I felt it was time to get married. Stupid or what?'

'Not really. There are worse reasons.'

'And better. But that's in the past now. I don't suppose you've managed to find out anything about Prince?'

'I told you I might not,' I said. 'But I've spoken to a friend of mine. He works on the local paper. He told me he'd put in a piece about him this Friday. I gave him your number. I hope you don't mind?'

She smiled for the first time since I'd arrived, and once again it transformed her face. 'Oh, that is good. I don't mind in the least. Thank you, Mr Sharman.'

'Call me Nick,' I said.

'All right, Nick, and you call me Sheila. I don't know how to thank you. I could never have done that.'

'It's a pleasure.'

'I was up at the dogs' home again last night.'

'No good?' I said.

'No.'

'Listen, Sheila,' I said. 'Don't take this the wrong way, but maybe you should think about getting another dog.'

'Yes, I know. But I can't help thinking that one morning Prince'll come scratching at the door to be let in for his breakfast.'

'I hope so, Sheila,' I said. 'I really do.'

'But it's been a long time.'

'Dogs are amazing creatures,' I said. 'You never know.'

'No, you don't, do you?' she said. 'More tea?'

I took another cup and sat and chatted until well past eight when I told her I had another appointment, said my farewells and that I'd keep in close touch, and left.

11

I went to the car and drove to Brixton once more.
I met Day as arranged and we settled into the pattern of the last couple of nights. A few drinks,
nothing excessive, and a chat. We were like old
friends by then, although he still refused to divulge
much about his past. Naturally we talked about
Sector 88, and the meeting on Sunday. And my
going. Shortly before eleven we drank up and
headed for the station. The night was chilly and the
streets were quiet. Our footsteps echoed between
the buildings as we went. Stan, the night security
man let us into the building. He nodded at me and
said something inconsequential to Day. After a few
seconds we went through to the production office to
get coffee, and for Day to collect his post.

That night there was the usual thin sheaf of envelopes which Day put into his jacket pocket unopened.
He explained that he liked to read his mail when he
got home from work in the small hours. There were
also four packages. One was a cardboard album
envelope. The other three were Jiffy bags. Two were
twenty inches by twelve, with printed-out address
labels and stickered with the names of major record
companies. The other was eight by ten. His name
and the station address were neatly typed on a small
oblong white label on the front. He opened one of

the larger Jiffys and pulled out a boxed set of Lightnin' Hopkins CDs.

'All right!' he said. 'Excellent. I've been waiting for these.'

'Good stuff,' I said.

'The best,' he replied and reached for the bag with the typed label. He pulled off the tape that sealed the end, and squeezed the edges of the envelope so that the flap opened like a mouth, and stuck his hand inside. He looked puzzled at what he found and pulled it out. At first I thought, as you might think, as you *do* think when something is such a surprise, such a shock, that you're imagining it. My eyes wouldn't actually believe what I was seeing in his hand, and my brain refused to compute what my eyes saw. I thought it was plastic or rubber. A joke shop fake. Anything but skin and flesh and gristle and dried blood.

He screamed then, in that quiet office with only the sound of the old Mel Torme record being broadcast drifting through the speakers to disturb it, and dropped what he found himself holding on the desk in front of me. He went to wipe off the sticky gunk of blood and hair that stuck to his fingers on his jeans. Then he realised what he was doing and stopped his hand six inches from his leg, stood and kicked back the chair he was sitting on so that it bounced off the wall behind him and tilted and fell on to the floor with a crash, and ran out of the office towards the nearest toilet. I could hear him retching through the two closed doors between us.

I knew exactly how he felt. I sat transfixed and stared at the thing he had dropped on to the desk next to the box of CDs. It was a human ear. Small. A child's or woman's. Where it had been hacked off there was a rind of dried blood and blond hair.

Through the pierced lobe was a silver ear ring. Attached to it by a smaller link was a tiny red cross. It was plastic or bone dyed crimson. I wasn't going to touch it to find out which.

As I sat there Day came back into the room. His face was green. Really green. I've never seen anyone's skin that colour in my life. His eyes had sunk into their sockets and there were black circles around them. His hair was sweaty and the fringe was sticking to his forehead. He looked as if he'd been in the pub all day ODing on Jack Daniel's with lager chasers. 'Are you all right?' I asked in a voice that I hardly recognised as my own. What a stupid question. It would be a while before either of us was all right again.

He nodded as if it hurt to move his head. 'Get Security,' I said. He looked at me as if I'd started talking in a foreign language. 'Peter,' I said, 'get your security man. Now.' He shook his head, then nodded again and went to the desk closest to the door and picked up the telephone and punched out a three-figure number. 'Stan,' he said when it was picked up at the other end, 'get into the production office.' His voice sounded like he'd been kicked in the throat, but it didn't tremble or shake.

There was a pause. 'Yes,' said Day in answer to a question I couldn't hear. 'Get in here, Stan. Now.' There was another, shorter pause then he lost his cool. 'Fuck that shit!' he screamed. 'Get in here.' And slammed down the receiver.

The security man was through the door in less than ten seconds. Something of the way Day felt must have got through to him. I would have been surprised if it hadn't. Day pointed at the desk and Stan's eyes widened. 'What the . . . ?'

'Call the police, Stan,' I said, and looked at the

clock on the office wall. 11.10. Fifty minutes to air time. Tony Bennett was singing about the good life through the speakers.

Day looked at the clock too and picked up the phone again. He seemed to have regained some of his professional composure. He tapped out another three-digit number. When the phone was answered, he said: 'Tim?' A pause. 'Come down to the production office, will you? Fast.'

By this time Stan was on another phone. He was stuttering and gesticulating. I lit a cigarette. It tasted like death. It was death in a way, I suppose. I sucked down the smoke and wished for something alcoholic. Day took the packet out of my hand and lit one for himself. It was the first time I'd seen him smoke.

Tim, who I later discovered was the newsreader, arrived and Day grabbed him. He showed him the ear and Tim blanched. Just then the police started hammering at the front door and Stan split to answer it. Tim offered to take Day's show, but he declined. Like I said, a real pro. Besides, something big was happening and he obviously wanted to be around.

Stan brought the police through to the production office. The station was just around the corner, and I suppose Sunset Radio was quite important as far as local politics/community liaison was concerned. Also I imagine ears don't get sent through the post every day.

There were six coppers altogether in the first wave. A lot more were going to show up as the night went along. Three were uniform, three plainclothes. Obviously they'd been hanging around the station when the call went out, and all wanted to get in on the act. One of the plainclothes knew Peter Day. He was a Detective Sergeant by the name of Charlie Harper. Apparently he'd been on the show a couple of times fielding questions mainly asked by angry black people and women who thought that the police were racist, sexist, fascist thugs. Perhaps they were right, or partly right. Perhaps some policemen were. But the next time you get an ear through the post, I bet you call the cops before you call a black radical feminist group.

Stan took one more look at what had been in the bag and left.

Harper went straight to the desk and looked at the ear. He was a youngish thirty-five in a crumpled suit, with the face of someone who'd seen it all. He shook his head and went over to Day. 'You look like shit,' he said.

'I feel worse.'

'But not as bad as whoever belonged to that,' said Harper, and gestured towards the desk.

Day didn't reply.

Harper looked over at me, still sitting in the chair I'd been sitting in all along, feeling about as much good in the situation as a spare prick at a wedding. Less, in fact. 'Who's your friend?' he asked.

'Nick Sharman. He's a private detective,' replied Day.

'So you're Sharman,' said Harper. 'I've heard all about you. What are you doing here?'

'I'm helping the station on another matter.'

'Helping? I suppose that's one way of describing what you do. Stay there, I'll talk to you later.'

I did as I was told. But somehow my eyes kept coming back to that ear lying on the top of the desk in front of me. Another of the plainclothes guys was a scenes of crime officer, soco. He went out to his car and brought back a black leather briefcase from which he took out a pair of thin rubber gloves. He opened the Jiffy with a pair of long tweezers. He was a witty type of guy in his own way. 'You Pete Day?' he asked.

Day nodded and lit another of my cigarettes. I did the same.

'Bit early for Christmas presents.' The soco squinted into the envelope and said, 'There's a piece of paper in here.'

'Let's see it then,' said Charlie Harper. 'Don't piss about, Jack.'

He put the tweezers into the envelope and pulled out a piece of paper. It was stained with blood and a paler, lighter liquid which had dried an obscene rusty yellowy-pink on the paper. I felt my guts rumble and had to look away. The smoke suddenly tasted sour in my mouth and I stubbed out the cigarette.

Jack unfolded the paper carefully with rubber-covered fingers, only touching it at the edges. He read it and grunted. 'Fan mail, Pete,' he said. 'Looks like you've got a friend.'

'Read it, Jack,' said Harper patiently. You get used to clowns in his business. If not, you don't last long.

Jack cleared his throat, like he was about to make an Oscar acceptance speech. ' "Dear Pete," ' he read, ' "you didn't believe me tonight when we talked. I was very upset by your attitude. I only wanted to be friendly. Maybe you'll believe me now. I'll call you again soon." It's signed John. Well, not signed, it's all typed. Same machine as did the label on the bag it came in, by the looks of it.'

'Christ!' I said. And it all came back to me. John. John from Stockwell. The crazy who'd called on Monday night and told Day that he enjoyed killing people.

'You know this John?' asked Harper, looking first

74

at me then at Day. The other coppers were all looking at us too, as if we might have arranged for the
ear to be delivered. Like a pizza.

'I don't *know* him,' said Day. 'He called the show.
First on Monday, then again last night.'

'Do you remember what he said?' asked Harper.

'He said he liked killing, the first time. I cut him
off.'

'Seems he took it personally,' said Jack, pulling
off his rubber gloves and reaching for the telephone.
'And cut something off himself. It might be better
to humour him in future.' Then to Charlie Harper,
'I'm going to get this over to forensic. It'll make
their night.' Then to no one in particular, 'How do
you get a line out on this?'

'Dial nine,' said Day. 'Then the number you
want.'

'What did he say last night?' Harper asked.

Day explained that John had told him he had sent
him a present. He gestured at the ear as he said it.
But he had thought that John was referring to the
box of shit that had come from Sector 88.

Harper said that he knew all about *that*.

'So it looks like two separate groups are sending
you things through the mail,' Harper concluded,
with a look that said: What's it like to be Mr Popular? 'Do you remember anything else about the
calls?'

Day shook his head. 'No. But my engineer might
think of something. I only spoke to the guy for a
few seconds. He was just another nut. Do you know
how many of those phone in each week?'

Harper said nothing.

'It'll be on the log, won't it?' I said. I was trying
hard to make some useful contribution to the
situation.

'Do what?' Harper said.

'He's right,' said Day. 'We record everything that goes out on air. We keep the recordings for three months. In case we want to repeat something, or there's a complaint or a court case or something. The calls will be on Monday's and last night's tapes. You can hear them for yourself.' He looked up at the clock. It was seven minutes to twelve. 'I'm on soon.'

'Are you sure you're up to it?' said Tim the newsreader.

'This bloke's going to call me,' said Day. 'I'd better be there . . . Sergeant?' He looked over at the policeman for confirmation.

Harper looked at the other officers then back at Day. 'Can you handle it?' he asked. 'You've had quite a shock.'

'He wants to talk. To talk to me.'

'If he calls,' I said. 'You were pretty rough on him last night.'

'*If* he calls, he'll want to talk to me,' said Day. 'And I think he will. He might get mad if I'm not there.'

'And God knows how he'd behave if he got mad. Huh, Pete? He might do something really desperate,' said Jack who was hanging on the phone and still examining the ear that lay on the desk as if he didn't want to part with it. Like a kid with a new toy. Personally I wished he'd just put it in an evidence bag and get the thing out of the room.

Harper made up his mind. 'Do it, Peter,' he said. 'But I'm going to be in the studio with you. If he calls we'll try and get a trace on the call.'

Whenever they try stunts like that in films, it always works. In real life it rarely does. Men like John are suss enough to use a public phone and by the time the police get there, the receiver will be swinging at the end of its cable like a hanged man. I looked at the ear, and Harper, and Tim, and Peter Day, and Jack, and the other coppers in the room, and I felt the horror again. I wondered how Peter Day could bear to do it. The last thing I'd've wanted to do right then was to talk to some crazy fucker who sent parts of bodies through the post like greetings cards.

Jack stayed in the office, and Harper ordered two of the uniforms to secure the room after he'd taken the ear to forensic. The rest of us went up the stairs to the studio. Day, Tim and Charlie Harper took the lead, and the other two coppers were close behind. I was last.

Stretch was leaning against the door to the engineer's booth next to Studio Two. 'Cutting it fine, bro,' he said. I don't suppose he knew he'd made a joke. Even the sight of the coppers pounding up the stairs didn't faze him. He just shrugged and went into his booth. Day leaned his head in after him.

'Let's get this show on the road, Stretch,' he said. 'There's a whole lot of shit going down. It's a different kind of show tonight. Load up some music. I'll talk to you in a minute.' Stretch nodded and began to sort through a pile of CDs on his desk, but never asked why.

Our little posse trooped into the studio behind Day. The clock said three to eleven. 'Fast' Eddie Felton, who DJ'd the previous show, was wrapping up. He had no idea what had been happening downstairs, and sounded perfectly normal. Tim went up to his cupboard to read the news. Day sat at the console and slipped a pair of headphones round his neck. Two to twelve. Eddie signed off and on came a commercial for a local carpet shop, followed by another for a car dealer in Clapham. One to twelve. A station announcement and a promo for the breakfast show. Thirty seconds to go, and a short promo for the programme, and Tim came in smoothly with the headlines. The studio was full of people. Too full for Day, and there was too much noise. 'Shut up,' he ordered. We did. He was captain of the ship, and he knew it. 'Right,' he said. 'It's too crowded in here. I feel like shit. This is not going to work. Charlie, Nick, you stay. The rest of you, get out. The switchboard's next door.'

'Why him?' said Harper, gesturing to me.

'He's a friend,' said Day, and looked at me with eyes that were full of such desolation I had to look away. 'I need a friend right now.'

'OK,' said Harper reluctantly. 'But, remember, if this John character calls, keep him talking.'

'He'll call,' Day said.

'Frank,' said Harper to the other plainclothesman, 'get in the other room on to the switchboard and make sure that the phone people know what's going on. We don't want to miss this joker, and we haven't got much time. You know what the code is?' He was referring to the special codes that the police use when they need co-operation from Telecom. Frank nodded, and he and the other uniformed officer went in to join Stretch.

Day flipped the toggle on the intercom and said, 'Stretch, these gentlemen will be needing your help. Just do what they say. They'll tell you why. OK?'

Stretch didn't look happy about his domain being invaded, but nodded nevertheless. Day knocked the toggle off, and I saw Frank speak to Stretch and get straight on to the phone that went through the station's main switchboard. Tim finished reading the news and went on to the weather. Stretch was talking on the phone-in switchboard, and flipped down the toggle on *his* mike and came through to Day's headphones. I picked up the spare set and held them so that both Harper and I could listen. 'There's people calling in already,' he said.

'Anyone named John?' Day asked.

Stretch shook his head behind the glass.

'What music you got on the deck?'

'*Moonglow.*'

The theme from the film *Picnic*, starring William Holden and Kim Novak, 1956. I could play *Trivial Pursuit* for money.

Upstairs, Tim introduced the show and, without introduction, Stretch cued in *Moonglow*. As the tune played we watched him answering the phone. I could see his lips moving but couldn't hear his voice. As the lush strings of the record faded he flipped down his mike toggle and said, 'I've got that geezer on the dog. John.'

Day looked at Charlie Harper and said, 'Told you.' The policeman stood up and went and opened the studio door and whispered something to the other uniformed copper who was standing outside. Then he turned to Day and pointed his index finger at him. Day looked through the glass into the control room. 'Stick him through, Stretch,' he said. 'Let's boogie.' He was hanging tough. Pretending to be cold and hard. But he was shaking like a shitting dog, and I'd seen that look in his eyes when he'd said he needed a friend. I heard the click of the connection in my earphones and Day pushed up the volume on his mike and said, 'John?'

'You sound strange, Peter,' said a voice I recognised as the caller from the two previous nights. Even now, I can still hear that voice inside my head.

'Frog in my throat, John,' said Day. 'Thanks for

79

calling. How are you tonight?'

'Fine,' he replied. 'Nice tune you were playing. It quite takes me back.'

'Me too, John. Me too,' said Day. 'So speak to me. Share your thoughts.'

'Did you ever see that film, Peter?' said John. 'The film that music came from.'

'Yes,' said Day.

'I saw it when I was a kid,' said John. 'I was in love with Kim Novak then.'

'Is that so?' said Day. He glanced over at Harper and me, and I saw that look in his eyes again.

'She looked like Kim Novak,' said John.

'Who?'

'You know who.'

I remembered the blond hair and blood on Day's fingers and tasted vomit in the back of my throat. I could tell he remembered too by the way he instinctively wiped his hand on his trouser leg.

'Don't you, Peter?' said John after a moment, and his voice was as distant as the Milky Way, and as close as a lover's kiss.

'I know,' said Day. 'Who was she, John?'

'Just someone I met.'

'Where?'

'In the world, Peter. There are a lot of people like her. In the world. Have you told the police?'

I was beginning to wonder what this conversation sounded like to the listening public. They probably thought Day was off his rocker. 'What do you think, John?' he asked.

'I think you have. I think they're in there with you trying to trace this call. Tell them to dream on. You'll never catch me. But now I think we've spoken enough for tonight. I'll call you again tomorrow. Have a nice night. Sweet dreams.' And we were listening to dead air. Then the dialling tone. Day closed the transmission mike, and slipped in the cart for a thirty-second commercial, and that was that. He pressed down the toggle on the internal mike.

'Stretch, cue up some music. You drive me. Just tell me what you're going to play and I'll introduce it. I think I'm going to have to talk to Mr Harper here. Choose mellow kit. Keep it sweet and low. Did you get that call on tape?'

'Every word,' Stretch came back. 'Is it true?' The copper in other room must have told him.

Day nodded through the glass.

'Heavy shit,' said Stretch.

'Music,' said Day. 'Close down the switchboard. Let reception take all the garbage.'

Stretch nodded then his voice came through the speakers. '*Blue Velvet* by *The Clovers*.'

'Good choice,' Day said, and re-opened the transmission mike. 'Tonight is a different kind of night,' he said. 'I'm not going to take any more phone calls this evening. I think that one was enough. So no more talk, just music. Music like they don't make any more. And first off, the mellowest version of *Blue Velvet* from Atlantic Records, New York City 1955, *The Clovers*.' The music started and he cut the mike.

'Very good,' said Harper. 'You're a pro.'

'That's my job,' said Day. 'I feel like I've just gone ten rounds with Mike Tyson. When this show is finished I'm going to collapse. Any luck with tracing the call?'

'I'll find out.' Harper stood up and went outside.

Day looked at me. 'Fuck!' he said. 'Why us?'

There was no answer to that. Harper came back and answered Day's and my enquiring looks. 'No,' he said. 'He's still out there.'

'That's a pleasant thought,' I said.

Somehow Day got through the next hour. Stretch chose the music just right. He timed it and the commercials perfectly. He worked out that if he played a long track about four minutes to one, went straight into a commercial break, then the news and weather, more commercials and back for another long track, Day could get an eleven-minute break off air around the hour. At four minutes to exactly Day introduced *Careless Love* by Ray Charles and left his chair. He was sweating and begged me for another cigarette.

Tony Hillerman was waiting in the corridor outside. He didn't look like the happiest man in the world. Someone must have called him in or else he'd been listening to the show. All three of us walked along to the fire exit, climbed the back stairs to the roof and Day and I lit a cigarette each. Charlie Harper followed us a minute later. I leant against part of the air-conditioning unit that towered over the roof and tried not to listen as they talked at Day. I looked across the railway lines towards town. The night was cold and getting colder.

He was out there, John or whatever the hell his name really was. John the ear cutter. Maybe he was asleep. Maybe he was listening to the sweet music that Stretch was playing. Maybe he was stalking another victim. Or maybe he already had one in some blood-stained room that echoed with her screams, drowning out the sound of Ray Charles on the radio.

12

Hillerman had nearly gave himself a coronary. He demanded to know why Day had let John from Stockwell on air. He tried to explain, but Hillerman wouldn't listen. Charlie Harper butted in and shut him up.

'I asked Peter to talk to him,' he said.

'This is my station,' said Hillerman. 'I'm in control of programming.'

Programming! I ask you.

'Leave it, Tony,' said Day. 'I wanted to take the call.'

'Do you realise this could close the station down?' Hillerman retorted.

'I doubt it,' said Day, throwing the cigarette down on the roof and crushing it with his shoe.

'Just you wait and see,' said Hillerman, rather petulantly I thought.

'I'll do that little thing,' said Day. 'But meanwhile I've got a show to finish.' We went back, and he and Stretch put together a music programme as they went along. Meanwhile, downstairs all hell was breaking loose. The first call came from one of the tabloids. Someone had telephoned a reporter after hearing the show, and he had telephoned a contact at Brixton police station. The word was out around the corridors and the reporter came straight on looking for someone to talk to. Tony Hillerman took the call. He tried to squirm out of telling the truth, but a mixture of clever questioning by the reporter and Hillerman's own stupidity let the story out. By six a.m. Sunset were reporting on the hourly news bulletins a censored version of what had happened.

An hour later the street outside was full of reporters and radio and TV news teams. Peter Day and I were still in the building waiting for the results of a hastily convened board meeting. Though why I should have bothered to wait, I don't know. I just thought that Peter needed someone in his corner. Plus, of course, I'm naturally nosy.

The board decided to pull the programme immediately. They pulled Day too. 'Fully paid leave of absence' they called it.

Meanwhile Charlie Harper arranged for all the station's post to be re-routed and checked by the police before it got to the building.

After Day heard that he was off the air, he, Harper and I sat in the production office. Harper got on the phone to the police laboratory. When he was finished, I asked: 'So?'

'So what?'

'So what did they find out?'

'Now why should I tell you? You shouldn't even be here by rights.'

'Would you rather I was outside talking to the press?' I asked.

Harper gave me a dirty look.

'Well, would you?' I pressed.

'Obviously not, *Mr* Sharman.'

'Look, I'm on your side,' I said. 'I'm being paid by the station to look into another matter . . .'

'I *am* aware of why you're here.'

'Fine. And I'm telling you that all this is too heavy

for me. I'm not going to step on anyone's toes, but I think Peter deserves to know what's going on at least. He helped you out by talking to this loony and now he's paying the price. If you want me to go, I will, but he'll only tell me as soon as we see each other again.'

Day nodded confirmation.

'OK,' sighed Harper. 'The ear came from a white blond female. Aged between twenty and twenty-five. Probably between five foot and five foot four. Blood type A. In good health . . . Well, she was.'

'Until?' said Day naïvely.

Harper looked him straight in the eye. 'Until someone cut her ear off, of course.'

Day looked sick. 'She was still alive when he did it?' he said incredulously.

'So they think,' Harper said.

'Christ!'

'Pleasant thought, isn't it?'

'Would that kill her?'

'It wouldn't improve her health.'

'And they can tell all that from her *ear*?' said Day, looking at me. I nodded.

'From a lot less apparently,' said Harper.

'Any prints or forensic on the envelope?' I asked. Harper shook his head. 'Posted London West 1,' he said.

'Have you heard the original calls?'

'Yes,' said Harper. 'I've had a cassette made.'

'What do you think?'

He shrugged. That said it all.

'I want to go home,' said Day.

'Me too,' I agreed. 'Is that all right?' I asked Harper out of politeness. We both knew he couldn't stop us.

'Sure. We'll be in touch if we need you.'

Day and I left by the back way. There were a few reporters and cameramen at the door. The cameramen snapped off a couple of photos, but we dodged the reporters and made a run for it through the market that was just coming alive. I parted from Day in the Brixton Road.

'Let me know what happens,' I said. 'I'll talk to Hillerman later. See if he wants me to stay on the job.'

'I do,' said Day.

'We'll see,' I said. 'Don't worry, I'll be about. If you need me – call.'

'I'll do that.'

I shook his hand and went to find my car. The last I saw of him he was slouching down the road in the direction of Stockwell. I went home and took the phone off the hook. I didn't want to talk to anyone unless I instigated the call.

The story broke in the late editions of Thursday's papers. It was front page in some of the more sensational ones. Sunset got a lot of publicity that day. So did Peter Day. Even I got my photo in the press, looking smudgy and bleary-eyed as I left the studios with him. Some of the papers reported that his show had been dropped. Where they'd got that snippet of information from so quickly, no one knew.

I called Hillerman at eleven. I hadn't bothered going to bed, I knew I wouldn't be able to sleep. I'd just lie there and think about the ear that had come through the post. I had a terrible job getting through to Sunset. The first half a dozen times I tried the lines were all engaged. Eventually I got through to the switchboard, and when I'd explained who I was, they put me through to Sophia. She'd lost a little of her cool since our last conversation.

'How are you?' I asked.

'I don't know. I'm numb. I can't believe it.'

You should have been there, I thought. 'It's bad,'
I said.

'You saw it?'

'Yes. I was there when Peter opened the package.'

'Christ!' she said. 'How is Peter? I can't get
through to him. He's got his machine on.'

'He's not very happy about being dropped from
the station. Especially after finding what he found,
and talking to the bloke on the air.'

'I don't blame him,' she said. 'That's one of the
reasons I want to talk to him. I think the board are
being far too heavy.'

'I agree,' I said.

'What about you? How are you feeling?'

'Personally or professionally?'

'Both.'

'Personally – lousy. Professionally – that's why
I'm calling. I need to know if I'm still on the case
or not. Or if Peter getting suspended means I'm not
working for you any more.'

'You'll have to talk to Tony. I'll put you through.'

'Thanks,' I said. 'I hope I'll be seeing you again.'

'I hope so too,' she said. 'Good luck.'

There was a click, a short ringing tone, then
Hillerman said: 'Yes.'

'Sharman,' I said.

'Ah.'

Ahs' I don't like. 'Good morning,' I said.

'Don't you believe it. This has been the worst
morning of my life.'

I sympathised then said, 'I'd like to know if I'm
still working for you or not?'

'Why not? You've been paid.'

'But under the circumstances . . .'

'I don't see what difference it makes.'

'But what about Peter Day?'

'What about him?'

'He's been suspended. No more shows. So no more parcels from Sector 88. And with the other thing, the police will be looking for them now *very* seriously – even though I doubt they sent the ear. But I also doubt that you'll hear very much more from them. The other business makes it too risky for them to get involved.'

'That's the general consensus from the police too. And as you so rightly said, they'll be looking for them properly now, if only to eliminate them from enquiries.'

'So do you need me?'

He paused. 'Look,' he said after a moment, 'I hear what you're saying. Just sit tight for now and I'll get back to you.'

'That's fine by me,' I said. 'I'll wait for your call. I'm sorry that it ended like this. If you want your cash back, no problem. I haven't spent much. If not, I'm here.' We made our farewells and hung up.

So that was that. For then at least.

13

When I touched down at the office, there were three messages on the answerphone from Chas, each more urgent than the last. I phoned him right back.

'I've been trying to get you all morning. Your phone at home is always engaged. What the hell are you up to?' he yelled when I got through to his extension at work and identified myself.

'Nothing,' I replied.

'Nothing. *Nothing!* You promised me the hot poop, as you put it, if anything broke. Next thing I know your face is all over the national press. Ears! *Ears*, for Chrissake, are being sent through the post. And what do I get from you? Sweet FA.'

'Calm down, Chas,' I said. 'It was as big a surprise to me as it was to you. And by the way, it was just one ear.'

'Oh, yeah?'

'Yeah. I was there when Peter Day opened the package.'

'Were you?'

'I was.'

'So tell me.'

So I did. Maybe I shouldn't have, but there you go. I gave him nothing that the other papers hadn't already got. Just a bit of eye witness stuff.

'Listen,' I said when I'd finished, 'don't for fuck's

sake quote me on this. An unnamed source is good enough. I might still be working for these people and they're good payers. Don't screw me. I probably shouldn't be talking to you at all.'

'OK, Nick,' he said. 'But who's this John geezer? Sector 88 or what?'

'No,' I said. 'Nothing to do with them, I'm sure of that. Just a freelance. Someone who's got it in for Day personally. He didn't take John seriously the other night when he said he liked to kill people. He more or less forced Day to tell him to prove it. Then he did.'

'So you reckon there's two lots of people sending stuff through the post?'

'Yes.'

'Amazing. This bloke Day must have something to rub so many people up the wrong way. Can I get to meet him?'

'Dunno.'

'I hear he's been kicked off the air.'

'You hear right.'

'Are you going to see him?'

'I don't know. Like I say, I don't know where I stand at the moment.'

'It's a bastard,' said Chas. 'I can't get through to him, see. I've got his number, but when it isn't engaged, he's got the answerphone on, and he's not returning my calls. If you *do* get to see him, tell him to get in touch. I'm a sympathetic kind of guy. Tell him I won't stitch him up.'

'If I speak to him, I'll pass on the message.'

'Do that, Nick. By the way, are we still going to this meeting on Sunday?'

'I don't see why not.'

'You haven't told anyone about it?'

'No. Well, only Peter Day.'

'Good. We don't want Fleet Street down there *en masse*. This is a local thing, and it should be dealt with locally.'

'And sympathetically,' I said.

'Of course.'

'And if you happen to get a job on the *News Of The World* because of it, that's no more than you deserve. Right?'

'But of course. Look, I've got to fly. I've got an appointment with a word processor. We're going to press soon and I've got to finish my story. Thanks for your help, Nick, I owe you one. I'll see you Sunday night in the pub, right?'

'I'll be there.'

'And if anything happens meanwhile – *anything* – call me here or at home.'

'I will.'

'And tell Day I want to talk to him.'

'I *will*.'

'I know, mate. Sunday then. And take it easy.'

I agreed that I would, and we both hung up. And that was more or less me for the rest of the day.

14

The next morning, Friday, the story was still running
but had been relegated to page three of the *Sun*
next to the topless model. Superb placement, I
thought. Real class. They had christened John 'The
Midnight Crawler'. I was sure he liked that, whoever
and wherever he was. All the papers I read reported
that Peter Day had been suspended from Sunset.

I bought the local paper as well as the nationals.
The story was front page there with a vengeance,
and on the centre spread too. Chas got the by-line
on the two-page feature. He used some of my quotes
but kept my name out of it, at least as far as naming
me as a source. However, the wire service photo of
me and Day leaving the station was much in evidence, and the story speculated on my involvement
and gave a little sidebar biography on my career
to date which didn't make for particularly inspired
reading. But then, it could have been worse, I
suppose.

As I looked through the rest of the paper in my
office that morning, I saw that, true to his word,
Chas had got the story of Sheila Cochran's missing
dog into print, complete with a fetching photo of
Sheila, and one of Prince too.

As I was reading the piece, the phone rang. By
coincidence it was Sheila Cochran herself.

'I'm just reading about you,' I said.

'I know. That's one of the reasons I'm phoning. I'm so grateful to you.'

'Don't be,' I said. 'I haven't done much for your money.'

'You've done a lot. Chas was so nice. We went out for a drink.'

'*Did you?* That's good. He's all right, is Chas.'

I could almost see her blush over the phone. 'I know,' she said. 'The other reason I'm phoning . . .'

'Yes?' I said.

'That is you, isn't it? In the photos with that disc jockey?'

'Yes,' I said.

'That was a terrible thing. That poor girl. Do they know who she was?'

'Not as far as I know.'

'How did you get involved?'

'I'm working, or I was working, I'm not quite sure which, for Sunset. An enquiry job. I was there when Peter Day got the parcel.'

'That's terrible.'

'It wasn't too clever.'

'I'm sorry. I don't mean to pry. It's none of my business.'

'That's all right.'

'It makes what I'm asking you to do look pretty unimportant.'

'Not at all,' I said. 'I'm still looking for Prince.'

'Will you have time?'

'All the time in the world, as from now.'

'I *am* grateful. I mean it.'

'I appreciate that,' I said. 'Not all of my clients are so forthcoming.'

'Well, I'll let you go then,' she said. 'I'm sure you've got things to do.'

'If I hear anything, I'll be in touch,' I replied, and

with that we said goodbye and both hung up.

I felt lousy and went for a drink, then home.

Early that afternoon Peter Day rang.

'What's up?' I said.

'I've had a call.'

'What kind of call?'

'From Charlie Harper.'

'And?'

'They want me down at Sunset.'

'Why?'

'He wouldn't say, but I didn't like the way he asked. Will you come with me? It may be nothing but . . .'

'Sure I'll come,' I said. 'I'm just vegetating here. I'll pick you up if you like.'

'That would be good. He said I'd have to run the gauntlet.' He gave me his address, and I went and collected him.

Run the gauntlet was right. There were twenty or more reporters and news teams waiting in the street outside the radio station when we arrived. We had our pictures taken again and did the usual 'No comment' to the questions that were thrown at us. There were two coppers on the main door, and they wheeled us straight in. There was a security man I'd never seen, and a uniformed police constable on the reception desk. The policeman phoned through, and a minute later Harper appeared at the door through to the back. He looked pale and serious. He gave me a dirty look, but that was all.

'Come on up,' he said, like he owned the place. We followed him through and up to Tony Hillerman's office which now seemed to be part of the police station. Where Hillerman was I had no idea. Harper sat behind the desk. 'There's been another,' he said.

'What?' said Day.

'Another parcel for you.'

'In the post?'

'No. Delivered by messenger here, three hours ago. But we can't trace the messenger service. We think John himself delivered it.'

'Christ!' said Day. 'What was in it?'

'Someone's finger.'

'Oh, Jesus. The same woman?'

'No.'

'You're sure.'

'As sure as we can be. This one belongs to a black woman.'

'Christ, where is it?' said Day, looking nervously round the room as if it might be lying on a blotter somewhere waiting to bite him.

'At the lab. There was a note with it.'

'What did it say?'

'I've got a copy. The original's being tested to see if we can get anything out of it.' Harper passed Day a sheet of paper. I looked over his shoulder. The note was neatly typed again. It read:

IF HE'S NOT BACK ON TONIGHT THERE WILL BE MORE
MEAT

'Pleasant,' I said, speaking for the first time.

'You feel like going back on the air?' Harper asked Day.

'Not really.'

'But will you?'

'Sure. If I must.'

'Good. It's been OK'd with your bosses. They're not happy, but . . .' He didn't finish the sentence.

'I bet they're not,' said Day.

'The only caller we'll let through is John, if we can be sure it's him.'

'What do you mean?' Day asked.

'There've been over twenty "Johns" phoning through already today. They're loving it out there.' He gestured towards the window. 'Fucking nutters, every one of them. But we have to check. Just imagine how many we'll get tonight when they realise you're back on the air.'

'Stretch'll know. If anyone can recognise the voice, it'll be him. He'll be working the switchboard, won't he?'

'I was going to put one of my men on,' said Harper.

'Don't,' said Day. 'Use Stretch. He knows what he's doing.'

Harper concurred, but he wasn't happy.

'Who took the parcel in?' I asked.

Harper looked slitty-eyed at me. 'One of the constables on the door.'

'So you had John and let him go?'

'Maybe,' said Harper.

'Did you get a description?'

'Crash helmet and leathers.'

'That narrows it down.'

Harper looked from me to Day and back again. 'Does he always have to be here?' he asked.

'Yes,' said Day emphatically.

With that we left it and went and found Hillerman. He was even more pissed off than when he'd been dragged out in the middle of the night. He'd not only lost his office, he'd lost control of the station. He was sitting in one of the small rooms off the production office. He dismissed Sophia when we went in. She smiled at us as she went out.

'Close the door behind you,' Hillerman said to her as she left. She did as she was told, but rather harder than was really necessary. 'You've heard?' he asked.

We both nodded.

'You're back on air tonight,' he said to Day. 'And don't go getting any inflated ideas of your own importance, Peter. They'll catch this bloke in a couple of days and all this will be forgotten.'

'I won't,' said Day.

'Right. Usual time tonight, and don't talk to the press. Come in the back door. We've got extra security on as from now. Go out that way too. And, Nick . . .'

'Yes?' I said.

'I want you to be here with Peter. You are still employed by us. I want you to look after him. Is that all right with you, Pete?' he said, as if I didn't matter at all.

'Suits me fine,' Day said. 'I was going to ask him to come with me anyway. You don't mind do you?' he said to me.

'It'll be my pleasure.'

'Thanks.'

We went out the back way as Hillerman had said. Since Thursday it had been cordoned off, and two more uniformed policemen were on duty. We ploughed through the waiting reporters back to my car. I took Day home and arranged to collect him later.

So that hadn't been that after all.

15

I arrived at Peter Day's flat at ten-thirty, as arranged. The street outside was deserted. No journalists doorstepping. Which simply meant they hadn't got his address yet. If this thing carried on, they would.

His flat was on the top floor of a three-storey purpose-built block. Very nice it was too. Obviously Sunset Radio paid their staff well. I rang through on the entryphone. Day's voice sounded strangled when he answered, as voices always do on those contraptions. I identified myself and he buzzed me through the front door. I took the tiny lift up to the third floor.

Day was standing at the door to his flat when I arrived. 'Come on in,' he said. He looked old, and very tired.

He stepped back to allow me entry, and I went into the warm interior of the flat, down the tiny hall in the direction of the sound from a television set. It was in the living room. The local news was on. The picture on the screen was of the front of Sunset's building. It was a very attractive room. Made even more so by the fact that Tony Hillerman's secretary Sophia was sitting on a sofa upholstered in dark blue material. She was upholstered in dark blue also. Which made it a perfect match.

I stopped in the doorway. 'Good evening,' I said. 'Hello, Nick.'

I walked further into the room and Day came in after me. 'I hope I'm not disturbing anything,' I said. Tact, see, I could give lessons.

Sophia looked at Day, and he looked back at her, and they both smiled. 'No, Nick,' said Day. 'We're old friends, Sophia just came round to check that I'd eaten today.'

'Sorry,' I said. 'No offence.'

'None taken,' said Day. 'I'm flattered.'

'And have you?' I asked.

'What?'

'Eaten.'

'A pizza.'

'You really should look after yourself better, Peter,' said Sophia, and got up from the sofa and went over to him. I could see why he had been flattered. She stood at least a head taller than he, and the healthy look of her contrasted with the pallor of his skin.

'Are we going?' I asked.

'Yes,' said Sophia. 'And I'm coming too.'

'Have you got a car?' I asked.

'Yes.'

'Shall we go in yours?' I said. 'Mine's a bit obvious, and a little on the cramped side.'

'Certainly,' said Sophia.

'You are going to stay until the end of the broadcast?' asked Day.

'Of course,' she said. 'I wouldn't leave you without a lift home.'

'That wasn't what I meant,' he replied.

'I know, Peter,' she said, and touched his arm solicitously.

I waited whilst they put on their coats and we

went back down to the street. Day left the TV and the lights on. Just for some sign of life when he got back home alone. I know that feeling. Sophia's car turned out to be an anonymous maroon Rover, which was fine.

She drove us over to Sunset and we arrived just before eleven. We went in the back way. Two coppers were keeping it clear. Inside the place was crawling with more policemen. They'd pretty well taken over the production office. There were a lot of station staff about too, according to Day. They obviously knew they were in on something, something big, and they didn't want to miss a moment of it. I could see they didn't know how to treat Day. To be honest, I didn't know how to treat him myself.

He returned their greetings and a uniformed copper asked him to go straight upstairs to Tony Hillerman's office. Day asked me to go with him. Sophia told us she'd be in her new office if she was needed.

When we got upstairs Charlie Harper had company. There was an older man with him, sitting behind Hillerman's desk. Harper had been relegated to the secretary's chair. He introduced the older man as Chief Inspector Lambert. He was a sour-faced individual with receding grey hair cut very short, wearing a grey suit, white shirt and regimental tie. He didn't look happy to see us, particularly me, or in fact to be sitting where he was sitting. He didn't make any attempt to shake hands.

'I've been put in charge of the case,' he said without preamble. 'And I'm very unhappy about the way things are going.'

'Why?' I asked, I thought somebody had to, and looked at Harper who said nothing, just looked exaggeratedly at the ceiling.

Lambert ignored me. 'I don't like you talking to this lunatic,' he said to Day.

So that was the way it was going to be.

'Nor do I particularly,' said Day. 'But what else can I do? You know what happened when he read that the show was being taken off.'

'I know,' said Lambert.

'If I'm not on tonight to talk to him, he'll do it again.'

'You seem very sure,' said Lambert.

'That's because he's crazy.'

Lambert looked at Harper who said, 'I think he's right.'

'It wasn't my idea that some bloody lunatic should latch on to me,' said Day.

'The kind of show you do, it was only a matter of time before something like this happened,' said Lambert.

'Bollocks!' retorted Day. 'I do a show. That's all there is to it. OK, so I insult people and cut them off, and maybe I do ask for the loonies out there to call in, but I never encouraged this one. Christ, what do you think I am? He's the one who's breaking the law, not me. I'm just trying to help.'

'He's right,' said Harper. 'This John character is stark raving mad. Peter is our only link to him. Lose that, and God knows what he might do.'

Lambert looked disgusted. He sat still for a moment, thinking. 'OK,' he said eventually. 'Do it.'

'I'll talk to you in a minute,' Harper said to Day. We took that as a dismissal, and left the office.

Outside, I said, 'The new boss doesn't think much of me, that's obvious.'

'Ignore him,' said Day. 'You're working for us, and right now they need us more than we need them.'

I wasn't entirely sure of that, but declined to say so. 'Thanks, Peter,' I said, and we went downstairs for coffee. There was a pile of opened letters and parcels in Day's pigeon hole. He didn't look inside them. He didn't even touch them.

There was so much traffic in the production office that another coffee machine had been installed. I helped myself to a cup. It tasted just as bad as the coffee from the old one. I looked at the clock. It was 11.15. I sat at a vacant desk to drink my coffee, and Day sat opposite. We didn't speak. Before I'd finished my cup, Harper came in and pulled up a chair. 'Sorry about that,' he said. 'New broom and all. Lambert's not too bad. He just needs to put the stamp of his authority on the squad. And he doesn't approve of you being here,' he said to me.

'He made that pretty clear,' I said. 'But I've got a broad back. Did you find anything out about the girl?'

'Girl?'

'The finger.'

'Sorry. Yes. A black girl. But I already told you that. The same age as the last one. About five foot to five foot four. Blood group O. No record of the one fingerprint he left us. Healthy. The finger was chopped with a heavy sharp instrument, like a butcher's cleaver.'

'In other words, she was alive when he chopped it off?'

He nodded. 'But like the other one, the shock could have killed her. There was certainly no trace of anaesthetic in her blood or the first one's.'

'That's sick,' I said.

'It could get worse.'

I looked over at Peter Day. His colour had

worsened and he held his stomach. 'Are you all right?' I asked.

'I'll survive,' he replied. His voice sounded distant.

'You look terrible,' said Harper.

'Thanks for the compliment.'

'You know what I mean. Look, if you can't go through with this . . .'

'Yes, I can,' Day interrupted. 'I have to.'

'Only if you're sure,' said Harper.

'I am.' Day sat back and breathed deeply. 'I need a cigarette,' he said. 'Have you got one, Nick?'

I nodded.

'Come on then.' He looked at Harper. 'If you need us, we'll be on the roof.'

He said nothing in reply, and Day and I got up, left the office, and went upstairs. We said a quick hello to Stretch who was hanging about in the corridor again. He made no comment about how Day looked, just asked: 'You cool?'

'Chilled,' Day replied.

Stretch smiled. 'You need to be. There's been a whole bunch of Johns called up already. They're coming out of the woodwork. They can't wait for the show to start.'

'Recognise anyone?' I asked.

'No, man. He's not called yet.'

'He will,' said Day.

'You're sure,' I said.

'Very.'

'How?'

'I just am. Don't ask me how. I expect he'll call when the first record's on. Right now I need a cigarette. I'll catch you in a minute, Stretch, my friend.'

'What are we going to play him?' Stretch seemed to have the right idea. Treat things as normal. As normal as possible.

'Sam Cooke,' Day said. 'Something sweet. *A Change Is Gonna Come*. Got it handy?'

'Sure. I'll dig it out for you. We just going to play music again tonight?'

'Yes. Apart from his call.'

'I thought so. I've got some stuff together.'

'Thanks, Stretch,' said Day. 'I appreciate it.'

'It's my job, man.'

We left him and went out on to the roof. Day went over to one corner and threw up. 'Are you OK?' I asked.

'I'll be fine,' he replied. 'Got that ciggie?'

I took out the packet, opened it, and handed him one. I took one for myself, and lit both of them. We smoked in silence, and then as time was getting on we went back downstairs.

Tony Hillerman, Charlie Harper and Chief Inspector Lambert were all waiting for us in the corridor. Hillerman was looking happier than he had for days. He grabbed Day by the arm and took him out of earshot of the rest of us. He pulled him close and whispered into his ear for a moment. Then they parted, and Day came back. We went into the studio.

'What was all that about?' I asked.

'Christ knows. He thanked me for coming back, as if it wasn't him and his cronies who took me off air in the first place. Suddenly my show's hot. The advertisers are queueing up to get slots on it. He tells me that he's sure the ratings will go through the roof if this carries on. Disgusting, isn't it?'

I was about to agree when the two policemen came into the studio. 'We're going to sit in with you,' said Lambert. 'We've got engineers plugged into the phone lines. If he rings, try and keep him talking so that they can trace the call.'

Day nodded. 'Is there anything in particular you want me to say?'

'Busk it,' said Harper. 'There's nothing much you can say that'll reach someone as far gone as this one. Try and get him to open up about himself. Maybe get some clues as to his location or anything about himself. With a bit of luck he might give something away. Keep him talking as long as possible. If we can't trace the call, something might come across in the background. A clock striking, or a plane going over, or a train going by. Anything that might help pinpoint his location. Otherwise try and appeal to him to give himself up. Tell him he needs help or something. It's all up to you, Peter. Just go with the flow.'

Stretch stuck his head through the door. 'Pete,' he said. 'Show time.'

'Sit down and be quiet,' Day said to us, his spirits suddenly revived by the thought of returning to the airwaves. The three of us did as we were told.

I sat in the guest's chair and put on a spare pair of headphones. I could hear Tim doing the weather from his studio. After he was finished, he introduced the show. Stretch counted down from five and Peter was off.

'Good evening, London,' he said. 'Peter Day back again with *Day at Night*, after a short break. A different kind of show again, I warn you. Mostly music, with just one call. I expect you've been reading about what's been going on down here. If you haven't then get a paper in the morning and you'll find out. Here at Sunset we seem to have been chosen as the outlet for one man's madness. It wasn't our choice, but we're stuck with it. Somewhere out there is someone with a grudge against the world, and he's chosen this station and this show to vent it. I won't go into details, and I won't make any further judgements, as I believe they may make matters worse. What I will do is play a record, and at the end of it I believe he may speak to us. I hope I'm wrong but I don't think so. Anyway, I've chosen a song that echoes the way a lot of us feel right now.'

Day pointed through to Stretch, who pressed the button on one of the CD players beside him, and Sam Cooke started singing. I slipped the headphones off my ears.

'Was that OK?' Day asked no one in particular as he did the same.

'I don't know,' said Lambert. 'I hope the crack about madness doesn't start him off.'

'You did fine,' said Harper reassuringly.

Through the glass I could see Stretch on the phone. He was shaking his head and cutting off callers one by one. Just before the song came to an end, he turned and tapped up something on the keyboard beside him. 'It's him,' Day said, and pulled the headphones up again. He turned up my mike. As the song ended he said, 'Now we go to the phone. Hello, John.'

I didn't want to listen, but I knew I'd have to, so I put the cans against my ears.

'Call me The Midnight Crawler,' the caller whispered in his unmistakable voice.

'John's shorter,' said Day.

'All right, Peter, you can call me John. Nice tune. I remember it. And, Peter?'

'What?'

'I'm not as mad as you think.'

'Aren't you?'

'Are the police tracing this call?'

Day looked over at Lambert. He shrugged.

'What do you think, John?' Day asked.

'I think they are. Ask them how mad I am when they can't catch me.'

'I'll do that, John,' said Day.

'I know you must have got my message today because you're doing the show.'

'I got it.'

'Did you like it?'

'No, John, you know I didn't.'

'I'm sorry,' he said. 'I'll try and do better next time.'

'I hope there isn't a next time, John.'

'There will be, Peter. Count on it.'

'Why me?' Day asked.

'What?'

'Why pick on me to talk to. To tell.'

'Because you're on the radio. You're important.'

I thought Day was going to laugh at that. 'No, John, I'm not.'

'You are to me.'

'Do you live round here, John?' Day changed tack.

If he was hoping to throw John, he was disappointed. 'I live everywhere,' he replied.

'I think you do, John. I think you're a local boy.'

That narrowed the field down to men who lived within the radius of the station's signal. How many? A million, two, more? Who knew?

'There are other stations that broadcast in the area, John. Bigger stations,' Day said. 'Why didn't you call them?'

'I like the music you play.'

'That's very flattering, John.'

'Play me another tune.'

'What?'

'Play me another tune now, Peter. If you don't,

108

you know what I'll do. And I'll be listening.' With that, the line went dead.

'OK, John,' Day said to empty air, and made a signal to Stretch who pressed the 'Play' button on his second CD player. The sound of Fats Domino singing *Blue Monday* filled the phones. Day pulled down the live mike fader, took off the headphones and tossed them on to the console. 'OK?' he asked.

'Well done,' said Charlie Harper. 'You've got him hooked.'

'And he's got me,' Day said.

'It works like that. Don't worry. We'll get *him* soon.'

'I hope so,' said Day. 'I really do.' But he didn't sound optimistic.

Lambert jumped up and left the room.

'Do you think the trace worked?' I asked.

'I don't know. I'll find out,' Harper said, and left too.

Day spoke to Stretch on the intercom. They did the show off the cuff again. I think it was more of a strain than Day liked to admit. I stayed with him and Sophia joined us too. At one o'clock when the news was on we went out and found Charlie Harper. The police hadn't been able to trace the call. 'He used a public telephone. When our blokes got there, he was gone. He could be anywhere.'

'Jesus!' I said. 'How long is this going to go on for?'

'Until it stops,' said Harper. 'That's all I can tell you.'

16

Sophia drove us back to Peter Day's flat. She stopped the car outside and kept the engine running as we got out.

'Are you coming in?' Day asked her.

'No,' she replied. 'I need my beauty sleep.'

'You, Nick?' he said.

'For a bit,' I said. I knew how he felt.

'Are you sure?' he said to Sophia.

She nodded. I knew how she felt too. The whole thing was getting too weird.

'OK,' he said. 'Thanks for coming by. And the ride.' And he walked off towards the entrance to the flats.

I looked at Sophia. She looked at me. 'Do you think I should . . . ?' she asked.

'It's all right,' I said. 'I'll look after him.'

'It's just that . . .' She didn't finish.

'I know,' I said.

'You're sure he'll be all right?'

'Course he will. Listen, I realise that it's probably totally the wrong time and place, but are you doing anything tomorrow night? Tonight? Saturday night?'

'What would you say if I said that I was seeing my boyfriend?'

I shrugged. 'Then I'd say that you were seeing your boyfriend.'

'And if I said I was seeing my husband?'

'You're not wearing a wedding ring.'

'Fiancé, then.'

'You're still not wearing a ring. So are you?'

'What?'

'Seeing whoever?'

'No,' she said.

'How about a drink? Dinner?'

She hesitated, then smiled. 'All right. Why not?'

'Why not indeed? Where do you live?'

'Clapham.'

'I know a good restaurant round there. What's your address? I'll call for you.'

She told me. I thought I knew the street. If I didn't, what is the *A-Z* for?

'Seven?' I said.

'Fine,' she replied, and put the car into gear.

I watched as she drove off in a cloud of exhaust smoke, then I followed Peter into his block. He was waiting by the door. 'Come on up for a drink,' he said.

'Sure.'

We went up in the lift and into his flat. There was an old film on the TV. French, complete with subtitles. He poured out two large scotches, we sat in front of the box, and he turned the sound down. I watched as two heavy-looking geezers flapped their lips nineteen to the dozen, and, according to the print at the bottom of the screen, said just, 'Let's go.' I hate subtitles. I always feel I'm missing something.

'What do you think?' Day asked, interrupting my thoughts. At first I thought he was talking about the film. Then I realised he meant John. I was getting tired. Too many late nights.

'I think that this one could run and run,' I said.

'There's a lunatic out there determined to make his mark.'

'He's succeeding,' said Day.

I nodded agreement, and a fresh wave of exhaustion rolled over me like a black tide. I swallowed my scotch and said, 'Peter, I've got to go. I need my bed.'

'Have another drink.'

I shook my head. 'No,' I said. 'Listen, keep in touch over the weekend. I'll be about if you need me.'

I knew he needed me then, but I couldn't handle it. I made my farewells and left. I went downstairs, got in the Jag and drove home.

The telephone was ringing when I let myself into the flat. The bell had the tired sound of one that had long ago given up any idea of being answered.

I lifted up the receiver and said, 'Hello.'

'Nick, at last.' It was Chas. 'I've been trying to get you for hours. What's been happening?'

'There's been another one,' I said. 'But then you know that, don't you?'

'Sure I do. Tell me what happened.'

'Am I your sole source of information?'

'No. But you seem to have the knack of always being around when these things arrive.'

I told him that I hadn't been. He asked me a slew of questions, and I answered them to the best of my ability although I didn't know if Lambert and Harper would approve, but by then I was too tired to care.

When I'd finished my story, Chas said, 'Thanks, mate. I do appreciate this. I owe you several.'

'I know you do,' I replied. 'Now I've got to get some sleep, I'm knackered. I'll see you Sunday.'

'No problem,' he replied, and hung up.

I dropped the phone on to its cradle and undressed. I was unconscious as soon as I hit the sheets.

The phone woke me at just past seven. I'd been asleep maybe three hours. I fumbled the instrument into bed with me. 'What?' I said.

'Mr Sharman? Nick?'

'Yeah?'

'I'm so sorry to disturb you this early. It's Sheila Cochran here.'

I was suddenly awake. 'Yeah? Hello, Sheila. What's up?'

'Someone threw a couple of bricks through my windows this morning.'

'Do what?'

She repeated the statement.

'When?' I asked.

'About four this morning.'

'Have you phoned the police?'

'Yes. They just left. It took them two hours to get here.'

'Not bad,' I said.

'Listen, I know it's not your concern but . . .'

'Give me twenty minutes and I'll be there,' I said. I hung up, got up, dressed, ran my fingers through my hair, grabbed my address book and keys and left the flat. I was at her door in just over fifteen. The two front windows of her house were smashed. She was watching out for me through one and opened the door straight away.

'Nice mess,' I said. 'Have you got a cup of tea?'

'Of course,' she replied, and went into the kitchen. I looked at the damage, and the two half bricks that she'd saved for souvenirs.

I followed her into the kitchen. 'Eddie?' I said as

she poured me a mug of strong tea.

'Could be,' she said.

'Almost definitely. I'm sorry I stirred up a hornet's nest.'

'It wasn't your fault.'

'Have you been in touch with a glazier?'

'I don't know any.'

'I do,' I said and tapped my book. 'Use your phone?'

I took my tea to the telephone and called up someone I knew in the window business. The phone rang and rang, and I sipped at the cup that cheers. Eventually someone answered.

'Twenty-four hour glazing service,' said a voice I recognised.

'Not got you up, I hope, Monty?' I said.

'Who's this?'

'Nick Sharman.'

'Christ, but it's been a long time. What do you want?'

'Some glass fixing. A friend of mine had the vandals in.'

'What kind of glass?'

'Ordinary glass. House glass. I don't know.'

'Well, Nick, it's bit difficult . . .'

'Monty, your card says twenty-four hours a day service. When you answer the phone you say twenty-four hour glazing service. Now don't force me to go to the office of fair trading. Just get yourself over here.'

'I'm a bit short staffed.'

'Too short to do an old friend a favour?'

'Where are you?'

'Herne Hill. Just round the corner.'

'All right, Nick. As it's you, I'll come myself.'

'You're a diamond, Monty. And keep it cheap.'

'What do you want, blood?'

'No. Just a good job.' I gave him Sheila's address and hung up.

'He'll be here soon,' I said to her when I went back into the kitchen. 'Tell me what happened.'

She explained that she'd been woken at about four by a terrible noise, then another. She went downstairs and found the broken windows. There was no sign of anyone about. A couple of neighbours roused themselves and checked the street. She called the police and waited for them to arrive, which they did about two hours later. She told me that they didn't seem too interested in anything except a sit in the warm with a cuppa. When they left she called me. End of story.

'This is my fault,' I said.

'No, it's not.'

'Yes,' I disagreed. 'It's too much of a coincidence. I jumped on your husband with both my big feet, and a few days later – this. I'm sorry.'

'Don't blame yourself. It wasn't necessarily Eddie who did it.'

'Who else?'

'I was in the papers yesterday. Maybe it had something to do with that.'

'Maybe it did, but I doubt it,' I said. 'Did you tell the police about him?'

'I mentioned that we were recently separated.'

'Did you tell them where he lived?'

She shook her head. 'Do you think they'll do anything?'

'What, about Eddie or generally?'

'Both,' she said.

'No,' I said. 'Not if you won't push it. They'll put in a report, and that will be that.'

'So?' she asked.

'So, when Monty's been, and I make sure he's not going to charge you enough to rebuild the Crystal Palace, I'll take a wander round to Eddie's myself.'

'Do you think that's a good idea?'

'I don't know. But if I find him, and have a word, it might dissuade him from doing it again.'

'Don't get into trouble on my account.'

'I won't,' I assured her, and there was a ring on the doorbell.

Monty was outside with his son in tow and a Transit van full of glass and tools. He shook my hand, and then his head sorrowfully at the damage, and after the pair of them had been fortified with tea, too, they got down to measuring up for windows.

I persuaded Monty to give Sheila a good discount, wished them all a good morning and drove over to Kennington.

I parked the car on the outskirts of the estate again and walked to the block where Cochran had his flat. The place was a bit busier than on my last visit, but no one paid me any attention as I walked into the murky hole of the entrance hall. The lift still wasn't working, and I took to the stairs once more. I didn't meet anyone on the climb, but some of the shit on the landings was fresh.

I rapped on the metal door of the flat at just before nine-thirty. There was no answer. I hammered again, much harder, but still got no reply. I thought there was no point in hanging round so went back downstairs and drove home. What's another wasted journey in a life so full of them? I'd catch up with him eventually.

I was back in Tulse Hill just after ten, and the phone was ringing as I let myself in through my front door.

17

It was Peter Day. 'Did I wake you?' he asked.

'No chance of that,' I replied. 'I've been out on a couple of house calls already this morning.

'To do with . . . ?'

'No. Another matter. So what can I do for you?'

'The police want to see me.'

'Not another?' I said.

'No. Nothing like that.'

'Thank Christ. What then?'

'Harper reckons I might know more about John than I think.'

'Like?'

'Like, I might know him.'

'You might at that.'

'I know a lot of people.'

'Exactly. I don't think anyone's suggesting you're bosom pals. But he picked on you for some reason.'

'That's exactly what Harper said.'

'Copper mentality.'

'I told him I'd only come down if you could come too.'

'I bet he liked that.'

'He wasn't bothered.'

'Then I assume Lambert won't be there.'

'I don't think so. I told him I didn't want to go to the police station. He agreed. We're meeting in a pub, and he's bringing someone else with him. So will you come?'

'When?'

'This lunchtime. The Horns Tavern in Clapham Road. The saloon bar at one.'

'OK,' I said.

'Thanks.'

'See you there.'

'Right,' he said. 'Bye.'

I sat around the house until it was time to leave, and drank coffee and smoked a few cigarettes. I was at the pub dead on time but Peter Day had beaten me to it. He had the remains of a pint in front of him on a table in a quiet corner of the bar. I went over and joined him.

'Want another?' I asked.

'Lager,' he replied, and I went to the bar.

It was a good pub for a meet, The Horns. Not too busy, no jukebox or pub games, just soft jazz on a discreet sound system. Harper was punctual too. He came in before the barman had finished serving me. He was with another bloke. Younger, dressed in a smart suit and a clean shirt. The other bloke's hair was slicked back like someone who worked in an ad agency. In fact he looked like that kind of geezer altogether, not like a copper at all although I assumed he was. I asked what they wanted to drink. Harper asked for a beer. The other one, whom Harper introduced as Detective Constable Jim Prescott, had an orange juice with ice. I paid for the drinks and we carried them over to the table. I lit a cigarette. Day had one too. Both coppers refused. Charlie Harper got straight into it.

'Jim here has a degree in behavioural psychology,' he said. 'He's one of the brave new breed of coppers you might have been reading about. He'll be my guv'nor within a couple of years.'

Prescott looked modest but didn't argue.

'He's been building up a profile on our man,' Harper went on. 'You know him best, Peter. I thought you might be able to add something. And you've been there from the start too, Sharman. You might have some input on this.' So Day was Peter and I was Sharman. That's the way it was to go.

'Fair enough,' I said. 'As long as I'm not treading on any corns. Lambert's, for instance.'

'You just leave him to me,' said Harper.

'You know everything I know,' said Day. He was beginning to look sick again.

Harper looked at him. 'Maybe. Maybe not. Listen to what Jim's got to say.'

Jim Prescott cleared his throat. 'On the surface, not much,' he said. 'But every time he sends in a piece of body or speaks to Mr Day here, he gives away more clues about himself.'

'For instance?' I asked.

'For instance that he exists,' said Jim Prescott, and appeared serious. I looked at Harper. He didn't budge. Prescott held up his hands. 'Don't laugh,' he said. 'If he hadn't phoned the programme, we wouldn't have any idea what he was doing. Right?'

I had to agree with that, so I nodded.

'Second, he's male,' Prescott continued. 'With an ego. He thinks that he's smarter than us.'

I couldn't disagree with that either. Perhaps Jim Prescott could have something.

He took a notebook from the inside pocket of his suit jacket, opened it and went on, 'We've listened carefully to the tapes of the calls he's made to the radio station. There's nothing in the background. Yet. But there's still time. If he keeps calling you we'll get something, I'm sure. But he has told us how old he is.'

'Yes?' I said. 'When?'

'Last night. If not exactly how old, at least he's given us an idea. Mr Day played a record by Sam Cooke.'

I nodded.

'*A Change is Gonna Come*, to be precise.'

I nodded again.

'He said that he remembered it. Not knew it, remembered it. I looked it up. The song was released in nineteen sixty-five, as a B-side to a record called *Shake*.' This time it was Peter Day's turn to nod his head. 'It wasn't a big hit,' said Prescott who seemed happy to have our undivided attention. 'Didn't make the top forty, in fact. So it would be logical to think that he was listening to a lot of music around then. Obscure music. Or fairly obscure. I've assumed that he was about twenty at the time, so it's safe to assume he's in his mid to late forties now. And there was his comment about Kim Novak. Being in love with her when he was a kid. She was around in the fifties. In fact, that film came out in fifty-six. About the time you'd expect someone in their forties to have had an early adolescent crush on a film star. You see what I mean?'

I did.

He went on, 'And that fits the pattern of serial killers in the States where most research has been done – mainly because they have more than we do. Plus it's roughly Mr Day's age. Not that I mean to be personal. You see, it's safe to assume again that if he wanted to tell someone what he was up to, he'd choose someone of his own ethnic type and age. So we assume he's white. Also he's up and about late in the day. We know that because he listens to the show on a regular basis. He told us that the first time he called.

'He's probably a loner who lives alone. Not in a block of flats or shared dwelling, if he's doing the killing at home. If he does live in plain sight of a load of neighbours he must have access to somewhere to do the killings. But I favour the fact that he lives alone in a house. I don't know why, I just do. Once again it fits the sort of pattern we know about. He lives locally, at least within the usual range of the station – even though he was loath to admit it last night. He calls himself John from Stockwell, so we can safely assume his name isn't John and he doesn't come from there. Unless, of course, he's doing a clever double bluff, but I doubt it. He knew what he wanted to say the first time he called you. The way he said it, he was waiting for you not to believe him. It was almost as if he was lying in wait for you.'

'Very good,' I said, but when I looked over at Day he didn't look very happy about it. But then, who would be? 'Anything else?' I said.

'Sure,' said Prescott. 'He used a butcher's cleaver or similar on his second victim. Now that I like.' He was really getting into it, and didn't even realise what he was saying. 'A butcher with a van would be perfect. Bloodstains on the vehicle and his clothing easily explained. Trouble is, it's *too* neat. Still, we'll go some way down that road before we give up on the theory.'

'A restaurant worker?' I said. 'Late nights. A butcher's knife. Bloodstains.'

'Very good, Mr Sharman,' said Prescott. At least I was 'Mr' to him. 'I like that. I like that a lot.' He made a note in his book. 'Now as for the victims . . . No ID on either so far, but a lot of people go missing in London every day. By the way he talked, I'd guess they were prostitutes. The way he said "out in the world" and the reference to meat in the

second letter. It all fits. And the meat bit combines
prostitutes and butchery in one. Not that I'd stake
my life on it.' He laughed at his own pun, then
reddened, cleared his throat and continued. 'Now
if we concentrate on south London, we're talking
Waterloo, Brixton, Streatham, Bedford Hill,
Balham, Croydon, Clapham Common. Lots of
places where a great many young women could go
missing before anyone suspected or cared what was
happening. Also, you've seen him, Mr Day.'

He looked up, surprised. Prescott saw the look.
'I don't say that you know him, although it's quite
possible that you have spoken. It's just that he's
watched you and I bet you've seen him too. Maybe
just in passing, but you've seen him nevertheless,
I'd put money on it. So you see, he's beginning to
take shape. Every time he calls you in future you
must try and get him to tell you more about himself.'

'Like what?' Day asked.

'Like anything,' Prescott replied.

'Well, I must say, I'm impressed so far,' I said.
Prescott smiled.

'But aren't you assuming an awful lot?'

'That's the nature of my job. But you'd be amazed
how many people fit themselves into patterns they
don't even know exist.'

I wasn't. I knew how easy it was to fall into a
routine.

'What happens if he's purposefully trying to lead
you astray?' I asked.

'It happens,' said Prescott. 'We just go down the
road until we come to a dead end. It takes patience,
but I've got plenty of that.'

'And what happens if he just stops calling?'

'He won't,' said Prescott confidently.

I admired his certainty. I wondered how many

knockbacks it would take to dent it.

'Do you think he's got anything to do with the earlier packages? The ones we assumed were from Sector 88?'

Prescott shook his head. 'No. Not a chance. You don't change from shit to bits of body. If you're going to cut someone up and mail them, that's what you do. There's no softening up process involved. Anyway, like I told you, this bloke's a loner, not a joiner. It's just coincidence.'

'Not a particularly pleasant one,' I said.

'No,' agreed Prescott. 'But a coincidence, nevertheless.'

'So where does this get us?'

'To here,' said Prescott. 'But I take it you agree with my theories so far?' Said as if it were impossible to do anything else. But he had a point.

'Yes,' I said. 'I do. But it doesn't help a lot. It still leaves an awful lot of people out there who could be John.'

'Of course it does,' said Prescott. 'But each time he calls, we narrow it down more.'

'And how many people does he have to kill before you get it down to a manageable level?'

Prescott looked at me sadly. 'That's the problem,' he said. 'I don't know.'

Then it was Harper's turn to speak. 'You're not on the air again until Monday, right?' he said to Day.

He nodded back.

'So, a bit of breathing space. Or at least, I hope so. What do you say, Jim?'

'Who knows,' said the constable in reply. '*I* don't think he'll send any more for a bit. He sounded pretty amicable as he rang off last night.'

Amicable, I thought, remembering the tone of

the conversation John had had with Day. If that was what Prescott called amicable, I'd hate to see him lose his temper.

'Anyway, there's no more post till Monday morning,' he went on with a certain ghoulish relish. 'And I doubt he'll try the motor bike messenger trick again. We'll be ready for him if he does.'

'Let's hope he doesn't,' I said, glancing over at Peter Day who was looking even worse. 'Do you need us any more this afternoon?'

Harper looked at Prescott who shook his head. 'No,' said Harper. 'We'll see you on Monday. Have a pleasant weekend.' And with that they drank up and left.

'Charming people,' I said as the door of the pub swung shut behind them.

'Do you mind giving me a lift home?' asked Day.

'It's on my way, Peter.'

I finished my beer, Day abandoned his, and we left the pub and went to my parked car. I drove him the short distance to Brixton. When we turned into his street there was a bunch of reporters and photographers hanging round the front door, and the ITN, LWT and BBC TV news vans were almost blocking the turning.

'Shit!' exploded Day.

'Is there a back way?' I asked.

'Yeah. Where they collect the rubbish. Straight on and right.'

I snaked the Jag between the parked trucks and accelerated to the end of the road, swung right, then sharp right again at Day's instructions, into a back entry lined with huge dustbins on rubber wheels.

'Terrific,' said Day as I braked the car to a halt. 'Going in with the garbage. I love this business.'

'It's the downside of fame,' I said.

'Isn't it just?' He hopped out of the car, then leant back in. 'Are you busy tonight?' he asked.

I nodded. 'Got a date.'

'Lucky you. You'd better go. You don't want to keep her waiting. Besides, that lot will be here in a minute.'

I gave him a half salute, and he slammed the door and went through a disreputable-looking door into the back of the building just as three or four reporters appeared at the end of the alley behind me. I hit the gas and the Jag fishtailed along the roadway, gained traction with a squeal of rubber. Straight away I had to brake to avoid shooting the other end. As the car slid almost to a halt, I spun the wheel to the left and accelerated down the main street.

I drove home and stayed there for the rest of the afternoon, waiting to go on my date with the lovely Sophia.

18

I got to the address she had given me at 7.05. I didn't want to appear too keen. I rang the bell for her flat in a tall terrace on a street that ran between Lavender Hill and Clapham Common. I heard noises from inside, the hall light went on, I saw a figure through the glass of the door, and she opened it.

'Hi there,' she said. 'Come on in.'

In the low wattage light I saw that she was wearing basic black. A short black dress and black tights, relieved only by a string of pearls around her neck, which were almost the same creamy colour as her skin. Her dark hair was a mass of curls, and she looked seriously good.

I'd put on a charcoal grey Hugo Boss whistle, a pale pink button-down shirt, a tie covered in a pattern of dark green leaves, and black leather Timberland loafers with thick rubber soles. I felt pretty seriously good too, in my own way.

I accepted her invitation and followed her up two flights of stairs to her flat door. I tried not to look at her buttocks moving under the thin material of her dress as we went, but failed miserably. But then, nobody's perfect.

She led the way into a small hall, and I closed the flat door behind us. It was warm inside, and the place smelled of her perfume.

'This way,' she said, and we went into the tiny living room.

It was neat and tidy, with two armchairs facing the TV set, a couple of free-standing black wooden bookcases full of books, magazines, records, tapes, videos, and a Sony midi system with two tiny speakers. A *Simply Red* album was playing at low volume, which was probably the best thing for it.

'Sit down,' she said.

I did as she said, and she asked me if I wanted a drink. I opted for a gin and tonic and she vanished into the kitchen to get it together. She came with two frosty glasses and took a seat in the chair opposite mine.

We toasted each other and drank. 'So, Nick,' she said, 'what's it to be?'

'I've booked a table at a place round the corner.' I told her the name of my favourite Thai restaurant which, by coincidence, was situated just a short way from her flat.

'I'm honoured,' she said. 'It's very expensive there.'

I didn't tell her that Sunset was paying. It's not really the done thing, if you know what I mean.

'I told them seven-thirty to eight,' I said. 'Is that OK with you?'

She nodded.

Time for another, I thought, and as if she'd read my mind she asked, 'Want a re-fill?'

'Don't mind if I do,' I replied.

She got up, collected my glass and vanished again.

After she came back, gave me my drink and sat down again, she said, 'So why did you ask me out?'

I hate questions like that. What the hell are you supposed to say?

'It seemed like a good idea at the time,' I replied after a moment.

'Did it?'

I nodded.

'And now?'

'Still seems pretty fair. Why did you say you'd come?'

It was her turn to hesitate. 'You seemed interesting.'

'Thank you,' I said.

'And . . .' She hesitated again. 'I don't know. This whole thing is so strange, I didn't want to spend all of the weekend on my own.'

'I shouldn't have thought you'd have much problem with that. I'd imagine young men are queuing up at your door to keep you company.'

'You'd be surprised,' she said.

'Would I?'

She turned the subject back. 'Why is this man picking on Peter, do you think?'

'I don't know,' I said. 'But our Mr Day seems to get up a lot of people's noses.'

'But this goes beyond that.'

'Oh, yes,' I agreed. 'The other stuff he was getting sent was bad enough. But this character John, or whatever the hell his name really is, is crazy. You can't expect logic from someone who cuts people up.'

She shivered.

'I'm sorry,' I said. 'Perhaps we'd better call a moratorium on the subject. Let's go out, have something to eat and forget about it. There's nothing *we* can do about it, after all.'

She nodded agreement, looked at her watch, put her glass down on the carpet and stood up. 'Well, if we're going, we'd better go. I'll get my coat.' And she swished out into the hall with a rustle of nyloned thigh on nyloned thigh. Erotic or what?

She came back carrying a big, black cloth coat with an extravagant collar which she gave to me to help her on with. I did the business, and inhaled a noseful of perfume and woman smell which did nothing to quiet my libido. Funny that. Until I'd seen her, on that first day, my libido hadn't been a problem for longer than I cared to remember.

She picked up her handbag and I followed her down the stairs, out of the front door into the chilly street.

'Shall I drive?' I asked. 'Or do you want to walk?'

'Let's walk,' she replied. 'It'll give me an appetite.'

She tucked her arm into mine and we set off.

The restaurant was only a few minutes away but I was cold by the time we got there, and glad to slide into the warm smell of cooking that greeted us.

I got my usual table by the window that looked out over Lavender Hill, and we ordered a gin and tonic for her and a Thai beer for me.

'Have you been here before?' I asked.

She nodded. 'A couple of times. I like it.'

'So do I. It's the best restaurant in London.'

For a split second I remembered the women I'd been there with before, and wondered where they all were now. Not a happy thought. More fuck-ups, down to me. More decent people I'd screwed in more ways than one. Maybe it was a mistake coming here. You should never go back.

She must have seen the look on my face.

'What's the matter?' she asked.

'Nothing,' I said. 'Someone walked over my grave.'

She pulled a face.

I pulled one back. 'Sorry,' I said. 'Memories.'

'Anyone in particular?'

'Not really.'

'Too many to count?'

She was uncomfortably close to the truth.

I shrugged. 'Not lately, that's for sure. I don't think I've been out with a woman,' I looked round the room, 'like this for – God, I don't know. It must be six months or more.'

'I don't believe it.'

'It's true.'

'So are you celibate?' she asked with a half smile.

Halibut, more like, I thought, but I find jokes about fish often don't go down too well with young women when you start talking about sex for the first time. 'Yes, I suppose I am.'

If I expected her to say something like 'what a waste', I was disappointed.

At that point the waiter brought our drinks, and we dived into them and the menus, and the moment was lost.

We ordered prawns stuffed with crab meat in a cream sauce with coriander for starters, followed by strips of chicken in hot sauce, a special mixed seafood dish in a pot, stir-fried vegetables and soft noodles. I asked for more beer, and Sophia had a Perrier with lime juice.

When the waiter had taken our order and left for the kitchen, I said, 'So, was the boyfriend you mentioned for real or just a myth?'

'A myth,' she said.

'I'm very surprised.'

'Why?'

'I would have thought . . .'

'That the only thing I wanted to do was settle

down with a nice boy of my own religion and raise a load of kids?'

'Not exactly.'

'But close,' she interrupted.

'Listen, I'm sorry. I was just making conversation.'

'Sure you were. No, Nick. I want to make something of myself. I'm twenty-three years old, and my ambition is to be a TV reporter. I came out of university, did some time on a local paper, then moved up to London and got this job with Sunset. Yeah, I know, making coffee for Tony Hillerman isn't my idea of a good career move either but . . .' She paused. 'But,' she went on, 'it could lead to all sorts of things. At least he keeps his hands to himself, which is more than I can say for my old editor. Tony asks me for my opinion on things. He's not as bad as he looks. I do a few items for the news. He doesn't want to lose me. I'm good at what I do. Sunset is going places. Maybe not the franchise they're after, but who knows? And I intend to go places with them. On my own. No one to tie me down.'

She saw the look on my face.

'End of speech,' she said.

I smiled. 'I get the picture,' I said.

'So *no* serious commitments.'

'How about light-hearted ones?'

It was her turn to smile. 'Every once in a while,' she said. 'How about you? Are you married?'

'Used to be,' I said. And I told her the whole sorry story. No embellishments, no bullshit. Just the truth about another failed relationship, and the inevitable casualties that follow.

'I'm sorry,' she said when I'd finished.

'Don't be,' I said. 'I'm sorry enough for both of us.'

Thankfully, that was when the food turned up.

It was excellent as always. I don't know who they have down there in the kitchen but he or she is a magician in the culinary department. We both dived into the meal and hardly spoke until our plates were clear.

'That *was* good,' said Sophia when she came up for air.

'Not bad at all,' I agreed. 'Another drink?'

'I'll have a gin.'

I got the waiter over, and ordered a reprise on the gin and beer, and lit a cigarette for each of us. We dawdled over our drinks, then a couple of coffees and liqueurs, so that it was almost eleven when I called for the bill.

'What now?' I asked when I laid my Access card on the saucer provided.

'What do you suggest?'

'Anything your heart desires.'

'It's been a tough week, Nick. And this has been a very pleasant interlude, but I fancy going home. Do you mind?'

I assumed that she meant alone. I didn't want to leave, but I wasn't about to force anything.

'Sure,' I said. 'It's been a tough week for all of us.'

The waiter returned with my card, and I signed the slip and asked for Sophia's coat. He was back with it in a flash, and it was his turn to help her on with it. We left the restaurant to fond goodbyes, and strolled through the dark streets in the direction of her place.

At the front door she said, 'I feel rotten letting you go like this. How about a coffee for the road?'

'If you can handle it.'

'I think I can just about do that.'

She let us into the house, and once again I

135

followed her upstairs and into her flat. She hung her coat on a hook in the hall and let me through to the sitting room again, then when I was sitting comfortably, went into the kitchen to put the kettle on.

I sat back and stared at a painting on the wall over the fireplace. The subject was a French marketplace. I got up to take a closer look. It was signed 'Sophia Haines, 1988'.

When she came back into the room carrying a tray, I said, 'Did you do that?'

She nodded. 'On one of my long vacations from university, I spent a month around Paris.'

'It's good.'

'Flattery will get you everywhere.'

'No, I mean it.'

'Thank you. I was quite pleased with it myself.'

'A woman of many talents.'

'You know how to get round me, Nick.' And she gave me a long look that set the hairs on my spine tingling.

I sat back down and took my cup of coffee. She found cigarettes in her handbag and gave one to me.

It was very quiet in her flat and she didn't break the silence with music or the TV, just sat and smoked and drank her coffee and looked at the picture she had painted.

'Penny for them,' I said.

'I was thinking about the strange things that bring people together. Two weeks ago I didn't know you existed, or you me, and now here we are.'

I didn't think she wanted an answer, so I didn't give her one.

'And all because of some horrible people out there.' She shivered again. 'Would you like to stay the night?'

At first I thought I'd heard her wrong, or else it was just wishful thinking.

When I didn't reply, she said, 'You don't have to knock me down in the rush.'

'Sorry. It was a bit of a surprise, that's all.'

'I don't want sex,' she said. 'No, sorry. That's not what I mean – maybe I do, I don't know yet. But I don't have anything here. You know what I mean?'

I did.

'I think my last relationship lasted about as long as a packet of condoms.' She smiled ruefully at the memory. 'And if you say you have some, I'll kick you out right now.'

I didn't as it happens, but if I'd had a gross of Featherlite in my back pocket I would have denied all knowledge at that point.

'No,' I said, 'I don't.'

'Good. I hate men who're too sure of themselves. I want you just to sleep with me. I think I need some human contact tonight. It's been a long time.'

'For me too,' I said.

'And you think you can control yourself?' she said, and looked over at me.

I nodded, with a smile. 'I think so.'

'I don't know if that's a compliment to your self-control or an aspersion on my femininity.'

'Neither,' I said. 'It's just the way it is. For now.'

'I think I like the last bit. I'm going to get ready for bed. I'll let you know when the bathroom's free.'

She was gone for about ten minutes. When she came back she'd taken off her make-up and changed into a floor-length nightie that was definitely *not* one for any self-respecting seductress's armoury. It was made of blue wincyette, with a pattern of pink roses on it, and it had a high collar that she'd buttoned to the top.

'Now you see the real me,' she said. 'The bathroom's on the left. The bedroom's on the right. Use the red toothbrush, it's new. See you in a minute.'

I left my jacket in the living room and went to the bathroom and used the new toothbrush.

When I was squeaky clean, I crossed the hall and went into Sophia's bedroom. She was lying tucked up in a large bed, supported by two pillows, wearing a pair of tortoiseshell glasses and reading a magazine.

I took off my tie and undid my shirt, and she said, 'Don't worry, I won't peep.'

'You're a flake,' I said. 'You know that?'

'It's been noted,' she said, eyes glued to the page.

I finished undressing down to my T-shirt and boxer shorts, and slid beneath the cool sheets next to her. They smelled of her perfume, and I could feel the warmth of her body next to mine.

She took off her glasses and looked at me.

'Why, Miss Smith, you're beautiful,' I said, and she laughed and turned off the light.

We lay next to each other in the faint illumination that came through the curtains from the street outside.

Sophia turned and moved towards me, and I put one arm around her as she nestled close. I had to turn slightly or else she would have speared herself on my erection, and she giggled. She kissed me lightly on the lips and turned away. I knew what we both wanted, but I also knew it would be fatal to rush her, so I just lay in the silence of her bedroom, punctuated only by the sounds of our breathing, and before I knew it I was asleep.

When I woke up I was alone, and the bedside clock read 9.30. I hadn't slept so well for years. I rolled over on to her side of the bed which still contained some trace of the warmth of her body and breathed in her smell off the pillow. I heard the door slam and she came into the bedroom in a puff of chilled air from outside. She was wearing a sweatshirt over Lycra pants and trainers.

'So you're awake,' she said. 'Kettle's on, bathroom's free, and by the time you're dressed I'll have some breakfast ready. What would you like?'

'You,' I said.

'I'm not on the menu this morning, but thanks for the compliment. It's a choice of muesli, bacon and egg, toast and coffee, or any permutation of the above. I've got the papers.'

'You're good, you know that?'

'Better than *you* deserve.'

'You know me so well already.'

'So what's it to be?'

'Bacon, eggs, toast and coffee,' I said. 'I'll skip the health food.'

'And you'll probably die a horrible, fatty death very soon.'

'But a happy one. Now get out of here and let me keep my modesty intact.'

She winked lasciviously at me, and left. I hopped out of bed, went to the bathroom, relieved myself, washed, cleaned my teeth and went back to her bedroom for my clothes. When I was dressed in shirt, trousers, socks and shoes I went looking for her. The flat was full of the delicious smell of grilled bacon and I followed my nose.

The kitchen was tiny and spotlessly clean. There were two places set on a table that let down from the wall in front of two high stools.

'It's a bit twee, I'm afraid,' she said. 'And rather small, but it's the best I can afford on my wages.'

'It's fine with me. You should see my place.'

'A bachelor's den?'

'Something like that.'

She served out the food, and I glanced at the headlines of the papers as she did so. She'd bought all the Sundays, and they all had articles about John, and Peter Day, and Sunset Radio. And me. Even the driest of the qualities.

'Still making news,' I observed as she sat down opposite me.

'I thought I'd better get everything.'

'You're going to have a busy day if you read this lot.'

'I've got nothing else to do. You?'

'I've got an appointment later. Apart from that, nothing.'

'What kind of appointment?'

'Strictly business.'

'Sunset business?'

I nodded. 'I'll tell you about it another time, all right?'

'The big man and his secrets?'

'Sophia, it's what I'm being paid for. If it's anything important, you'll be the first to know. After Tony Hillerman, that is.'

She nodded then said: 'Nick?' I lowered my forkful of food. 'About last night. Thank you for being so understanding.'

'It's a dirty job, but somebody's got to do it.'

'Seriously, I'm grateful. Most men would have tried it on all night, and sulked if I didn't give in.'

'I'm not most men.'

'I knew that when I asked you to stay. But you confirmed it. I like you, I really do.'

'And I like you, Sophia. But next time, if there is a next time, maybe I won't be such a gentleman.'

'And next time, if there is a next time, maybe I won't want you to be.' And she smiled, and I leant over the table and kissed her lips that tasted of the marmalade she was eating.

After we'd finished breakfast, I told her I had to go. I didn't want to, but nor did I want to spoil the impeccable reputation I had with her. I hoped she didn't want me to leave either. But I knew that if she wanted me to stay, we'd probably get into something neither of us would want to finish that day.

I begged a copy of the *Observer* for the crossword, put on the rest of my clothes and left.

We embraced at the doorway, and she made me promise I'd call her at the station the next day.

I agreed without hesitation. I was already looking forward to the next time.

19

I met Chas and his photographer at opening time in The Bull at Norbury as arranged. It was a cold and miserable sort of place, all dark wallpaper and reproduction leather furniture that was made of plastic. I suppose the brewery wanted to make the place look like something out of a TV adaptation of a Dickens novel. All it managed was to look like somewhere you wouldn't want to spend a Sunday evening.

Since my photo had been in the papers, I tried to look as different as I could without getting out my Sherlock Holmes disguise outfit. I hadn't shaved, wore a dark grey woollen hat pulled down low over my forehead and the tops of my ears, a pair of thick-rimmed glasses with slightly tinted, plain glass lenses, and a huge shapeless overcoat.

I think it worked because I had to go right up to Chas before he realised who I was. 'Christ!' he said. 'You look like a sexual pervert in that outfit.'

'That's the idea,' I said. 'What better way to infiltrate a bunch of Nazis?'

'It's all a bit over the top, isn't it?' said Chas, and introduced his sidekick. 'This is Piers. Piers, this is Nick Sharman, the Norbury flasher.'

Piers was a willowy youth who didn't look like he'd be much good in a ruck, which was possibly just what we were going into. But I said nothing. For all I knew, he might be a black belt in Kendo or Aikido or something equally exotic.

I shook his hand and said, 'I hope your camera's well hidden. We don't want any embarrassment at the door, do we?'

'Don't worry,' he said. 'I've played this game before. They won't suss me out.'

'I'll take your word for it.'

He smiled, and Chas went off to the bar to get me a pint of Guinness. Don't ask me why I chose Guinness to drink that night. It just seemed to go with the mood of the evening.

When he got back, he asked me if there was anything fresh on The Midnight Crawler as he needed an angle for his story in Tuesday's edition of the paper. I told him I knew as much as he did, which was true. I thanked him for putting in the piece about Prince, and asked him how his date with Sheila Cochran had gone.

He denied that it was a date.

I told him that wasn't what I'd heard, and I swear he blushed, hard-bitten news hound that he was.

'It was just business,' he said.

I told him that I believed him but the population of China probably wouldn't. He shut up and sulked for a few minutes, then revived when Piers went up to the bar for re-fills. At eight we went off to the Masonic Hall. It wasn't exactly buzzing, but a couple of hard-looking lumps were standing at the door checking everyone who went in.

We stopped, and they gave us the once over. 'What?' said the first lump, an acne-scarred veteran of many an encounter with a tube of Clearasil.

'We've come for the meeting,' said Chas.

'What meeting?' said the second lump, an older

man with a nasty scar the length of one cheek.

Chas looked up and down the street. 'You know,' he said.

'*We* know,' said Pizza Face. 'But do you?'

'Sector 88,' I said. 'Don't worry. Smithy sent us.'

'Who?' Scarface this time.

I grinned and winked through my glasses. '*Mr* Smith,' I said.

Scarface grimaced, then looked at his mate, and the pair of them patted us down perfunctorarily. I looked over at Piers but he was cool and they found nothing. Scarface gave us one more dirty look then stepped aside. 'In you go,' he said. 'But we'll be watching you.'

I grinned again. 'Thanks, mate,' I said. 'See you later maybe for a drink.'

I don't think my invitation got me to the top of his social calendar but he ushered us into the foyer of the hall anyway. There was a table set up in one corner. A handwritten sign propped up on it read: COFFEE HERE AT THE END OF THE MEET-ING. ALL WELCOME.

We went through to the main hall and found seats at the side of the hall. In front of the banks of seats was a stage, maybe three foot high. Across it were drawn a pair of red velvet curtains. Piers whispered that he would need to get closer for really good shots. I held him back. I didn't want to get too close to the main action. He pulled a face, but stayed where he was.

I looked round the hall. It was hardly standing room only. There were maybe forty people in a place that could hold two hundred comfortably. All men. I wondered what was on TV to keep the folks away from all this excitement.

We sat there for maybe ten minutes, and a further

ten or twelve people joined the merry throng. Then the lights dimmed and the curtains across the stage slid back with the whirr of an electric motor.

On stage was a table with four men seated at it. From left to right: a bullet-headed individual wearing a black shirt, white tie and sports jacket. Because of the table and the long cloth on it that brushed the floor of the stage on the audience's side I couldn't see anything below the waist.

Next to him, a studenty-looking geek with big glasses, a spotty forehead and an anorak with a ratty fur hood, over a polo neck jumper.

Next in line was a white-haired individual with a suit and tie. He looked one of those fake doctors in the TV adverts for aspirin.

As I watched, to sporadic applause in which neither Chas, Piers nor myself joined, he rose to speak. At the first screech of feedback from the PA system, I looked at the man on his right, wearing a brown bomber jacket over a white T-shirt. I looked away and then it clicked. I recognised him.

'Jesus,' I said, sank lower in my seat, and blessed the fact that we hadn't gone into the front row like Piers had wanted.

'What?' said Chas.

'The one at the end,' I said. 'In the bomber jacket.'

'What about him?'

'That's Eddie Cochran.'

'What? *Summertime Blues*?' asked Piers.

'No,' I hissed. 'The husband of the woman who lost her dog. The one in the paper. Sheila. Chas's latest squeeze.'

'Blimey,' said Piers. 'What's he doing here?'

'Well, he ain't selling ice cream for the interval,' said Chas. 'He's one of the Guv'nors.'

146

'Terrific,' I said. 'The most perfect little Nazi I've ever met . . . Piers?'

'What?'

'Can you get some shots of the committee, and him in particular?'

'I already have.'

'Good.'

'But I'm going to the loo, and when I'm down there I'll get some better ones.'

'Go on then,' I said. 'But be careful.'

He nodded, and did as he was told. 'When can I have the pictures?' I said to Chas when Piers had gone.

'Ten tomorrow morning. Come up to the office.' Then he changed the subject. 'I hope Cochran doesn't recognise you,' he said nervously.

'Why should he? He's only seen me once and I was Mr Clean that day.'

'I take back what I said about the way you look,' he said. 'If he'd spotted you, I doubt we'd have got out of here with our teeth.'

'A piece of piss,' I said. 'Right is on our side.'

'Oh, yeah?'

'Every time,' I assured him.

At that point, I tuned in to what the white-haired individual was going on about. It certainly wasn't National Socialism he was preaching, just the kind of far right politics you can hear any time in any bar in England. Unpleasant it might have been but Nazism it wasn't. More or less exactly what Chas had told me his undercover reporter had discovered. And no one had mentioned Sector 88 once. Except me. And there were no Nazi artefacts or uniforms in evidence. In fact, if it hadn't been for the heavies at the door, it might have been a meeting of the local wine-making club or rose growers' association.

Piers returned to his seat and gave me a wink. After ten more minutes of boredom, that seemed like ten days, I leaned over to Chas. 'They aren't going to get into anything heavy now. I reckon that the *real* dirt gets dished over coffee later. I can't risk staying and getting blimped by Cochran. What do you reckon?'

Chas looked at Piers who looked straight back and said, 'I've got everything I need. Anything else would just gild the lily.'

'OK,' said Chas to me. 'I reckon your man's the key to all this. All we needed was a positive ID on one of them, and we can work on that. I reckon it's about time to split.'

'Me too,' I said, and we stood up and shuffled out. A lot of heads turned but we ignored them. We went out into the foyer again and from there into the street. Scarface was still on the door.

'Not to your liking, gents?' he enquired solicitously.

'No,' said Piers. 'We thought it was an AA meeting.'

Scarface looked puzzled as we left the building and made our way back to the pub.

20

Chas ordered another round of drinks, and we went to a quiet table in the corner. The place had hardly livened up since we'd left. No strippers, no Karaoke. Nothing much, but a few dour-faced individuals peering into their drinks as if the secret of life might be contained inside them.

I knew better. I'd gazed into enough glasses myself to know that all you got was a layer of scum on the inside. But maybe that *was* the secret of life, and I never knew it.

Piers swallowed his beer quickly, and then told us that a darkroom beckoned if he was to get Chas the photos by the next morning. We shook hands all round, and he left.

'So what do you reckon?' said Chas after he'd gone.

'I reckon that Eddie Cochran may very well have something to do with sending nasties through the post to Sunset Radio,' I said.

'Why him?' Chas demanded.

'It fits. He's such a little turd.'

'But you don't think he's the Crawler, though, do you?'

'No,' I replied. I hadn't told Chas abut Jim Prescott and his behavioural theories, so I expounded a few for his edification.

He nodded as I spoke, and when I'd finished, said, 'Pretty good. A psychologist I spoke to pretty well said the same.'

'Great minds,' I said modestly. 'But I love Eddie for the other stuff. The little git got right up my nose.'

'You could well be right,' agreed Chas. 'But someone will have to prove it. I'd like to see him go down for something myself. If only for lobbing bricks through his wife's window.'

'You like her, don't you?' I said.

'I suppose I do. If you hadn't been there tonight, I'd've been tempted to chin him.'

'Save your strength, son,' I said. 'He'll get his. I'm going to talk to one of the coppers in charge of this whole thing tomorrow morning after I collect those snapshots. If I can find any connection, however small, between Eddie and the parcels, they'll make life so uncomfortable for him, he'll wish he'd never heard of Sector 88.'

'You think you can?'

'What? Find a connection? I'll try my best. But I don't want you putting your oar in.'

'There's nothing I can do.'

'Good.'

'But, Nick . . .'

'Yeah.'

'Promise me first crack at it?'

'Course. If it hadn't been for you, I would never have got this far.'

Chas smiled. 'Good enough,' he said.

With that we drank up and left to go our separate ways.

The next morning, Monday, I telephoned Sheila Cochran early.

'Are you all right?' I asked when she answered the telephone.

'As well as can be expected.'

'I need to see you.'

'Any time.'

'Aren't you at work?'

'I'm going to take a few days off.'

'Are the windows OK?'

'Yes. Your people were very good. That's one more thing I'm grateful to you for.'

'Don't be. It's my fault your husband did what he did.'

'If it *was* him.'

'I'm pretty sure it was.'

'Did you get to see him?' she asked.

'Not at his flat, but I have seen him. That's one of the reasons I want to see *you*.'

'Like I said, any time.'

'I'll be over in an hour or so.'

'I'll see you then.'

Next I telephoned Brixton police station and caught Charlie Harper at his desk.

'What can I do for you?' he asked.

'The original parcels to Sunset,' I said. 'Before John got in on the act. The shit and all that. Was there anything identifiable about them?'

'How do you mean?'

'Anything that might nail the culprit.'

'Hold on.'

I heard the rustling of paper and he came back on to the line. 'Only one thing,' he said. 'A thumb print. Or at least a partial one. Nothing known, though. We ran it through all available records, and came up with a blank.'

'Say I brought you a set of prints, you could make positive identification, couldn't you?'

'What *are* you up to now?'

'I don't know. It's a hunch. A flyer. But you could?'

'I imagine so.'

'Right. Are you about today?'

'I'll be around.'

'Then I might have something for you later. If I do, I'll bring it in, OK?'

'Right now, *anything* is more than we have.'

'All right, Sergeant,' I said. 'Keep a light in the window.' And I hung up.

I got shaved and dressed and hit the road to Herne Hill. I was at Sheila Cochran's address just after nine. She answered the door immediately. I could smell something cooking, and it smelled good.

'Hungry?' she asked.

'I could be.'

'Bacon and eggs, tomatoes and fried bread.'

'Sounds wonderful.'

'Go in and sit down then, and I'll get you some breakfast. Then you can tell me what brings you round here so early.'

I went into the kitchen. The table was set for one.

'It's been a long time,' she said, 'since I cooked breakfast for a man.' Prior to yesterday it was a long time since anyone had cooked breakfast for me, apart from in a greasy cafe. I could get used to the idea.

'From the way that smells,' I replied, 'you haven't lost the knack.'

She smiled, and broke two eggs into a pan. The bacon was warming on the grill with two halves of tomato and a fried slice. Within half a minute she'd flipped the eggs over easy, added them to the plate, and put it in front of me.

'What about you?' I asked.

'I've eaten, but I'll have a cup of tea with you.'

She went over to the dresser and warmed the tea pot, put in a couple of tea bags and added boiling water. Then she put milk into two cups, and turned to me.

'So?' she said. 'Tell me everything.'

I asked her a question instead. 'Did Eddie ever have anything to do with politics?' I said.

'What?'

'Politics,' I repeated.

'What kind of politics?'

'Ultra right-wing,' I said round a mouthful of bacon.

'Well, he was a skinhead when I met him.' She looked at me. 'I know. You must think I was mad marrying him. I don't know why I keep saying that.'

'I've met some perfectly delightful skinheads,' I said.

'But I'm afraid Eddie wasn't one of them. Why do you ask?'

I told her. The whole story.

'I don't know,' she said, when I'd finished. 'He was always vanishing. Sometimes for days on end. He could have been anywhere. Doing anything. He certainly never mentioned it to me. But then, he wouldn't, would he? I've voted Labour all my life.'

'No,' I said. 'With that sort of background, I doubt that he would. Has he ever been in trouble with the police?'

'Never,' she said positively. 'Why?'

'It was just a thought. Have you got anything here that might have his fingerprints on it?'

'*What!*'

'His fingerprints,' I repeated. 'Something glass or plastic or metal that only he touched.'

'You're serious, aren't you?'

'Yes. Of course, if you don't want me to pursue it . . .'

'Oh, I do. It's just a bit of a surprise, that's all.'

'I know. And I'm sorry.'

'Don't be. I'm not trying to protect him. If he's done something wrong, he deserves all he gets. I might have something upstairs. Cough mixture. He bought it last winter. The bottle's still upstairs in the medicine cabinet. I've never touched it. Would that do?'

'That would be fine. As long as it hasn't got his name on it.'

'It wasn't prescription. Just a linctus.'

'Lift it up by the top,' I said. 'Don't touch the glass.'

She left the table and went upstairs. I heard her moving about, then her footsteps on the stairs, and she came back into the kitchen carrying a brown medicine bottle carefully by its plastic cap. She put the bottle on the dresser next to the tea pot.

'Have you got a bag I could put it in?' I asked.

She knelt down, opened the cupboard under the sink, delved around, and came out with a Tesco's carrier bag. I got up from my seat, took the bag from her, and carefully put the bottle into it.

'Thanks,' I said.

'What are you going to do with it?'

'Take it to the police station for comparison. It's probably nothing, but you never know.'

'Do you think he's got anything to do with those bodies?'

'No,' I said. 'If it's anything, it's the other stuff.'

'That's disgusting,' she said. 'Even I didn't think he was that bad. Sending . . .' She paused. 'Stuff like that through the post. It's horrible.' She shivered at the thought, and held herself tightly.

'Listen,' I said, 'it may not be him. It's just a thought.'

'Not a very nice one. Then, he wasn't a very nice man. More tea?'

I nodded and sat down again and she took my cup and refilled it.

When I'd finished, I took the bag and left, promising to keep in touch.

By then it was past ten o'clock, and I headed for Chas's office opposite Streatham Hill Station. I spoke to one of the charming blond receptionists at the front desk, who called through to him at his desk, and he came down to see me.

'Morning,' I said. 'Has young Piers come up with the goods?'

'He's just left. Come on up and take a look for yourself.'

I followed Chas through the maze of the building to the tiny cubby hole he called home. On top of the mess that he referred to as a work station were laid out two dozen or so photographs of various aspects of the Sector 88 meeting. There were some dark pictures of the bouncers. A good shot of the sign by the table, a whole bunch of snaps of the hall itself, and the audience, and, finally, at least fifteen photos of the committee members.

'These are good,' I said, shuffling through them.

'But there's better,' said Chas, and gave me a large brown envelope. Inside were three blow ups of Eddie Cochran, taken from the best group shot that Piers had got. The photo was black and white, sharp and clear.

'Brilliant,' I said. 'Can I have one?'

'Sure. Take whichever you like.'

I selected one and slid it back into the envelope.

'Thanks, Chas,' I said.

He shrugged in reply. 'I said I owed you several. That's one.'

I declined his offer of coffee. 'No, I've got to go,' I said. 'People to see.'

'Are you going to be at Sunset tonight for the late show?'

'When do I ever miss one? I'll be there.'

'Keep an ear out for any good angles. This is the story of a lifetime.'

'I will, Chas. But if those coppers find out I'm feeding you information, they're going to kick my arse from here to Christmas.'

'Then don't let them find out.'

'Sure,' I said, made my farewells and left.

21

I went straight round to the police station and
delivered the medicine bottle. I left the photo of
Cochran in the car.

Harper came out to see me personally. 'So, do
you have a name?' he asked.

I nodded.

'And an address.'

'Sure.'

'Want to give it to me?'

'He might be an innocent man. Let's leave it for
now.'

'But you think he might not be?'

'I've found that anything's possible in this world.'

'Then we'll give it a go.'

'It's a thousand to one against,' I said.

'At the moment, they're good odds.'

'Nothing turned up?'

'Not a sausage. And people in authority are getting impatient.'

'I just bet they are. So hope that this one comes
up trumps.'

'I'm giving you an awful lot of leeway,' he said.
'I could get heavy with you, you know.'

'I know.'

'I could keep you here until you tell me what I
want to know.'

'And I could drop this on the floor,' I said, referring to the bottle in the bag I was carrying. 'And if you do keep me here, there's a good chance Peter Day won't go on air tonight.'

'Fair enough,' he said.

'Anyway, I knew you wouldn't get heavy with me.'

'How?'

'You're a good policeman. Even I can see that.'

He smiled thinly. 'A case of it *doesn't* take one to know one.'

I smiled thinly back. 'I'd hoped you were never going to bring that up.'

He shrugged. 'Some things are meant to be. So where are you today?'

'About,' I replied. 'You'll probably get me at Sunset, or at my office, or at home.' I gave him my card with both phone numbers on it.

'And if you're not in any of those places?'

'Leave a message.' And with that I left.

My next stop was Sunset Radio. There were still reporters outside the front doors, but fewer than on Friday. I drove past, parked at a meter on the other side of the market, loaded it up with coins enough for a two-hour stay, and walked back to the station. I went in the back way again.

There were a few reporters and photographers in the entrance to the back alley when I got there. One was Piers.

We slapped palms like old mates, and he drew me aside.

'Photos all right?' he asked.

'Perfect,' I replied. 'I hope you haven't told anyone about them.'

'Not a chance. If they tie in with this lot,' he gestured at the building, 'I'm set to make a few bob.'

'The best of luck,' I said, and left him. But not before he'd captured me a couple of times for posterity with his motor drive. Some people are all business.

There were two bored-looking coppers standing by the back door talking to Stan, Stan, the security man. He was holding a clip board with a load of names typed on it.

'Morning, Stan,' I said.

He looked dolefully at me. 'You haven't caught anyone yet, then?' he said.

'Nor have the combined forces of the Metropolitan Police,' I remarked. But quietly. So that the coppers couldn't hear.

Stan cracked a smile. 'They're not very happy.'

'So, am I on the guest list?' I asked, nodding at the board he was holding.

'Yep. You're one of the privileged few. You can go straight in. This one's all right, boys,' he said to the two uniformed police, who just nodded.

Stan opened the door into the building and ushered me in.

I went looking for Sophia.

She was in a tiny room adjacent to Hillerman's new quarters. She looked all neat in a dark suit and black stockings, with her hair up and her glasses on the end of her nose.

I closed the door behind me so that no one outside could hear. 'That's my favourite fantasy,' I said.

'What?'

'Messing up a woman dressed like you are.'

'You're such an adolescent. And you dare!'

'I plead guilty as charged. Couldn't I just rumple your hair a little? Ladder one of your stockings?'

'Nick, stop it.'

'Why. Am I getting you hot?'

She sat back in her seat and laughed. 'What am I going to do with you?'

'I've got a few ideas. Meet me at the back of the bike sheds and I'll give you a demonstration.'

'Nick!'

'OK. Your loss.'

'You think so?'

'I know so.'

'So what are you doing later?'

'How much later?'

'After you've finished whatever you're doing today.'

'Sadly, that won't be until after Peter comes off the air tomorrow morning.'

'So?'

'So, I won't be through until about four.'

'So, come round.'

'You'll be asleep.'

'Wake me up.'

'All warm and tousled from your bed. Hair unkempt, and wearing nothing but a wincyette nightie. What a thought!'

Now it was my turn to get hot.

'Will you?' she asked.

'Course I will. I'd be crazy to turn down an offer like that. I'll be counting the minutes,' I said. Then I changed the subject. 'Is the boss around? I think maybe I'd better have a word.'

'He's next door.'

'Right. I'll see you later. What are you doing for lunch?'

'I thought I'd get something sent in. Those damn' reporters are getting on my nerves.'

'Sure you wouldn't rather have a drink?'

'You're a glutton for punishment.'

I let that one pass.

'Well?' I said.

'I could get away for an hour.'

I named the bar where I'd first met Peter Day, and we arranged to meet at lunchtime. So what with one thing and another, by the time I knocked on Tony Hillerman's door, I was feeling pretty chipper.

'Sharman,' he said when I entered. 'Got any good news?'

I declined to mention the free publicity he was getting, and Day's upward ratings spiral.

'Could be.'

'Tell me.'

'Not right now. Nothing's definite.'

'We're paying you.'

'So you are. Just have some patience. It's a long shot, but there's a name in the frame.'

'Who?'

I shook my head. 'Not until it's confirmed. I'll probably know later today, or tomorrow at the latest. You'll have to wait until then. Just in case it's a no-no.'

'Who's confirming it?'

I just grinned and shook my head.

He wasn't happy, but there wasn't a lot he could do about it.

'Will you sit in with Peter tonight? He seems to trust you,' he asked instead.

'He does,' I said. 'And I hate to say this, but the money you paid me last Tuesday runs out today.' Remember what I said about some people being all business?

He nodded. 'All right,' he said. 'I'll get Accounts to issue another cheque.'

'Terrific,' I said. 'That means I can eat tomorrow.'

He didn't rise to the bait.

As there seemed little more to add, I left and took a wander round the building. There was no sign of Peter Day, but then I hadn't expected there to be.

I looked at my watch. It was twelve-thirty. I decided to go and get a livener, and wait for Sophia.

I walked out through the back way, dodged the newspapermen again and ambled round the corner.

I sat in the bar and ordered a premium bottled beer at a premium price. I toasted Hillerman silently when it arrived, and sat back in my chair and watched the world go by through the big plate glass window that looked out over Acre Lane.

Sophia arrived shortly after one. She was the best-looking woman in the place. Not that it would have mattered if she hadn't been, but she was, and that's a fact.

I ordered a gin and tonic from the waiter at her request, and we both lit cigarettes.

'Can you tell me now?' she asked.

'What.'

'Last night? Your business?'

'I really shouldn't.'

'Go on.' Her eyes were alight with excitement and curiosity.

'Can you keep a secret?'

She marked a cross on her left breast with one red fingernail, and I was gone. Tough guy, huh? And remember, when I was on the force I signed the Official Secrets Act.

I told her about Eddie Cochran and Sector 88, although once again I didn't identify him by name. And I didn't say anything about Prince, in case she'd read the story in the paper.

When I'd finished, she said, 'That's amazing. You're so good.'

'Remember what you said about flattery?'

She giggled. 'Maybe you'll find out later.'

By then, she just had time for another drink before getting back to work, so I got a round in, and we sat and chatted inconsequentially until it was time for her to go.

That is if you think serial killers and Nazis inconsequential.

I walked her partway back to Sunset, and went to find my car. Of course it had been ticketed, but it was a legitimate expense so for once I didn't screw the thing up and throw it away.

I drove home and called Peter Day on the phone. His machine was on so I left a message to say I'd pick him up later to take him to work.

Halfway through, he picked up the phone.

I hate that. It's bad enough talking to a machine in the first place, but when a human interrupts, it always throws me.

'Hi, Peter,' I said when I realised he was there. 'Dodging the slings and arrows?'

'Something like that. The bloody phone is ringing every two minutes.'

'Unplug it.'

'I can't. You never know who'll call. I have to keep in touch.'

'Fair enough. Listen, like I was trying to say a minute ago, I'll pick you up tonight. That is, if you still want me to come in with you.'

'Course I do. You and Stretch and Sophia are the only ones keeping me sane.'

'That doesn't say a lot for your sanity,' I remarked. Which probably wasn't too tactful. But I thought after what we'd been through together, we were past tact. 'So I'll see you later.'

He agreed, and we hung up.

After that I just sat around the flat keeping myself company and thinking about Sophia's legs.

22

Just as my thoughts got interesting the phone rang. It was Harper. 'I don't know how you did it,' he said, 'but the thumbprint on the bottle you gave me matched the one we found on a plastic bag inside one of the parcels of crap that was sent to Sunset.'

Lucky for my professional reputation no one would ever know just what a coincidence it really was. I certainly wasn't telling. 'That slimy little bastard!'

'Friend of yours?'

'Not at all.'

'So give me his full name and address so that I can get a warrant.'

I complied with his request. When I supplied the name, he did the usual. 'Are you fucking me about? Because if you are, I'm not in the mood.'

'It's his name,' I said. 'Don't blame me. Perhaps it's partly what turned him into what he is. Everybody taking the piss.'

'OK,' said Harper. 'I believe you. Address?'

I told him. 'What time are you going in?' I asked.

'Dawn tomorrow. The best time.'

'Let me come with you.'

'*What*?'

'You heard.'

'Don't ponce about, Sharman. This is police business.'

'And if it wasn't for me, you'd be none the wiser.'
He paused. 'Why?'
'It's another job I'm on.'
'What kind of job?'
'I'm looking for a lost dog.'
'A what?'
'You heard,' I said again.
'I don't believe this.'
'Believe it. That's how I got on to Cochran in the first place. I want to have a shufti round his place myself. See if there's any evidence of it ever being there. Come on, Harper. The dog belongs to the woman who gave me the medicine bottle. His wife. Give us both a break and let me come with you.'
'You do what I say?'
'Without question.'
I could almost hear his brain working. 'All right, Sharman,' he said. 'But if my guv'nors get to hear about this . . .'
'Why should they?'
'With you about, lots of ways. But you can come. Are you going to be at Sunset later?'
'Looks like it.'
'I'll talk to you then.'
'You're working long hours.'
'You mean, you don't remember?'
'Sure I do,' I said. 'Sorry.'
I don't know why I apologised. I was getting to like Harper, I suppose. Bad mistake that. With a copper.
'I'll see you later, then.'

I got ready to go out. I wasn't expecting to get back till morning. In fact, it was looking like it might be quite a night. A possible call from a serial killer, and a dawn raid on a suspect's drum. Not to mention a romantic interlude with Sophia. I hadn't looked forward to so much action since I didn't know when.

I put on jeans, leather jacket and polished loafers. I stuck an old pair of Timberlands with a split welt into a bag. I'd been on early morning spins on premises with metal doors before, and it can be hell on a decent pair of shoes. I also took the photo of Cochran with me.

I got to Day's block at ten-thirty again. The press and TV had vanished, thank God. Obviously there was more gore to be had elsewhere that night.

I rang through on the entryphone and he buzzed me up. When he let me through his front door I noticed that he hadn't shaved, and that he stank of booze.

'Drink?' he said when we got inside.

I shook my head. He went to the sideboard and sloshed a good measure of Jack Daniel's into a big glass.

'Don't you think you've had enough?' I asked.

'What's it got to do with you?'

It was going to be one of those.

'Nothing. Nothing at all. But it could be a tricky show tonight.'

'They're all *tricky*, Nicky, my boy,' he said. 'All tricky. All fucking tricky. But what the fuck do you know?'

'Hey, listen,' I said, and opened my arms like I was surrendering, 'I know nothing. It was you that asked me here, remember? I could be tucked up with a good book.'

Or a bad woman, I thought.

He pondered my remark for a moment. 'Sure,' he said. 'Sure. I'm sorry. This thing's beginning to get to me.'

'Understandably.'

167

'But have a drink, eh?'

'OK, Peter,' I said. 'A small one. And why don't you make that one your last?'

He nodded and splashed bourbon into a glass for me. We toasted each other and drank.

'Nick,' he said at length.

'Yeah?'

'I . . . I . . .' He paused. 'Forgive me. Please.' And two tears slid down his face.

Shit! I thought.

'I forgive you,' I said. 'Shall we go?'

I've got to tell you, I really wasn't into male bonding that night. But nevertheless I went over and took his hand.

'It's crap, Pete,' I said. 'But you're doing well. No one could do better under the circumstances. And the more you talk to this creep, the closer Old Bill will get to catching him.'

'I know,' he said. 'It's just that I hate doing it.' He looked at me, and I thought he was going to say more, but he didn't.

'Sure you do,' I replied after a moment. And whatever he was going to say remained unsaid.

He sighed then said, 'Fuck it. Come on, let's go.'

I squeezed his arm and we went.

Harper was waiting for us when we got to Sunset. He was looking a bit peaky himself, if not positively haggard. It seemed the case was beginning to tell on everyone. Except lucky old Nick who was looking forward to his first fuck in an age.

It made me careless.

After Harper had given Peter Day his usual pep-talk and instructions, he excused us and dragged me off to a deserted office.

'Right,' he said. 'About tomorrow morning. You

can come in with us. But – I repeat, *but* – you obey my or any of my officer's orders, immediately and to the letter. Understand?'

'Course I do.'

'You keep out of the way at the back. And you only speak when spoken to.'

'All right. You won't know I'm there.'

'I hope not. Meet me at the station tomorrow at quarter to six. Be on time, or we'll leave without you.'

'I'll be there. I wouldn't miss it for the world. And by the way, this might come in handy.' I gave him the brown envelope containing the 10×8 print of Cochran's face.

'What is it?'

'Take a look.'

He opened the envelope and extracted the photo. 'Who's this?'

'Eddie Cochran.'

'Is that right? I suppose I shouldn't ask you where you got it.'

'You'd be wasting your time.'

'I thought as much. Now hop it . . . And, Sharman?'

'What?'

'You've done well. Maybe you were a better copper than I thought you were.'

'No. I was lousy. I do this to make up for it.' And I left him to himself.

I went up to the studio where Day was talking to Stretch. There were the usual police officers and engineers hanging around waiting for the show to start, in case John called.

'What did he want?' Day asked me.

'I think I've sorted out your Nazi mates,' I said.

'You have? How?'

'Diligence and hard work. And a lot of luck,' I replied.

'Well, that's something. I'd almost forgotten about them.'

'But they're no closer to The Crawler.'

'I wish you wouldn't call him that.'

'Sorry.'

Right then it was time to sort out the show, so Day went into conference with Stretch. It was to be music again. No calls unless John came through. I went downstairs for coffee.

I went back just before midnight and joined Day in the studio.

Nothing happened until almost two. Stretch had been answering the calls that came through the switchboard closely monitored by an engineer, but all we could see was him shaking his head and cutting off the callers. As if to mirror the mood, the music that he and Day had chosen was slow and mournful. Lots of blues tunes. Lots of songs about loss.

Then, just before the last record was ready to go before the two o'clock news, he took a call and pointed through to us.

'That's him,' said Harper.

Peter Day gave Stretch the thumbs-up, and the call was routed through into the studio.

'Hello, Peter. How are you tonight?'

'Not bad,' said Day in reply.

'I'm going to keep this short,' said John. 'You never know who could be listening in, do you?'

I looked through the glass into Stretch's booth where one of the police engineers was talking on one of those big professional yellow telephones that BT use. He was rabbiting away like mad to someone. Probably to another engineer at a switching station.

'Just a few night birds,' said Day.

'Like you and me, huh?' said John.

'That's right, John. Why don't you stay and chat awhile?'

'So that the police can trace this call? No chance. They're wasting their time. They must know that. I'm phoning to tell you there's another little present on its way to you. I don't want you to think you're being ignored. And, Peter?'

'Yes?'

'Remember that the best is yet to come.' And the line went dead.

The police engineer slammed his phone on the console on the other side of the glass in frustration, and Day went straight to the news which I imagined was being re-written even as Tim read it.

'This is no bloody good at all,' said Harper. 'We're never going to catch him at this rate. He's making fools of the lot of us.'

'And it sounds like he's got another one,' I said.

Peter Day put his head in his hands and sat very still.

I left the room for a smoke. As I went I touched him on the shoulder and he jumped at least two inches out of his chair.

I went upstairs to the roof and stood in the night and smoked. Harper had been right. This was no good at all.

The rest of the show was uneventful. I took Peter Day home afterwards. We hardly spoke during the short drive. When I dropped him off he said, 'Want to come in?'

I shook my head and said, 'No. Not tonight.'

'I understand,' he said, and got out of the car slowly, like an old man.

I watched as he went into the block, then I put the car into gear and headed for Sophia's.

23

When I got there she was up.

I gave a short ring on the doorbell and she came down within moments. She'd dumped the winceyette. Instead she was wearing a long robe of a silky material, and when she kissed me hello, and I embraced her briefly, it felt like not a lot else.

She looked at the bag I was carrying, with my old shoes in it.

'What's that?' she asked. 'Your laundry?'

'Funny. I'll tell you all about it in a minute.'

We went up and into the kitchen where I could smell fresh coffee. She poured me a cup and I accepted it gratefully.

'I set the alarm clock,' she said. 'I didn't want to miss you.'

'Did you hear the show?'

She shook her head. 'Did he call?'

I nodded.

'Was it bad?'

'Not really. He only stayed on the line for a minute. But Peter's taking it badly.'

'I know.'

'He was hitting the sauce in a big way earlier on. Crying. The full half hour.'

'I feel so sorry for him.'

'Me too. But what can we do? He's got his own

173

demons to deal with. Just like the rest of us.'

'I feel so helpless,' she said.

'Same here,' I replied. 'It's an impossible situation.'

It wasn't. I could have gone in and kept him company. I felt lousy enough about the way I was acting without justifying it to her.

Luckily she changed the subject. 'So what *is* in that bag?'

I told her about the spin I was going on. Once again her eyes shone with excitement.

'So you see, I've got to meet Harper at a quarter to six in Brixton,' I said when I'd finished and looked at my watch. It was almost four. 'I'm sorry, but I've got to go in an hour or so.'

'Can I come?' she asked.

'Are you serious? This isn't a party. It could get heavy.'

'No. I mean can I come before you go.' She blushed in a most attractive way. 'You know what I mean.'

I did.

'And I thought you were a sweet old-fashioned girl,' I said.

'I'm a sweet, old-fashioned, horny girl. I don't want to think about murders and Nazis and lost dogs. All I want is to go to bed with you.'

'You took the words right out of my mouth.'

'Come on then.' And she reached out her hand.

I put down my coffee cup. She gave my hand a gentle tug and I followed her through to the bedroom.

She slid off the robe, and I'd been right. She wasn't wearing much underneath. In fact, nothing at all.

I tore my clothes off and she came into my arms,

all warm and slippery. Our mouths met and she pulled me on to the bed.

Her skin was shiny under the soft light from her bedside lamp and I ran my fingers along the length of her just to make sure she was real. 'Don't wait,' she whispered. 'Just fuck me.'

So I did. And she did. Come, I mean.

When we were finished, I barely had time for another cup of coffee before I had to go and meet Harper.

She sat with me in the kitchen as I put on the old pair of boots I was going to wear.

'You will be careful, won't you?' she asked as I knotted the laces. 'I don't want to lose you so soon after finding you.'

'I'll keep well out of the way,' I assured her. 'This isn't my show. The big hairy coppers can collect any flak flying about. Me, I'm just going as an observer.'

'Make sure that's all you are.'

I grinned at her. A big stupid grin, like a dog that's just discovered a particularly juicy bone, that he'd buried and thought he'd forgotten where.

'Trust me,' I said.

She came over and sat on my lap. As she was wearing nothing but the tiniest pair of black lace panties it began to get steamy again and I peeled her off like banana skin.

'Sophie,' I said. 'Don't.'

'I hate being called Sophie,' she replied petulantly.

'Sorry.'

'I'll let *you* though. But only when we're on our own.'

'And I intend that we'll be on our own a lot in future,' I said.

175

'Good.'

I left just before five thirty. I wished that I could just curl up next to her in bed and sleep for a week. Alternatively I wished for a Black Bomber or the equivalent. But I had to settle for just coffee and a long, slow farewell kiss.

Mind you, the way she kissed, it wasn't a bad option.

24

I arrived at Brixton police station at a quarter to six and parked my car round the back in a residents' zone. Charlie Harper was hanging about behind the counter in reception. He was wearing a donkey jacket, jeans and Doc Martens. He was talking to two tough-looking younger men whom he introduced as DCs Phillips and Cook.

They had an unmarked Cavalier parked in the garage. Cook drove, Harper rode shotgun. I got in the back with Phillips. It was a short, unremarkable drive through empty streets with the sun rising in front of us. No one said much.

We rendezvoused with a dark blue Land-Rover on Kennington Road. Harper had a short natter over the R/T, and the 4WD vehicle fell into convoy behind us. We drove into the flats at six-fifteen and drew up outside the block where Cochran lived.

The four of us got out of the Vauxhall, and two huge men emerged from the Rover. One of them opened up the tailgate and handed a heavy-looking sledge hammer to his mate and took one for himself, plus an oversized jemmy that he slid into his belt.

'Who're they?' I said to Harper as we watched them tool themselves up.

'A couple of boys from the station. Rugby players. I'm not going to hang about all morning and wait

177

for our man to open the door. If he's not sharp, we're in. No messing.'

Good job, I thought, as we all hit the front door of the flats.

Harper tried the lift and I said, 'It won't work,' just as the doors opened.

'You haven't got the touch,' he said.

I tended to agree. But that's life. Mind you, Sophia might not have agreed, and I smiled at the thought.

The ancient machine ground into action and jolted its way up, and I hoped that we hadn't overloaded it with the six of us and the heavy tools, but eventually we got to the tenth floor and the doors squealed open.

We all exited the lift and stood in a loose group on the landing. Harper pulled the warrant and his ID out of the inside pocket of his jacket and rang the bell, then rapped smartly on the metal of Cochran's door. There was no answer. After half a minute he banged harder. Again no answer. He put his face up close to the smooth metal and shouted. 'Cochran, police. Open up. We have a search warrant. I'll give you fifteen seconds to come out or we come in.'

Once again there was no reply. Harper looked over at the two rugby players who were standing casually holding their hammers. 'Lose that fucking door,' he said.

The rest of us moved out of the way as the two hammer wielders smiled at each other in anticipation and moved to centre stage. I half expected them to spit on their hands but neither did. They stood one each side of the door, hefted the sledges, nodded to each other, and the one on the left gave the door a hefty smack between the two key holes that secured it. The metal boomed at the force of the blow and buckled slightly, then the one on the right whacked the metal between the hinges. More noise. More buckling. Then they really got into their stride. Alternately each one beat at the door until, with a screech of metal and a splintering of wood, it collapsed inwards. Nobody else in the flats paid any attention to the racket we were making. I expect they were used to it.

Harper was first across the threshold. He vaulted over the door and into the hall. The geezers with the hammers dropped them and followed him, closely followed by Cook and Phillips, with me bringing up the rear.

I heard a scuffle from inside, and Harper came out through one of the internal doors holding Cochran in an arm lock. 'Tried to give me a slap,' he said, pushing Cochran into the bear-like hug of one of the rugby players. 'Hold the little fucker.'

Rugby player #1 did just that. The rest of us went through to the kitchen to start the search. As I passed Cochran he spat at me. The man holding him twisted his arm cruelly, and Cochran made a noise halfway between a scream and a moan. I wiped the spittle off my sleeve but otherwise ignored him. Once inside the kitchen I stood by the sink out of the way whilst the professionals got on with the job.

Harper designated each man a room to search and let them get on with it. He sat at the kitchen table and lit a cigarette.

Within thirty seconds Cook came back into the room. 'Guv,' he said, 'come and have a gander at this.'

Harper got up and followed Cook out of the kitchen. I tagged on to his coat tails. Cook led us into the bedroom. It was quite a sight. Not very big, and made smaller by the amount of stuff jammed into it. The bed was a single, and unmade. The rest of the furniture consisted of a chest of drawers, a small bedside cabinet and a wardrobe. Every surface was covered with Nazi and survivalist artefacts and memorabilia, and loads more covered the walls. There must have been a thousand magazines in the room. They were piled everywhere. Dozens of different titles, but all to do with guns, knives, warfare and living rough off the land. There were model planes, cars, tanks and ships, both metal and plastic, either free standing or hanging from the ceiling. They were all German, with WW2 markings. One wall was lined with swords, bayonets, knives and guns. The firearms looked like replicas, but the bladed weapons were real enough. Another wall was full of pictures of WW2 German soldiers, vehicles, and loads of photos of Hitler, Goebbels, Goering and Himmler. But pride of place was saved for the flag over the bed. It was huge. Six foot by four at least. Black, with a white circle in the middle, and a huge red swastika in the centre of that.

Cook opened the door of the wardrobe. In amongst the ordinary clothes were several sets of greyish-khaki fatigues and a full dress German military uniform. Black with silver braid and red flashes on the revers. With it was an SS cap, complete with death's head insignia.

'Charming,' said Harper.

Just then Phillips came into the room. 'Better come and have a look at this, sir,' he said.

We all trooped out of the bedroom again and into the living room. It looked perfectly normal. No Nazi connections at all. Against one wall was a bureau with a drop-down flap. Inside were half a dozen small brown cardboard boxes with staples at the corners to strengthen them. Just like the ones that were used to send wedding cake through the post. Or dog and human shit. Also inside the bureau were a pile of polythene bags, a tablet of writing paper, and a black felt tip pen.

Harper smiled.

Then Phillips opened the top drawer of the bureau. Inside, nestling on top of a folded table cloth, was a Luger pistol. Unlike the ones on the wall of the bedroom, this gun had the deadly look of reality. Next to it was another brown cardboard box. Harper eased off the lid. Inside were a dozen or so 9mm brass-jacketed bullets. Harper took out a pen, inserted it into the barrel of the Luger and lifted the gun up. He looked at it, then smelled the breech and smiled.

'Gen?' I asked.

He nodded. 'And it's been used since it was last cleaned. Bring that shithead in here,' he said to Phillips. Then to me, 'You were dead right.'

Praise indeed.

Phillips went to the door, said something, and Rugby Player #1 came into the room holding Cochran by the arm. Harper turned and held out the Luger in his direction. 'Yours?'

Cochran said nothing. Harper cautioned him. The caution concerned sending obscene and threatening material through Her Majesty's Mail, and the possession of unlicensed firearms and ammunition. 'So do you have a licence for this?' asked Harper after he'd finished the caution.

Cochran did not reply again, and Harper smiled.

Suddenly Phillips exclaimed, 'Bloody hell, what's that?'

We all looked at him as one.

He'd pulled back an armchair in the corner of the room facing the TV and video hook-up.

181

Even further in the corner, and previously hidden by the bulk of the chair, was a dog. A tiny West Highland White Terrier, stuffed and mounted on a wooden pedestal.

'Christ,' I said. 'It's Prince.'

25

I went over to Phillips, and he stood back to let me get a better view of what he'd found. I knelt and looked closely. Indeed it was Prince. He looked just like the photo I'd been carrying with me, and around his neck was a red tartan collar, complete with a silver metal tag that had been engraved with his name and address, exactly as Sheila Cochran had described.

Whoever had done the taxidermy on the animal had been an expert. He had been set in a begging position, with his front paws almost touching his chin. So realistic was the pose that I almost expected him to give a bark at any second. His eyes were wide open and his tongue stuck out of the side of his mouth. But the worst thing, the really bad thing, was that when he'd been stuffed, a metal ashtray had been stuck or bolted to the top of his head. The tray was full of cigarette ends.

I stood up and turned to face Cochran. He was smiling evilly in my direction. 'I am right?' I said. 'That is Prince, isn't it?'

He confirmed with a nod. I made one step in his direction with my fist clenched before Phillips' strong hand caught my elbow. 'No,' he whispered. 'Sorry. Not allowed.'

I tried to shake him off, but I might as well have

tried to shake off a steel hawser. I stopped and opened my palms in a gesture of surrender. He let go.

'You are a nasty little fucker, aren't you?' said Harper conversationally.

Cochran didn't reply.

'What did you do that for?' I asked.

'I never could stand that poxy dog,' said Cochran. 'Noisy little fucker. But it don't bark at me no more. And it's handy when I'm watching the tele. I can open bottles on its teeth.'

'You took it from outside your wife's house?' I said.

He nodded.

'Then you killed it?'

'It just came apart in my hands.'

'Then you had it stuffed.'

He nodded again. 'You can have it if you want. Take it home to Sheila.'

'You're a bastard,' I said.

He shrugged as if to say: 'So what?'

Harper said to Rugby Player #1, 'Get your mate, and get this garbage down to the car. Cookie, you go with them.'

The two men obeyed, and left the room with Cochran between them. I heard some conversation from the kitchen where Rugby Player #2 had been continuing the search, then footsteps outside and someone trying to replace the metal door in the frame, then silence.

Harper said to Phillips, 'Better get some uniforms down here to make this place secure. I don't want any of this stuff going missing.'

Phillips nodded and left the room. From outside I heard him talking on his radio.

Harper said, 'It's going to give me great satisfaction to see that fucker go down for a while.'

'How long?' I asked.

He shrugged. 'Who knows? A couple of years. Depends on the judge.'

'He won't do six months,' I said. 'Fancy killing that poor little dog. What am I going to tell his wife?'

'That's your problem.'

'Yeah,' I agreed. 'Isn't it just?'

Phillips came back with evidence bags and put the gun and ammunition inside two of them. 'Reinforcements on the way, sir,' he said.

'Good,' said Harper. 'I'm going back to the station to have a chat with our mate. You stay here. Keep looking. You don't know what you might find. Get a lift back in the squad car. If anything floats to the surface, let me know. The more the merrier with this slag.'

Phillips nodded.

'You coming?' said Harper to me.

'Not in the same car as him,' I replied.

'You can go in the Land-Rover.'

'Can I have the dog?' I asked.

Harper shook his head. 'Not until it's been examined. It's stuffed, and who knows what's inside it. Sorry.'

'Can I have it when you're finished with it?'

'Depends. It's his property.'

'He stole it. And he did say I could have it. You heard him.'

'We'll see. Don't worry, I'll make sure it's not busted up too much. Mind you, I can't think why you want it. You can't give it back to his missus, can you?'

'I know,' I said. 'I just don't want him to have it.'

'Fair enough,' said Harper. 'Come on, let's go.'

And he picked up the bags containing the gun and ammunition and left the room.

We went out of the flat through the ruined door. On the landing, Harper stopped, turned to me and said, 'Looks like we've got a name for the second victim.'

'Yeah?'

'Yeah. Sandra Richards. An amateur whore. Her boyfriend reported her missing last night. She was last seen on Wednesday, plying her trade round the back of the Ritzy cinema. She'd never been nicked. That's why her fingerprint wasn't on file.'

'Any leads?' I asked.

'Not one. Poor cow. Looks like she got more than she bargained for that night.'

'Anything on the first one?'

'Not a thing. Anyway, thanks for this. At least we've had one result.'

He called the lift and we went down in it. The two hammer wielders gave me a lift back to Brixton to get my car. I knew I wouldn't be wanted in the station, so I told one of them to tell Harper I'd be in touch and got into the Jag and drove home. I was back by eight.

A busy morning.

26

On the way there, I picked up the latest copy of
Exchange & Mart. When I'd made some tea, I took
the cup to the table and found the 'Pets' section of
the paper. I ran down the columns full of advertise-
ments for pedigree dogs until I found a kennels that
sold West Highland Whites close by. It was located
in Penge and I gave them a bell straight off. A man's
voice answered after the third ring.

'Hood's Kennels,' the voice said. 'John Hood
speaking.'

'Do you have any West Highland White Terrier
pups for sale?' I asked.

'Yes,' said the voice. 'As a matter of fact I do.'

'Dogs?' I asked. 'Males, I mean.'

'Several.'

'Ready to leave?'

'Absolutely. Complete with pedigrees and vaccination certificates. Did you wish to purchase one?'

'It's for a friend,' I said.

'We don't usually recommend buying animals for
other people . . .'

'It's to replace a dog that died,' I interrupted.

'Ah, that's different. Did the dog die recently?'

'A matter of weeks ago.'

'Good timing.'

'I have a photo of the dog that died. Shall I bring

it?' A stupid question really, but I hadn't quite recovered from finding Prince in Cochran's flat. Not like that. It was disrespectful somehow. A denial of dignity.

'By all means. When do you want to come by?'

'This morning . . . Now.'

'We're open. I'll be here all day.'

'I'll be over in half an hour.'

He gave me directions from the town centre, and I hung up, went out to my car and headed south.

I found the place without much trouble. It was down a muddy road by some playing fields. Mr Hood turned out to be a portly individual in a Barbour, jeans and Wellington boots. He took me into the kitchen of his house adjacent to where the dogs were kept, and insisted on making a pot of tea.

I wasn't arguing. He passed round the Benson & Hedges, and we sat at the kitchen table.

'You said you had a photo,' he said. 'Although I can't promise a perfect match.'

I took out the picture of Prince and put it on the table in front of him. 'Attractive dog,' he said. 'What happened to him? If this picture's recent, he looks not much older than a pup himself.'

'An accident,' I said. 'Tragic. His owner's very upset.' I didn't bother to tell him that she didn't even know yet. 'So I decided to buy her another.'

'Good move. Unless, of course, she rejects the whole idea.'

'If she does, can I bring the dog back?'

'Of course. We're in the business of making both people and dogs happy. I'd rather keep my dogs than let them go to the wrong home.'

I liked Mr Hood a whole lot better after that. 'That's good to know,' I said. 'Can I see what you've got?'

Hood took me through to the kennels. They were small and warm. We walked past several dogs behind wire mesh screens until he found half a dozen pups cavorting around in a rather larger area.

'There you are,' he said. 'Take your pick.'

'Which one do you reckon?' I asked. 'I'm afraid you're talking to a novice here.'

He bent down and put his hands into the woolly mess of tiny animals and pulled out one. 'This is the chap for you,' he said. 'Three months old. A lovely dog. Feel that nose. Look at those eyes. Strong back, firm hindquarters, and a tail that never stops wagging.'

'You've sold me,' I said. 'What's the deal?'

Eventually, after some haggling which Mr Hood seemed to enjoy immensely, for two hundred quid I got the pup in a cardboard box lined with yesterday's *Guardian*, complete with pedigree and vaccination certificates, a wicker basket, a blanket, a cushion, a blue tartan collar with a blank silver metal tag attached, ready to be engraved with his name and address, six tins of puppy food, a doggy bowl, a packet of puppy chew, whatever the hell that was, a rubber bone and a red rubber ball that squeaked when it was squeezed.

Seemed fair enough to me. I paid cash, got a receipt, put the pup in the box in the well in front of the passenger seat of my car, the bits and pieces on the back seat, and the red rubber ball in the pocket of my leather jacket so that it didn't roll around inside the car.

Mr Hood and I shook hands and I headed towards Herne Hill again. Now came the bad bit.

I parked the Jag in front of Sheila Cochran's house and got out. I opened the front gate, walked up the path, and knocked on the door. Sheila opened it a few seconds later, and she knew. It must have been the look on my face.

'It's about Prince, isn't it?' she said.

I nodded.

'You've found him?'

I nodded again.

'He's dead, isn't he?'

For the third time.

'Was it Eddie?'

Once again, the nod.

'Did you see Prince?'

I shook my head that time. I wasn't going to tell her. Not then. Not ever, if I didn't have to.

'But you're sure.'

The fifth nod.

'Eddie's done something bad.' Not a question, a statement.

'Yes.' I actually spoke.

'Where is he?'

'Under arrest.'

'Because of that bottle I gave you?'

'Yes.'

'Poor Prince,' she said, and her face crumpled, and she leaned against the doorpost for support. I stepped forward and put my arms around her. She was like a woman without bones. I held her and she began to sob. I swear I patted her back, just like they do in films. Big waste of time if you ask me. How does that help?

I led her gently back into the living room. I put her into a chair and stood awkwardly by as she kept on crying. 'Tea?' I said.

She shook her head.

'I brought someone to see you,' I said.

She looked up at me through her tears. 'Who?'

'I don't know his name.'

She began to twig. 'Not another dog?' she said.

I made one of those gestures that I believe novelists call deprecating.

'Oh no,' she said.

'It seemed a shame not to make use of that dog flap,' I said.

'No, no, no.'

'I can always take him back.'

She said nothing.

'If that's what you want.'

She looked up at me again. 'I couldn't bear it,' she said. 'What happens if Eddie hurts this one too?'

'I don't think *he'll* be about for a bit. And even if he is, I don't think he'll bother you again. There's a certain Detective Sergeant at Brixton nick who's making Eddie his personal project. Something tells me he'll be a good boy in future.'

'I don't know, Nick. Hearing about Prince has come as a hell of a shock.'

'I'll take him back then,' I said. 'The man at the kennels said I could if you didn't want him. It seems like a shame, though.'

'Why?'

'Because I packed all his toys.' And I took the ridiculous red rubber ball that squeaked when you pressed it out of my pocket and did just that. It made the stupidest noise I've ever heard, and Sheila started to cry again. But not in the same way, and I knew I'd sold her on the idea. 'He's outside in the car,' I said. 'You can have a quick look at him before I take him away, if you like.'

She dried her eyes on a tissue and I took her out to the car. I lifted out the box and put it on the bonnet. 'He's probably wet himself,' I said, and opened the container. As it happened, he hadn't. The sports page of the *Guardian* was as dry as when

Mr Hood had put him in. The dog popped his head over the edge of the opening and panted at the pair of us.

Sheila lifted him out and held him close to her. 'He's so sweet. Don't you really know his name?'

'It's on his papers,' I said. 'But it's a bit long-winded to remember after such a short acquaintance. You could call him King if you like. That's a good name.' And I winced. That might not have been a very good idea, but Sheila took to it right away.

'That's great,' she enthused.

'So you're going to keep him?'

She looked up at me from under her eyelashes again. 'If you think I should.'

'I wouldn't have got him for you if I hadn't. And the man from the kennels agreed.'

'Then I'll keep him. But you must let me pay . . .'

I shook my head. 'No,' I said. 'He's a gift.'

'You're very kind.'

'I got him some bits and pieces,' I said, leaned into the car and brought out my booty. 'This way he'll be off to a fresh start.'

'That's wonderful,' she said. 'Bring that stuff in and we'll get him settled.'

And she did just that. She made me tea, and we sat and chatted as King roamed round, getting used to his new home. Sheila didn't ask me about Eddie Cochran again. That was good. Plenty of time for that later.

After an hour of playing gooseberry in a new love affair, I said goodbye to Sheila and King, and left.

27

I went straight home, took the phone off the hook and went to bed. I didn't wake up until almost five o'clock that evening.

When I did, it was one of those strange awakenings when even the most familiar objects seem odd. Alien. Nothing fitted.

I lay on my back in the dim light that filtered through the curtains, and tried to work out what day it was. What month it was. What year it was, for God's sake.

I rubbed the sleep out of my eyes and ran my fingers through my hair.

I got up, switched on a light and went to the bathroom. When I'd finished, I filled the kettle, switched it on, and put the phone back.

It rang within two minutes. It was Sophia.

'Where have you been?' she demanded. 'I've been trying to get you all afternoon.'

'Asleep,' I replied. 'Yesterday was a long day. What's up?'

'There's been another.'

'Another what?' Although I knew.

'Another parcel from John.'

'Oh, Jesus. He did say there was going to be. Where?'

'It was delivered to Peter's flat.'

'I don't believe it. What was it this time?'

'Another ear.'

'One of the same people?'

'No. It was a man's.'

'How's Peter taken it?'

'Not well.'

'Is he doing the show tonight?'

'Yes. But I don't know how much more he can take of this.'

'Me neither. Where is he?'

'At home.'

'I'll give him a ring. I hope he doesn't just jump into a bottle. Not that I'd blame him if he did.'

'Nor me.'

'Listen,' I said, 'I haven't even asked you how you are.'

'I'm fine,' she replied.

'What are you doing later?'

'How much later?'

'This evening.'

'Nothing.'

'Can I see you?' Right then I needed to badly.

'Of course.'

'At that bar where we had lunch? Say eight o'clock?'

'I'll be there.'

I made my farewells and hung up. Before I had time to pick up the phone again, it rang. It was Peter Day.

'I've been trying to get you for hours,' he said.

'Sorry, mate.'

'Have you heard?'

'Yes. Sophia just called. I'm sorry.'

'Not half as sorry as I am.'

'Why don't you get out of there? Check into a hotel or something?'

'I'm staying put.'

'He knows where you live.'

'So what? It's not me he's cutting into pieces.'

'Not yet.' As soon as I said the words, I regretted them. He didn't reply.

'Sorry, Peter,' I said.

'Don't worry. You're not the first to say it.'

'Can I come over?'

'Why not? Charlie Harper's here.'

'I'll be with you in half an hour. Tell Charlie I'd like to see him before he goes.'

'I'll do that. I believe you had a little excitement earlier.'

'You could say that.'

'Well, they can't say you didn't do what you were hired for.'

'That's true. Listen, I'll be there soon. We'll talk then.'

I made a cup of tea, got dressed and left for Brixton. I was at Day's flat by 5.45. The journalists and TV people were back with a vengeance, Piers included. Now wasn't the time to speak to him, so I pushed through the throng and had a word with the police constable guarding the front door. He radioed through to someone inside, then allowed me to enter.

I went up in the lift and found another constable outside Day's flat door. He let me straight through. Harper was waiting in the hall.

'In the kitchen,' he ordered. 'My guv'nor's talking to Peter.'

I went into the room and he followed, closing the door tightly behind him.

'Lambert doesn't know you were with us this morning.'

'Don't worry. I'm not going to tell him.'

'Good. Cochran's banged up nicely, and I wish this other bastard was too.'

'I'll second that. Is the little shit being co-operative?'

'Singing like a bird. Chapter and verse on who his mates are, and what they've done.'

'Great,' I said. 'So what exactly happened this morning?'

'Somebody, we don't know who, came by at about eleven. He left a package for Peter with the care-taker. He said he couldn't get any reply from the flat, so couldn't get into the block. The caretaker delivered it up here at eleven-thirty. Day took one look at the package and called us.'

'And?'

'And inside was an ear from a Caucasian male.'

'So John was telling the truth last night?'

Harper nodded.

'And he said the best was yet to come.'

'So he did.'

'I wonder what he meant by that? And how *did* he know where Pete lives?'

Before Harper could answer, the kitchen door opened and DI Lambert stood in the doorway.

'Oh, it's you,' he said with a scowl. 'Day told me you were coming.'

'I couldn't stay away.'

'I take it you know what's happened?'

I nodded.

'A terrible business.'

'Do you think Peter should stay here?' I asked.

'*I* don't. But he insists.'

'I'll have a word with him.'

'Do that. By the way, I understand we owe you a vote of thanks.' You could tell that it almost hurt him to say it.

I looked at Harper. His expression didn't change.

'That Cochran business,' Lambert went on. It was his turn to look at Harper. 'I expect you've heard about it.'

'I heard,' I said.

'Thanks,' said Lambert. Then to Harper: 'Charlie, I'm off now. I'll see you later.'

'Yes, sir,' said Harper.

'We'll liaise tonight.' And Lambert left the room. I heard the front door open and slam shut behind him.

'A man of few words,' I said.

'That was enthusiastic praise,' said Harper. 'Coming from him.'

'I'd hate to hear him tear anyone off a strip then.'

'You're right. Believe me. I'd better go too. Will you be at Sunset tonight?'

'S'pose so.'

'Right, I'll see you there. I'll just say goodbye to Peter.'

We both went out into the hall, and Harper opened the door to the living room. Peter Day was sitting in an armchair. He looked clean and sober, but when he shook my hand I saw that his was shaking badly.

'I'm off now,' said Harper. 'Are you sure you're up to it tonight?'

Day nodded.

'Right. I'll see you later. And you, Sharman,' he added.

'See you,' I said, and he left the room, and once more I heard the front door open and close.

Day went back to his seat.

'Peter,' I said, 'are you quite sure you want to go on with this?'

'I have to.'

197

'Why?'

'Because I do. It started with me, and it'll finish with me.'

Or be the finish of you, I thought as I looked at his face, which seemed even older and more haggard than it had the previous night.

'Do you want me to collect you tonight?' I asked.

'Please. You don't mind, do you?'

'Of course not.'

'Thanks.'

'Do you want to talk?'

He shook his head mournfully. 'No,' he said.

'Then I'll see you later.'

He nodded but said nothing, and I left.

Although I was almost a couple of hours early, I went round to the bar where I'd arranged to meet Sophia. I got a beer and asked for the food menu. I ordered a burger and chips with a side salad and blue cheese dressing. I sat in a window seat again as I ate and looked at the street outside, trying to ignore MTV on a screen above the bar and the noise of the punters around me.

When I'd finished eating I had a coffee, then another couple of beers, and as eight o'clock rolled around, I saw Sophia turn into the small courtyard outside. She stopped in the doorway and looked round. I caught her eye and she came over.

She looked at the bottles in front of me and said, 'Been here long?'

'A while,' I replied. 'I went and saw Peter, but he wasn't very forthcoming so I left. I'm picking him up later. Drink?'

'I'll have what you're having.'

I caught the waiter's eye and ordered two more beers. 'So how are you?' I asked.

'Better for seeing you, but worse for what happened today.'

'It certainly is no joke,' I said as the drinks arrived.

'This bloody man seems to be able to come and go as he pleases, and the police can't do a thing.'

'They can't be everywhere at once. He pops up and then vanishes. That's the way it is. They can't read his mind.'

'Can't *you* do anything?'

'Me? No. All I can do is keep Peter company.'

We were silent for a long minute. Eventually she broke the silence and asked, 'How did it go this morning?'

I told her. She was horrified at what Cochran had done to Prince, but relieved that he was in custody. When I told her I'd bought Sheila Cochran a puppy to make up for the loss of her dog, she touched my hand and said, 'You're a nice man.'

I swear I blushed. 'I don't think you'll have any more trouble from Sector 88.'

'That's a relief at least. You're quite the detective, aren't you?'

'Sometimes I surprise myself. But it was mostly luck. That's probably how they'll catch John. If they do.'

'You think they might not?'

'Sometimes these people just vanish. Stop whatever they're doing and go back to a normal life.'

'There's a thought. His definition of normal. I wonder if we'll ever be normal again, any of us?'

'I don't know,' I said, and looked at her face. It wasn't a bad view.

'I'll be glad when those bloody reporters stop hanging around.'

'You don't like them, do you?'

'No, I don't. One of them tried to chat me up today.'

I felt a pang of jealousy. 'Did you enjoy it?'

'No, I didn't. He was a horrible little lech. All sweaty and stammering.'

'I expect he'll want you to pose for him.'

'Fat chance. Will you come round later?' she asked, changing the subject abruptly.

'If you want me to.'

'Of course I do. I even brought you these.' She delved into her handbag and brought out a key ring with two keys attached. 'The Yale opens the front door, and the Chubb's for my flat door,' she explained. 'Now don't lose them.'

'You're a trusting soul.'

'With you I am.' And she leaned over and kissed me on the cheek.

After all I'd seen and heard over the past week it was a relief to sit and talk to someone who was still capable of trust. The next two hours flew, and before I knew it it was time to drop her off and go and collect Day. I must confess I wasn't looking forward to the night ahead at all.

28

We arrived at Sunset at eleven. Day hadn't said much when I collected him from his flat, or on the subsequent short drive to the station. I was getting fed up with the whole thing. How much longer could it go on?

When we got to the production office, there was an envelope waiting for me. It contained a cheque for twenty-one hundred quid. It answered my question. Another week.

I stuck the cheque in my jacket pocket and got a coffee. Day vanished upstairs. I didn't follow him, just ignored the 'No Smoking' signs and lit a Silk Cut.

There was a message from Harper that he'd be late, if he got there at all. I didn't blame him for not showing up. It must have been as frustrating for him as it was for me to be on the scene of crimes as horrendous as the ones perpetrated by John, or The Midnight Crawler, or whatever he was calling himself that day, and to be so powerless.

At five to twelve I joined Day in the studio. He ignored me, but not in the way he'd once done. Like my presence made him uncomfortable. It was almost as if he didn't want me there at all which was fine by me, but not what he kept saying. And at three hundred nicker per I would have been crazy to walk out and leave the whole mess behind, much as I might want to.

I sat quietly as Day and Stretch ran the show. It was warm in the studio and I kept finding myself nodding off. Eventually I left the room on the pretext of going to the Gents, but I didn't, and I didn't go back. Instead I went downstairs for more coffee to wake myself up.

The speakers in the production office were turned down low. I was alone. Just me, a plastic cup of sweet brown liquid and a packet of cigarettes. I sat on the edge of a desk and thought about visiting Sophia after the show.

I was hardly listening when a record ended and John came on air. I think I must have missed the first couple of sentences he spoke. But as his voice registered I came awake, almost dropping my coffee on to my lap. I put down the cup, dropped my half-finished cigarette into it, and ran back to the staircase.

I reached the top and went along to the studio. There was a copper standing outside trying to get in.

'What's the matter?' I demanded.

'He's locked the door,' the uniform said in exasperation. 'And he's going crazy in there.'

'Christ!' I said, hesitated, then turned and went into the engineer's booth. Stretch was in there with another copper. They were arguing fiercely. The copper wanted to take the show off the air, Stretch wouldn't let him. The big black man made the copper look puny by comparison, so it was no contest.

I looked through the glass into the studio. The lights were very dim in there, and I saw Day, his face illuminated by the green glow from the computer screen, hunched over the control panel speaking into the mike. I was trying to listen to what was coming over the speakers and said to Stretch and the policeman: 'Shut up, the pair of you.'

Miraculously they did.

'. . . Why don't you just stop calling me?' I heard Peter Day saying in a voice that was close to breaking point. 'Just leave me alone, you bastard.'

'That's not nice, Peter,' said John. 'I've told you before about calling me names.'

'Shut up, you murdering little creep,' said Day. 'I've had about all I'm going to take from you.'

'Don't you believe it,' said John. 'I'll tell you when you've had enough. Just me, do you understand?' John sounded calm on the surface, certainly calmer than Day, but I could sense an underlying hysteria, as if he was about to crack.

'No,' said Day. 'No. *I'll* tell you when I've had enough. And that's now. Do you hear?'

'I hear you, Peter. But it makes no difference.'

'Cut it off,' said the copper. 'Pull the plugs.'

'No,' I said. 'Don't do it, Stretch. He's beginning to break.'

'They both are,' said Stretch.

'I know. That's a chance we've got to take. This thing has got to stop, and maybe this is the only way.'

'No. Cut them off,' said the copper.

'Your guv'nor won't thank me if you do,' I said.

'And he won't thank me if that mad fucker starts slaughtering people willy-nilly because some arsehole DJ can't control himself. And I was here, and did nothing about it.'

I looked at Stretch, and he looked back at me, but the decision was taken out of our hands.

'I warned you before that the best is yet to come,'

said John. 'And what I said was true.' And he cut himself off.

The electronically reproduced words hung in the air like smoke. He'd said them with such chill certainty that I knew he meant every one of them.

I looked through the glass and saw Day pull the faders down, cutting the station off the air.

He put his head in his hands and I wondered just what the hell he'd done.

29

'What happened?' I demanded. The switchboard was lighting up like a Christmas tree, and Stretch switched it off and put a record out on air before he answered.

'Peter freaked out.'

'I gathered that from listening to him. Why? I mean, was there anything in particular?'

'No. The loony came on. I switched him through, same as usual. Peter had locked the door and then just turned on him.'

I looked through the glass partition again. Day was sitting slumped in his seat. 'Talk to him, Stretch,' I said. 'Get him to open the door.'

'I'll try,' he said. 'Wish me luck.'

He touched the toggle that worked the mike into the studio, and said. 'Peter, are you OK?'

Day didn't move. Or speak.

Stretch repeated the question.

Still no answer from the dim interior of the other room.

Stretch looked at me and I said, 'Let me have a go.'

He made an 'It's all yours' gesture at the mike.

I flicked down the toggle and said, 'Peter, it's Nick. Why don't you open up and let me in?'

I saw Day's head move in my direction, and he nodded.

The record ended and Stretch cued another. I left the booth and walked down the short length of corridor to the door of the studio.

I heard the click of the lock as I arrived and the door swung open slightly.

I pushed it further and went inside. Day was standing by the console. His face was in shadow.

'Are you all right?' I asked.

He didn't reply.

'Peter?'

'Christ! I blew it, didn't I?' he said wearily.

'Don't say that. You've been under incredible pressure the last few days. I'm surprised you've managed as well as you have.'

'Thank you *so* much.'

Obviously I was taking the wrong track. Mind you, as far as he was concerned, probably any track would be the wrong one at that precise moment.

'Do you want to go home?'

He nodded.

'Can I give you a lift?'

'I'll get a cab.'

'Please yourself.'

'I will. From now on, I will.'

'I'll be going then,' I said.

He didn't reply, so I left him and went back to find Stretch. He was in his booth. Everything was switched off, but I could hear music from the speakers.

'What about the show?' I asked.

'Tim's doing it from the other studio. How's Peter?'

'Rough. He's had it. I doubt if he'll be talking to John again.'

'What's he doing?'

'He's going to get a cab home. Looks like it's all over.'

'What about you?'

'I'm going to split too.'

'Well, I'll see you around,' he said, and put out his hand. I shook it.

'It's been interesting.'

'You can say that again.'

But I didn't. I just walked downstairs, out the back, got into my car, drove to Sophia's flat and let myself in with the keys she had given me.

She was sitting in the kitchen when I arrived, dressed in jeans and a man's denim shirt. The radio was on, tuned to Sunset.

She stood up as I walked in the door.

'Nick,' she said, 'what happened?'

'Did you hear the show?'

'Yes. It was awful. I tried to phone, but there was no answer on any of the lines. If you hadn't arrived I would have driven over. Where's Peter? How is he?'

I answered the latter question first. 'Bad,' I said. 'He went home in a cab. He doesn't seem to want me around any more.'

'Should I call him? Should I go over?'

I shrugged. 'I don't know. I don't think he wants any company right now. He thinks he blew it.'

'What do you think?'

'I think that if he hadn't let go, he would have gone crazy.'

'Do you think I *should* call him?'

'Why not?'

'Pour yourself some coffee, I won't be long.' She came up and kissed me lightly, then left the room.

I did as she said, poured a cup of coffee, added milk and sugar, and sat down in the chair she had vacated. It was still warm. I felt as tired as I'd ever done in my life. Tired and old and sick of the things that people were capable of doing to each other.

From another room I heard her talking. She was gone for as long as it took for me to finish my drink. When she returned there was a troubled look in her beautiful eyes.

'You were right. He is bad. I said I'd go and see him, but he doesn't want to see anyone.'

'I told you.'

'He sent his apologies to you. He said he was very rude, and he's sorry. He'll call you soon.'

'He knows I'm here?'

'I told him. I'm not ashamed of your being here.'

'I'm very pleased to hear it. Coffee?'

She nodded, and I poured out two cups and handed her one. We both sat at the kitchen table opposite each other.

'Is this the end, do you think?' she asked.

'The end for Peter talking to The Midnight Crawler, that's for sure. When Harper hears what went down tonight, he won't be pleased.'

'Do you think the killing will stop?'

'Because of Peter? I doubt it. If anything, it might get worse.'

She paled, and I reached over and placed my hand over hers. Her skin was very cold.

'Don't worry,' I said. 'Believe me, it won't help.'

She tried to smile with little success. 'What do you want to do?' she asked.

'Go to bed with you,' I replied. 'And try to forget about all this crap.'

She looked over at me, and smiled again. This time a bit more enthusiastically.

'Good idea,' she said. 'I'll race you for the duvet.'

We got up, linked arms, and went into the bedroom. The bedside lamp glowed in one corner and the sheets were turned down. I pulled her close and kissed her, feeling the curves of her body through the shirt. I closed my eyes and rested my head against hers. Although I was trying to forget, I could still hear John's voice going through my head.

She began undoing my shirt, and we moved over to the bed and collapsed on it. As she undressed me, I did the same to her.

She was wearing white underwear, and by coincidence so was I, but anything further from a pair of virgins I couldn't imagine.

She squirmed all over me, her hands at first freezing on my body, then gradually getting warmer. I undid her bra, and allowed her breasts freedom, and watched as the nipples puckered when exposed to the air. Then I pulled her panties down, and stroked the smoothness of the skin of her buttocks and slid my fingers into the warmth between her legs.

We kissed for what seemed like hours until neither of us could stand it, and we joined together. And only then was I able to dismiss John's voice from my mind.

She woke me at seven-thirty.

'Good morning,' she said, and handed me a cup of coffee. She was naked.

I looked at the clock next to the bed. 'God, but you're an early bird,' I said.

'Some of us have got to work.'

And it all came flooding back and I groaned.

She slid back beneath the sheets and nearly lost the cup as she started to kiss me.

'I thought you were going to work,' I said.

'This is work,' came her muffled voice from under the covers. 'Shall I stop?'

I put down the coffee and pulled her up next to me.

'I think you'd better,' I said. 'Or else productivity

is going to hit an all time low.'

'I'd say you were producing something very nice, very well.'

'Stop it,' I said.

She pulled a mock solemn face and said, 'Quite right, Nick. I'm glad you're the kind of man who takes *my* job seriously. Now I'd better get dressed.'

'Can I watch?'

'You've got eyes, haven't you?'

She hopped out of bed and began to dress. She put on a tiny black bra and matching pants, black tights, a black blouse, a dark blue suit with a very short skirt, and black, heeled shoes. As she was finishing her make-up in the mirror, I said, 'Doing anything tonight?'

'Going out with a dishy bloke.'

'Really?'

'Really.'

'Anyone I know?'

'I doubt it.'

'What does he do?'

'He's a private detective, very macho.'

'A real stud.'

'In his youth, I think he probably was. He's a bit past it now.'

I threw a pillow at her.

She was ready by eight-fifteen, pulled on her black coat, checked her handbag and came over and kissed me again.

'You can let yourself out when you're ready. There's food in the fridge and yesterday's loaf in the bread bin. Call me at the office later. But not too much later.'

I wanted to say 'I love you' as she went, but I restrained myself. Instead I just said, 'Take care.' And with a swirl from the skirts of her coat she was gone.

30

I got up about fifteen minutes later, pulled the bed-clothes straight, and went to the bathroom. When I was finished, I got half dressed and wandered into the kitchen. There I found enough warm coffee to make another cup, which I heated up and drank with a couple of slices of toast and marmalade. I washed up the few dishes, dried them, and put them away. Then I went and finished getting dressed, got my keys and split.

As I opened the front door, I met the postman on the step. He handed me half a dozen letters. Two were for Sophia. I separated hers from the rest, and put them on a small table in the hall that was obviously there for that purpose.

On the way back home I stopped off at Sheila Cochran's place. She was just getting ready to take King out for his morning constitutional. She looked years younger and smiled easily. She told me that Chas was becoming a regular caller, and blushed as she said it. King was all over the shop whilst we talked, banging around our legs for attention and obviously as much in love with his new mistress as she was with him.

I left them with a promise to call again soon, and continued my drive home. I was in the house by ten-thirty, had a shower and shave, changed into an old pair of jeans and a soft tartan work shirt and gave the place a lick and a promise to keep the dust and clutter at bay.

I wasn't feeling ecstatic, mainly because of Peter Day's behaviour the night before, but I was feeling pretty good, all things considered, mainly because of Sophia. When I picked up the phone to call her at midday all that changed, and I don't think I've felt pretty good since.

I got through to the switchboard and asked for her by name. The operator said that she didn't think she was in yet, and I got the first feeling in my stomach of something being wrong. I asked to be put through to Tony Hillerman and tapped my fingers on the table where I kept the phone as I waited to be connected.

Eventually he answered. He sounded harassed and short-tempered.

'Hello, Tony,' I said. 'Nick Sharman. How are you?'

'Busy,' he replied.

'Is Sophia there?'

'No, she bloody well isn't! She hasn't come in yet today. Christ knows *where* she is.'

'But you were expecting her, weren't you?' The feeling of wrongness increased.

'Of course I was. There's a mountain of stuff here to be dealt with. And with what happened last night, I'm up to my ears. How could you let Peter Day do that?'

'I'm not his keeper. I was hired to sort out Sector 88, which is exactly what I did do.'

'I know, I know, I'm sorry,' said Hillerman. 'And I haven't had a chance to thank you properly.'

Properly? He hadn't thanked me at all.

'Forget that,' I said. 'I was paid to do the job. I don't need any thanks for doing it. Just tell me where Sophia is.'

'I've told you already, I don't know. She's probably gone off shopping or something and forgotten the time.' The bad feeling was getting worse all the time, and I gripped the phone hard until the plastic cut into the skin on the palms of my hand.

'Has she ever done it before?' I asked, amazed that my voice sounded so calm in my ears.

'Well, no, but . . .'

'And she didn't do it this morning.'

'How the hell do you know?'

'Because I was with her when she left for work. She didn't say anything about shopping or anything else.'

'You were *what*?'

'You heard. I was at her flat when she left for work, and only for work.' I was suddenly realising what was happening, and the pain in my guts was almost unbearable. 'Listen,' I went on, interrupting whatever he was saying, 'I'm going round to her place to check she hasn't gone home, then I'm coming to Sunset. I want to see you the minute I get there.'

'How will you get into her house?'

'I've got keys. I'll be with you soon. Maybe she did change her mind and go off somewhere. I hope so. But if she didn't I want the police in on this immediately. You'd better try and get hold of your friend Harper.'

'He's not being very friendly after last night.'

'Just get him,' I said, slammed the phone down, and left on the run.

I drove to Clapham fast and entered the house before twelve-thirty. Sophia's letters were still on the table. I took them up to the flat. It was just as I had left it. I tossed the mail on the kitchen table and went through each room just to make sure she wasn't there. I went outside and checked the street,

213

and those nearby. I found her car parked around the corner. The bonnet was stone cold. As soon as I saw it sitting there, I knew, I positively knew, that something very bad had happened. Part of my mind tried to tell me that it wouldn't start, and that she'd taken a cab or a bus somewhere. But I knew that if it hadn't started, she would have simply come back and bullied me into giving her a lift to work.

I went back to my car and drove the short distance to Sunset. I was outside Hillerman's office by one-fifteen. Harper was with him. They were both drinking coffee when I walked in.

'Is she here?' I demanded, although I knew that she wasn't.

Hillerman shook his head.

I turned to Harper. 'What are you doing about it?'

'We've circulated her description to every officer in the area.'

'A fat fucking lot of good that's going to do!' I said, then I hesitated. I didn't want to articulate my fears, but I knew that I'd have to sooner or later. 'You know what I think, don't you?'

The pair of them looked at me.

'Jesus!' I exploded. 'What the fuck is the matter with you? *He's* got her.'

'We don't know that,' said Harper, although he obviously knew who I meant.

'And we don't know he hasn't,' I said. 'And you're sitting around here on your fat arses drinking coffee.'

'Listen, Sharman,' said Harper, 'we don't know that anything's happened to her. She could be anywhere.'

'But she's not anywhere, is she? She was on her way here when she left me.'

'Just calm down and tell what you know.'

I stood in the room and told them what had happened that morning. I told them about finding her car, and their expressions got more gloomy. I gave Harper a description of what Sophia had been wearing. As I told him, I could see her getting dressed in front of me, and the pain in my stomach turned like the blade of a knife. When I'd finished he got on the phone to Brixton police station to pass on the information.

Whilst he was talking, Hillerman tried to tell me that Sophia would turn up soon, none the worse, with some story about taking the morning off.

That really pissed me off, and I told him so in no uncertain terms. He half rose from his chair and I told him to sit down again or I'd knock him down. It was that sort of conversation.

Harper hurriedly wrapped up his phone call and tried to calm the situation. I wasn't having any of it. My stomach was knotted into lumps and I wanted to hit someone. Anyone. And Tony Hillerman seemed as good a person to hit as any. But there was no point. It would have been a waste of energy.

'Has anyone spoken to Peter Day lately?' I asked.

'I've been leaving messages for him all morning,' said Hillerman. 'His answerphone's permanently on.'

'I'm going round there,' I said. 'She just might have gone to see him. I know she was worried about him last night.'

'She hasn't been there,' said Harper. 'I checked with the officers who've been on duty outside.'

'I'm going anyway,' I said. 'He might know something. I'll check back with you.'

And with that, I left.

My stomach was churning and I could feel the muscles in my arms and legs shaking as I drove to

Day's block of flats. I parked the car just round the corner and walked through the small crowd of newsmen. Piers was there, but I only acknowledged him briefly before going up to the front door. There was a uniformed man on duty. He stepped forward and I told him who I was, and he let me through. Maybe Harper had told him know I was coming. Maybe not. If he had tried to stop me, the mood I was in, I would have knocked him out.

The front door was open, and I went up in the lift and rang Day's flat bell. At first there was no answer, but I persevered and eventually he answered. He was looking even worse than when I'd last seen him, if that were possible. I didn't care how bad he looked. I was past caring.

'What do you want?' he asked, blocking the doorway with his hip.

'I need to see you.'

'What about?'

'Can I come in?' I asked. I was amazed at my patience.

Reluctantly he allowed me to pass, and I went straight into the living room. It was quiet in there, and I turned to face him as he followed me in.

'Have you seen Sophia today?' I asked.

He shook his head. 'No. Why?'

'She's disappeared.'

'*What*?' His face registered amazement. 'What do you mean, disappeared?'

'Exactly what I say. She hasn't been to work today.'

'Maybe she's ill. Gone off somewhere . . .'

'No. You know I was at her place last night. She told you on the phone. She left for work this morning at eight-fifteen, and never got there.'

'What are you saying?'

'I'm saying that she left her flat and vanished. Her

car's still parked outside. No one's seen her since. You know what I'm saying?'

'John?' That one word summed it all up. His face crumpled and he sat down in an armchair, hard. 'My God,' he said. 'You don't think . . . ?'

'I think that he said the best was yet to come last night. I say he knows us, but we don't know him. I say that he's got her.'

'Oh, Jesus.'

'Oh Jesus is right. You know what it means if he's got her, don't you?'

He didn't answer, just put his face into his hands and started to sob.

I didn't have time for all that.

'If he took her because of what you said to him last night . . .' I didn't finish the sentence, just turned on my heel and left.

I went back past the policeman and the reporters and got into my car. I drove to Sophia's place and phoned Sunset. Harper was still there. He'd heard nothing. I promised to keep in touch.

I stayed in her flat for hours, walking round, smoking cigarette after cigarette and drinking coffee. Every hour or so I got in touch with Harper. Still nothing.

When it got dark I got into the car and drove round the streets of south London looking for her, although I knew that I'd never find her. I knew where she was, but I also knew that it was pointless going home, the state I was in. As I drove I kept the car radio tuned into Sunset, where Tim was once again doing the midnight to three in the morning show.

As the night got older I kept checking in with the police and at her place, but she was nowhere to be found.

John didn't call the radio station that night.

31

A Jiffy bag containing the little, ring and middle
finger of Sophia's right hand was mailed to Sunset
Radio, first class, special delivery from Brixton main
post office sometime on Wednesday afternoon.

The parcel was routinely intercepted by the police
when it was delivered on Thursday morning. The
first I knew about it was when Charlie Harper
phoned my place at nine-thirty that morning.

I'd fallen asleep on the sofa fully dressed sometime around 7 a.m. I came awake with a start as the
telephone rang. I was stiff, my eyes felt grainy and
my mouth tasted of the remains of fifty cigarettes.

I felt around for the phone and said, 'Yes?'

'Nick, Charlie Harper here.' It was the first time
he'd ever used my Christian name. It should have
warned me.

'What?'

'Bad news, I'm afraid.'

I was suddenly wide awake.

'Tell me,' I said, but I knew.

He told me what had happened. I sat and listened
and felt my whole body go cold.

'Where is it now?' I asked when he'd finished.

'At the lab.'

'I want to see it.'

'I don't think that's a very good idea.'

'I don't care what you think.'

He was silent. Then he relented. 'You know where to go, don't you?'

'Sure.'

'I'll meet you there in half an hour.'

'I'll be there. And you'd better tell them, no jokes. No pathologist's humour, or there'll be trouble.'

'No jokes, Nick.'

'And, Charlie . . .' I think that was the first time I'd used his Christian name to him too. I couldn't remember.

'Yes.'

'She's dead, isn't she?'

He didn't answer right away.

'Isn't she?' I repeated.

'They're not sure.'

'She is,' I said. 'And, Charlie?'

'What?'

'You'd better get him before I do.'

He made no reply, and I put down the phone.

I closed my eyes and a black cloak of grief covered me. I fumbled for the first cigarette of the day, lit it, then stubbed it out in the overflowing ashtray.

I went into the bathroom and looked at myself in the mirror. I didn't like what I saw. My eyes were rimmed with red and I needed a shave. My face had a greyish tinge and my hair was sticking up from my head.

I splashed water on to my face and pulled wet fingers through my hair to tidy it. Why, I don't know. I wasn't going out on a date. Or maybe I was.

I went back into the kitchen, opened the fridge and found some juice that was just past its sell-by date. I took a mouthful, but I knew if I drank any more I'd throw up.

I took my jacket, left the flat, got into my car and drove to Lambeth mortuary. Attached was the path lab. Harper was waiting in the little room they laughingly called reception when I arrived.

He took me through to a room that smelled of death. On a stainless steel counter was the Jiffy bag. Next to it was a polystyrene cold box. A young bloke in a white coat that hadn't been properly laundered, so that the front was dotted with old blood and chemical stains, was standing by the counter. He looked at me, and I looked at Harper, and Harper looked at the bloke who lifted the lid of the cold box. Inside, it was packed with dry ice that steamed as it was exposed to the warmer outside air. Not that it was much warmer, but warm enough. He brushed the steam aside with his hand. A silver-coloured specimen tray was embedded in the ice. Resting on the tray were the contents of the Jiffy bag.

I couldn't look at first, but I plucked up courage and walked over.

Lying neatly on the tray were the three fingers, still attached to each other by a web of skin. The finger nails were scuffed and broken, the deep red varnish peeled back in places. On the middle finger of the three was the distinctive ring with the black stone in a gold surround. The skin was grey, and where the cut had been made the flesh was black and puffy with a thick scab of dried blood, and I could see splinters of white bone that had been crushed by the blow that had severed her fingers from her hand.

I remembered the short time that I had spent with her, and how I'd kissed those very fingers, and what it had felt like when they touched me. I bit down hard on my lip until I tasted blood.

I looked away. I wanted to cry, but nothing came.

I looked over at Harper. He seemed embarrassed. So did the bloke in the white coat.

I turned my back on the remains of Sophia. The smell of chemicals was getting to me. I tasted the juice in the back of my throat and went to one of the three sinks that were mounted on one wall and puked up a thin bile that lay on the bottom of the sink until I rinsed it away.

I took a mouthful of water from the tap and spat it down the plug hole.

I felt Harper's presence behind me.

'Are you all right?' he asked.

Stupid question really. It was going to be a long time until I was all right. A long time, and a long bitter road to travel.

'I'll survive,' I said. 'I've got to get out of here.'

The bloke in the white coat closed the cold box, and the three of us left the room. In the corridor I touched the pathologist's sleeve.

'She's dead, isn't she?' I asked.

He looked from me to Harper and back again. 'We can't be sure. Not one hundred per cent.'

'What per cent *can* you be sure?'

He looked uncomfortable as he answered. I don't know why. It was all part of a day's work to him. 'Ninety. Ninety-five,' he said.

'That'll do,' I replied.

Harper and I left the bloke and we walked together out of the building, and I leaned on the wing of a car parked in one of the bays next to the mortuary and lit a cigarette. It tasted like shit, and I dropped it on to the ground and crushed the hot coal with the toe of my shoe.

'You're not going to do anything stupid, are you?' he asked me.

I shook my head. I didn't want to talk to him any more. What was the use?

32

I got back home, unplugged the phone, and made a pot of tea. The old standby. When in doubt get the tea bags out. I drank maybe half a dozen cups as I paced the short distance between the walls of my flat. One, two, three, four steps. Turn. One, two, three, four steps. Turn. Over and over again. The walk only punctuated by the lighting of cigarettes and the stubbing out of same after a few puffs.

I thought about Sophia as I walked. No one else. And the sense of loss washed over me like dirty water. I wanted to break everything in the room. To cry out at the unfairness of it. To cry at all. But no tears came. Although it was bright daylight outside, to me the sky was dark. The world had taken on a knife edge of sadness, and I doubted I would ever shake it off.

As I walked, I cursed the world.

At noon I plugged the phone back into its socket and rang Chas. He'd heard. I knew by his tone that he'd also heard I was involved in more than a business sense with Sophia.

I told him what I'd seen. I wanted it to be in the next day's paper. I don't know why really. I just wanted to talk, and Chas was enough of a friend but also distant enough from me for him to be the ideal person to talk to.

'Do you want me to come round?' he asked when I'd finished.

'No thanks,' I said.

'Perhaps you shouldn't be on your own?'

'I've had plenty of practice,' I said.

'How about tomorrow? I'm not working.'

'Maybe,' I said. 'Call me. And make sure that bastard knows that some people will *never* stop looking for him.'

'I will,' he said, and we hung up.

I looked at the kettle, and then at the vodka bottle a quarter full sitting on the sideboard, and mentally flipped a coin. The vodka won.

I poured a drink, using more of the dodgy juice from the fridge, and was sitting down on the sofa with yet another cigarette when the phone rang. Wishing I'd unplugged it after talking to Chas, I picked it up.

It was Peter Day. I'd almost forgotten about him.

'I just heard about Sophia,' he said. His voice seemed to come from another, unhappier place. If that were possible.

I didn't know what to say in reply, so I said nothing.

'Can you come over?' he asked.

I wasn't up to more grief, and said so.

'No,' he said. 'There's something here you should know about.'

'What?' I asked, mystified.

'I can't tell you on the phone. Nick, please come over.'

I looked at the vodka, then around the room I was sitting in, and decided maybe going out would be the best thing I could do. I feared that ghosts would walk the carpet with me if I stayed. Too many ghosts.

'OK,' I said. 'I'll be with you in a little while.'

'You'd better come in the back way. The press are here in force again.'

'I'll do that little thing, Peter,' I said, and hung up the phone.

I finished the vodka and orange in one swallow and left.

I got to his place and parked in the back alley. There was a Panda car across the back door of the flats. As I walked up to it a policewoman got out. When I told her who I was, she leaned into the car and used the radio. When she re-emerged, she said, 'You can go in.'

'Thanks,' I replied, and did. I went through the door and up the back stairs to the top floor. I rang the bell and Day answered. As soon as I saw him I knew something serious was up.

'Come in,' he said.

'What?' I asked, when he'd shut the door behind me.

He took me into the living room and picked up a bunch of cassettes off the table.

'I want you to listen to these,' he said.

'What are they?'

'Just listen and you'll find out. I'll be in the kitchen.'

He walked out and left me alone. The stereo was switched on.

There were five tapes in all. C30s. Answer machine tapes manufactured by Panasonic. Each one was neatly numbered on a white strip, with the day and date next to the number. Except the last one, which just had a number.

The first one was dated the previous Friday. I put it into the jaws of the machine and pressed the button. There was a faint hiss from the speakers, and I adjusted the volume. When the message began I recognised the voice immediately, and felt the hairs on the back of my neck rise.

The voice belonged to John.

33

'*Peter, you know who this is, don't you?*' said John's voice, low and insinuating. '*I hope you're alone. But then you usually are, aren't you? I am too. That's one of the reasons why I chose you. Are you surprised I know your telephone number at home? Don't be. I know a lot about you. More than you can imagine. I know where you live. Perhaps I've even been inside your flat.*'

I wondered if he had, and what effect it must have had on Peter Day to hear him say it.

'*Don't worry, Peter,*' the voice went on. '*I'm not going to hurt you. Not you. I'm your friend. I want you to believe that. Even though when we spoke on Monday night I got the impression you didn't like me. You cut me off, didn't you? That wasn't friendly. And you didn't believe what I said, did you? You cut me off again on Tuesday. I think you got me mixed up with someone else, didn't you? I don't think you'll make that mistake again. Not since you got what I sent you.*

'*I brought you another present today. Delivered by hand. That's quite funny if you think about it. Have you seen it yet? Even if you haven't, I'm sure you know about it. There'll be more, Peter, I promise you. There's plenty more meat where they came from. It's like a great big supermarket out there, and I just choose what I want and take it. People are stupid, Peter. But not you, I'm sure. I've been listening to you long enough to know that.'*

I switched off the machine and took out the tape. Friday. The day after the show had been taken off the air, and the black woman's finger had been delivered to Sunset.

Shit! I thought.

I put the tape back in the machine and pressed the 'Play' button again. That dreadful voice continued. *'Eventually you'll learn to love me, Peter, I'm sure,'* it said. *'In time. And we both have plenty of that. I'm going to make you a star, you see. In fact, I'm going to make both of us stars. I've already started, haven't I?*

'Did you read about us in the papers? You must have done. We made quite a splash, didn't we? I like the name they've given me, don't you? "The Midnight Crawler." How apt. I'm saving all the cuttings. You should too. Maybe one day you'll write a book about it. We're going to be famous. You'll be on TV. I look forward to watching that. We're going to get to be good friends, you and I. Really good friends.

'I know they tried to take your show off, Peter. I read that in the paper too. But I think they'll change their minds now. Maybe they already have. Maybe that's where you are now, or are you at your local pub? The next time you're in having a drink, look round. I might be there. I might even send you over a bottle of Beck's or a scotch. That's what you like to drink, isn't it? I might be the bloke sitting right next to you at the bar. Anyway, wherever you are now, this will be waiting for you when you get home. If you haven't spoken to anyone at the radio station today, I suggest you do right away. But, Peter, don't tell them about this message. Don't tell anyone.

Especially not the police. I want this to be our little secret. Don't try to be clever, will you? You see, I'll be watching you constantly from now on. You don't know who I am, but I know you. Everywhere you go, I'll go. So keep looking over your shoulder.

'I'll call you again at home soon, but I don't want to talk to you. Just leave the answering machine on all the time. I'm so glad you've got one. It was something I had to make sure of. The only time I want us to speak to each other is on your show. And tell the police not to bother tracing the calls. They'll be wasting their time. But then I'm sure they know that already.

'I'm going now. Remember what I said about telling no one about this. And remember another thing, Peter. Nothing's for nothing. I'm going to make you famous just like I said, whether you like it or not. But I'm going to want something in return. I'm not sure what yet, but I'll know it when I see it. I'll call you tonight at the station, same time. You'd better be there, or it'll be the worse for someone.

'Play me some pretty music, Peter, and I'll know you want to be friends. Goodbye till then.'

And that was the end of the message.

I hit the 'Stop' button. I felt cold and sweaty. The sound of his voice made my flesh crawl, like he'd touched me with freezing fingers. I went over to the sideboard and poured a large scotch. My hand was unsteady and the neck of the bottle rang on the rim of the glass. I drank most of it in one swallow, and poured another and went back and re-wound the tape and listened to the message again. As his calm voice filled the room, I sat on the sofa and drank the second scotch.

It was him all right. The Midnight Crawler. I knew that he'd like the name.

229

I ejected the first tape and put the one marked with a '2' and dated the previous Saturday into the slot. I pressed the 'Play' button again.

It was the same voice.

'*Hello, Peter,*' it said. '*I knew you'd be back. I was so pleased to hear you last night. But calling me mad won't do. It won't do at all. I think I might have to teach you a lesson. But never mind that now, we've got better things to talk about. I hope this call isn't being traced, Peter. I do so hope that you're being good, and doing as I say. I'm taking a big chance trusting you, Peter. A very big chance. But I think you're the kind of man who'll appreciate that.*

'*I won't stay long today, I just wanted you to know that I'm thinking of you, Peter. I'll be listening on Monday. Have a pleasant weekend. Bye.*'

And there was the sound of the phone being hung up.

I picked up tape number '3'. This one had been made on Tuesday. Two days ago.

'*Hello, Peter,*' said the voice. '*I've found what I want from you.*'

I listened carefully.

'*Something I think you hold dear. It's a fair swap. Something you hold dear, for being famous. Don't you agree? Or maybe you don't. You won't know until it's gone. I'll talk to you later. Bye bye.*'

Followed by a click and dead tape.

Sophia. Could it have been her he was referring to?

I leaned forward and picked up the next tape. As I moved I felt sweat, cold and slick, under my clothes. I looked at the door and wondered about going to find Day. But my curiosity won and I put the next tape on to the machine. It had been made on Wednesday, after Day had freaked out on air.

230

And the day that Sophia had vanished.

John's voice was different now. Harder, but there was a hysteria in his tone if you listened for it, and the mode of the message had changed.

'Peter, why did you say those things? You had no right. I thought we were friends. I send you things and you say that to me. You're just like my father was. A horrible, wicked man. That's another reason why I started to call you. You reminded me of him. He was never my friend. He hated me too. I thought you might be different. But I was wrong.

'I thought if we could be friends, it would make up for all the years he treated me so badly. But you're the same as all the rest. The same as him. You don't want my friendship. You don't want my love. Neither did he. Well, he's gone now.'

As he spoke, his voice got higher and more fragmented.

'I'm going to pay you back, Peter. I intend to make you sorry that you've treated me with such disrespect . . .'

There was no more speech on the tape. Just silence punctuated with breathing. Then not even that, until the inevitable click and the sound of the dialling tone, then the machine cut it off.

There was one more tape. It had just '5' marked on it. I knew it had been made today. It started abruptly.

'You haven't got many friends, have you, Peter? I'm not surprised, the way you treat people. But I know you've got one. Or at least you had one. Because I've got her now, and I'm going to send her back to you piece by piece. You should get the first piece today. She's a beautiful woman, your friend Sophia. Or at least she was. I'm afraid she's not so beautiful now. And it's all your fault. I hope you

231

remember that. She's dead, you bastard, and you killed her.'

And with that, the last of the tapes finished.

Dead, I thought. Although deep down I'd known it all along. Since the day she'd disappeared. Dead, but not forgotten. And I knew that I'd never rest until her murderer was caught.

I sat holding the glass with the remains of the scotch coating the bottom. I could feel it slick in my sweaty grip. I squeezed it tightly until I knew that one more ounce of pressure and my hand would crush it and send shards of sharp glass into my palm. To cut and slice and gouge, and the pain of the wounds might take away some of the other pain I felt. I wanted to do just that. To feel the pain and see the blood flow. But I resisted the temptation, and eased the pressure, then I swirled the few drops around, swallowed them, and placed the glass very carefully on the low table in front of me.

I collected the tapes together neatly, in order of their being made, and lined them up on the table next to my empty glass.

I wondered if Sophia's voice was on any of them, with a last message for Peter Day, and briefly I thought about going through them all to find out.

But I resisted that temptation too, switched off the machine and left the room.

34

When I walked back into the kitchen after listening
to the tapes, I was so angry, I wanted to hit Peter
Day. To drag him out of the chair that he was sitting
in and smash his head against the kitchen wall until
his skull fractured like an eggshell.

I was so angry that I wanted to punch him low
down in the gut where it really hurts, so that he'd
throw up all down his shirt. Or clap my hands hard
across both ears and possibly rupture an ear drum.
Or kick him between the legs and make it impossible
for him to stand up or sit down comfortably for
days. Or anything.

But I didn't. What would have been the point?
He had to live with what he'd done, and I knew that
it would bring him more pain than any that I could
inflict on him with my fists or feet.

'Outstanding,' I said as coldly as I could. 'You do
realise that you're responsible for Sophia's murder,
don't you?'

His face appeared to collapse upon itself. 'No,'
he protested.

I wanted to hit him again, but held myself in
check. Once I started I didn't think I'd be able to
stop. 'Yes,' I said.

'But there's nothing on those tapes that tells
anyone who he is.'

'Don't be so fucking stupid!' I exploded. 'Maybe there's not, but he told you what he was doing. What he was going to do.'

My anger bubbled up like a well of bad water.

'And he almost certainly made the calls from where he lives or works. They weren't made from a call box. If the police had been able to put a trace on the line, they might have been able to catch him days ago.'

'You don't know that.'

'I don't *not* know it. That's not the point.' I threw up my hands in sheer exasperation at the man. 'How the hell could you do it, Peter? Is having your picture in the paper, and your voice on the radio, more important than catching this fucker? He's been *killing* people. Don't you understand? Christ, you saw some of what he's been doing. You touched it. I saw your face. He's been killing people and mutilating them. God knows how many. And even when he got hold of someone you cared about, you still did nothing. What kind of person are you?'

I closed my eyes and breathed deeply. I was coming close to losing it, and it would be worse for him if I did.

'I told *you*,' he said.

'Too late,' I said back. 'Too late. I want you to call Harper now. Get him down here with his blokes in case there are any more calls. Although God knows after what you said the other night, I doubt it. He's gone right over the edge now. You can hear it by the way he's talking.'

Just looking at him filled me with disgust, and I went over to the sink and found a clean glass on the draining board and filled it from the tap. Good fresh London water that had probably been filtered through at least a dozen people's kidneys before I drank it.

I stood by the kitchen window staring through the slats of the venetian blind that was pulled down tightly, thinking about the messages I had been listening to, and looked at the street outside as I drank. I could feel a tremor of anger in my fingers as I raised the glass to my lips.

I thought about everything John had said on the tapes, searching desperately for a clue to his identity as I idly gazed at the small group of journalists and photographers and the occasional sightseer standing outside, waiting for something, anything, to happen. I looked for Piers but he wasn't there. He must have been on another story.

'Are you going to call Harper or am I?' I said.

'I'll call him,' said Day tiredly, and I heard him get to his feet behind me.

'Do that,' I said, and as I said it, outside on the pavement, one photographer turned to speak to another, and as he did so the lens of his camera caught a ray of the afternoon sun and flashed into my eyes like a signal, and I thought once more of John's words.

'*I'll be watching you constantly from now on. You don't know who I am, but I know you. Everywhere you go, I'll go. So keep looking over your shoulder.*'

'From now on' he'd said. And that had been Friday. The day after the story broke in the media.

And then I remembered Sophia saying that one of the photographers had tried to chat her up. When had that been? Monday? Tuesday? I couldn't remember. But I was sure it must have been just about the time that John had found what he wanted to take from Peter Day.

And I knew where John was. Suddenly I just knew. I was looking at him right then. He was outside watching the block. One of that group down there in the street was the man who had kidnapped

Sophia and killed her before or after mutilating her body.

I dropped the glass into the sink where it smashed into a thousand pieces, turned, shoved Peter Day out of my way and ran out of the flat, shouting as I went, 'Get Harper. Now!'

I hit the button for the lift, but it wasn't on Day's floor, and I was in too much of a hurry to wait, so I took the stairs, three or four at a time, risking the chance of a broken ankle or a recurrence of my old foot trouble as I went.

I slowed as I reached the foyer. I didn't want to frighten my prey. I turned the handle, opened the front door and stepped calmly out on to the shallow front steps of the building where the policeman guarding the place stood in solitary splendour.

He turned and looked at me. A look that said that he was aware of who I was, and didn't like it much. 'Do you know this lot?' I asked.

'Do what?' he asked suspiciously. He was about twenty-two, with very white skin and a very dark beard that he had to shave so closely he'd cut himself at least twice that morning.

'The journalists,' I said, but I knew it was pointless even as I said it. What would he know? He came on duty, stood around, then went back to the section house to have a laugh with his mates. He was just a kid.

'Know 'em?' he said. 'I don't *know* 'em. They're just there. Every bloody day. Bunch of bloody vultures, wasting my time. If I had my way, I'd run the lot of them back where they belong.'

That was a good attitude, I liked that, and thought I might be able to capitalise on it. 'I think one of them's the killer,' I said.

'Killer?' He looked perplexed. Who could blame him.

'The bloke who's been cutting up bodies and sending them through the post,' I said patiently, as if to a five year old.

'Why do you think that?'

Good question. But the explanations would take too long.

'Could you check their credentials?' I asked.

I just knew he was going to say, 'Do what?'

'Do what?' he said.

'Their credentials,' I said patiently again. 'I think one of them isn't really a journalist or photographer at all.'

I looked at the group bunched up on the other side of the brick wall that separated the garden of the block from the pavement. They were smoking and chatting and casting covert glances at the pair of us. They just looked so right, standing there, that I wondered if maybe I was wrong. Maybe it was one of the smattering of the general public who had stopped to see what all the non-excitement was about. But then if one of them was always there, even a copper as stupid as this one was fast turning out to be, might get suspicious. No. If he was there at all, he was one of them.

'I don't know,' he said. 'I should call in.'

'Call in then,' I said. 'Speak to Sergeant Harper. Better still, get him down here to do it himself.'

The constable drew himself up to his full height. 'I'm quite capable of looking at their credentials myself,' he said.

So do it, I thought.

He grinned, all of a sudden, and looked about twelve years old. 'And it might break the monotony.' And miraculously he moved from where he was standing in the direction of the press corps.

I stayed on the steps as he walked out on to the pavement and buttonholed the nearest journalist.

'Excuse me, sir, could I see some form of identification, please?'

The journalist looked amazed. 'Why?' he said.

'Just a formality, sir. Purely routine.'

'Don't be stupid. You know who I am. I don't have to show you anything,' said the reporter. 'I'm here doing my job.'

Bad choice of phrase. And he shouldn't have called the copper stupid. The young constable drew himself up to his full height again. 'And I'm here doing *my* job, sir. One part of which is to keep the thoroughfare clear. If you can't or won't show me identification, I must ask you to move along.'

I thought the reporter was going to laugh in the copper's face. 'This is crap and you know it,' he said. 'We've been here for days, and no one's asked us to move.'

'There's always a first time, sir,' said the policeman.

The journalist pulled open his jacket to show a laminated pass tagged to his shirt pocket with the word 'Press' prominently printed on it. He shoved it in the policeman's direction. 'Happy now?' he said.

Wrong attitude. The copper might have been young and stupid, but he had his fair share of self-importance. He glanced briefly at the badge then said, 'Any other form of identification, sir? I could run one of those off on my John Bull Printing Set.'

As the small altercation continued, I watched the rest of the press crew. One nondescript forty-something, with long thin blond hair, a leather jacket and jeans, who was standing slightly apart from the rest of the gang with a camera slung round his neck and a cheap-looking canvass holdall hanging from one shoulder, was looking very closely at the policeman and the journalist arguing. He shuffled from one foot to the other then caught me looking at him.

Our eyes met for a moment, then he broke the contact and began to walk away from the rest of the group. I went down the steps, through the gap in the wall and followed him.

He glanced over his shoulder and began to walk faster. I did the same. He began to run. Now, as you might have gathered, running is not my strong suit. The old wound in my foot, and the metal plates and screws that hold the bones together, don't make me a natural contestant in the London Marathon. But I broke into a run too. I glanced behind me and the young copper was standing looking at my retreating back in amazement.

The blond man turned the corner. There was a motor bike parked twenty yards or so down the road and he was mounting it, ignition key in hand, as I turned the corner after him. I speeded up as best I could but I knew that I'd blown it. I should have waited for Harper and reinforcements instead of enlisting the aid of the constable. I shouted something at the man. God knows what, or what good I thought it would do. He ignored my shout and hit the starter, pushed the bike off its stand and, with a roar from the engine, headed in my direction. I ran into the road, as if that would do anything but get me killed, and he aimed the bike straight at me. I moved closer to the kerb, out of the way, but he pushed the machine into a sideways skid, and I had to jump to avoid being hit.

As I dodged the back wheel of the bike, which if it had made contact could have broken most of the bones in my legs, I stumbled, lost my balance, and fell on to my knee. I put out my hands to save myself, but kept falling, and my head hit the kerbstone with a crack that knocked me dizzy. I sat up, shaking my head to clear my vision, and blood filled my eyes. I tried to clear it away so that I could see the number plate of the bike. But as I scrabbled at my face with fingers that felt like lead, the rider expertly straightened the machine out of its skid and accelerated away with a crackle from the exhaust in a cloud of blue, noxious smoke. All I could see through the red veil that clouded my vision was a blur of yellow and black, and he was turning the corner out of my sight.

35

As I sat there with blood dripping down my face and the front of my shirt, and the motor bike turned left down a side street, the young copper pounded round the corner. He looked at the bike as it vanished, then at me, and ran towards me.

'Was that him?' he asked.

'Yes.'

'Jesus! They'll have my bollocks for breakfast for this back at the station,' he said, helping me to my feet.

'Did you get the number?' I asked.

He shook his head. 'Did you?'

'No,' I said.

'Oh, fuck.' Which was exactly how I felt about it too.

'Are you all right?' he asked me.

'I'll survive,' I said. 'Have you radioed in?'

'Yes,' he said. 'Sergeant Harper is already on his way. He got a call from inside the flat a few minutes ago.'

'You'd better tell them about him,' I said, gesturing at the corner the motor cycle had turned.

The young copper did as he was told. He operated his radio and said, 'Alpha 231 to Sierra Bravo. Alert all units. Be on the look out for a black motor cycle being ridden by a male IC1. Blond. Early forties.

No crash helmet. Wearing a leather jacket and jeans and carrying a tan bag. No registration number of the cycle. Last seen turning into Marshall Street, SW9. Heading south. He's a suspect in a murder case.'

He got an affirmative back in a crash of static.

Fat chance, I thought. I'd've bet serious money he had his crash helmet in the bag, and by now he was street legal.

'You're a bit of a mess,' said the young copper. 'That cut on your head looks bad.'

He reached into the pocket of his tunic and pulled out a snowy white handkerchief, neatly folded into a square. He gave the handkerchief to me, and I put it against the wound on my forehead. That gesture, giving me his handkerchief when he needn't have bothered, a little bit of common humanity amongst all the cruelty and wickedness I'd seen and heard about over the last few days, affected me more than I would have thought possible. The knife of pain turned in my stomach so hard I almost doubled up. I felt terribly weak all of a sudden, and the copper must have seen something of it because he gripped my arm in his strong hand, and led me over to a low wall nearby.

'Sit down,' he said. 'Before you fall down. You took a nasty knock there.'

I did as I was told. I felt a right mess. I was covered in blood, and when I looked down at my trousers, there was a rip in the knee and I could feel more blood running down my leg, and the palms of both my hands were cut and rubbed raw. That bastard John. This was another one I owed him.

From the distance I heard the whoop of sirens.

Against the copper's advice I stood up and we walked back to the corner of Day's street, and as we turned into it two police cars came in from the opposite end.

They skidded to a halt, their doors opened and a bunch of police got out, uniformed from one car and plainclothes from another. I saw Harper straight away, and he saw me. He broke away from the rest and headed in our direction.

'What's going on?' he demanded. 'What happened to you? And what was that message we just got over the radio all about?'

I looked at the uniformed constable, and he looked at me. So many questions. Where did we start?

'I think we had him,' I said. 'But he got away.'

'Who?' said Harper, as if he knew but needed to hear it confirmed.

'John from Stockwell,' I said.

'What!' exploded Harper.

'Sorry,' I said.

'*Sorry*?' said Harper. 'You stupid fucker!' Then he turned to the constable. 'What do you know about this?'

'Just what this gentleman told me,' he replied. Meaning me. 'And then what I saw. He chased someone. He got away on a motor bike.'

Harper turned back to me. 'So tell me.'

I gave him a precis of the day's events so far. When he heard about the tapes I thought he was going to have a heart attack. When he heard how John had got away, I was almost sure he would.

'And neither of you got the number of the bike?' he demanded. We both agreed sheepishly.

'Two trained observers,' he said apoplectically. 'And neither of you can get a simple number down!'

'He was turning the corner of Marshall Street when I got there,' said the uniformed constable. 'I

243

only saw him for a split second.'

'I was being dumped on my head,' I said. 'The sod was trying to maim me for life.'

Right then, I think, Harper wouldn't have been the least upset if the attempt had been successful.

'OK,' he said. 'Let's try and salvage something from this mess.' He beckoned a plainclothes copper over. 'You,' he said, 'take him,' he pointed his thumb at the constable, 'in the back of the car. Get a statement. Everything he remembers. Then you,' this time he spoke directly to the constable, 'back to the station. I want a full report of this fiasco on my desk when I get back. You – ' he pointed at one of the uniforms who had arrived by car – 'get on the door of the flats. No one in or out without my say so. The rest of you, each grab a gentleman of the press. I want to know what they know about our friend who got away. Anything. And no excuses.'

They all got busy. The press boys were already asking questions and firing off cameras in all directions. I wondered how they were going to feel when it was their turn to be interrogated.

'And as for you.' Harper looked directly at me, and I could see specks of foam on his lips and the blood vessels of his face like road maps under the skin. 'Inside. Up to Day's flat. I want your statement while I listen to these tapes.' He grabbed another uniformed officer. 'Come with us and write it up.'

The officer nodded, then added 'Yes, sir' smartly when he saw Harper's face redden in anger again, and we all did as we were told.

Harper, the uniform and I went up to Day's flat in the lift. As it trundled upwards, Harper said to me, 'Do you want the surgeon to have a look at that cut on your head?'

I shook it, and winced.

Harper gave me an unsympathetic look. 'I suppose *Ms* Brody,' he accented the prefix heavily, 'is still sitting at the back of the building?' he said to the uniformed officer who was with us.

The uniform nodded.

'Is she on her own?'

'No. I think Bob Davies is with her.'

'Then get her upstairs with the first-aid box and see what she can do with this man's head.'

When the lift doors opened and Harper rang Day's flat doorbell, the uniform got on his radio.

Day opened the door to us.

The uniform took me into the kitchen where the remains of the smashed drinking glass still lay in the sink, and Harper took Day into the living room where the tape machine was, and closed the door firmly behind them.

There was a ring at the front doorbell and the uniform answered. The policewoman who had allowed me entry at the back door stood in the doorway holding a white metal box with a red cross on top. She came into the kitchen and looked at me.

'Hello again,' I said.

She barely nodded a reply then said, 'Looks like you've been in the wars.'

'Looks like it.'

She put the box on the kitchen table, opened it, took a fresh pair of thin latex gloves out of their cellophane packet and put them on.

'Nothing personal,' she said. 'Body fluids. You know.'

I nodded, and the uniformed male officer sniggered nastily.

She gave him a dirty look.

'Let me see,' she said, referring to my face.

I took the handkerchief away from the cut and she examined it closely.

'Why is it always me that has to do the patching up?' she asked nobody in particular.

'The feminine touch,' said the other copper. 'And you can touch me any time.'

The policewoman gave him another dirty look. She was tall and heavily built, with blond hair pinned up under her hat. She had a round face, blue eyes, and as she worked on the cut she caught her tongue between her teeth. She deftly cleaned the wound, applied antiseptic that stung like hell, pulled the skin tight, and applied a couple of butterfly plasters. Then she covered the whole thing with gauze and taped it down.

'You should see a doctor,' she said. 'You could use some stitches.'

'I'll think about it,' I replied.

'Please yourself. That's all I can do for now. But I warn you, you're going to have a lovely pair of shiners.'

The male uniform sniggered again. Obviously any reference to pairs, with a woman present, was his cue for a good laugh.

The policewoman shook her head at him sadly. 'I'd better get back downstairs. Bob'll be wondering where I've got to.'

'Go on then,' said the male uniform with a leer. 'And don't do anything I wouldn't do in the back of that motor.'

'It's what you *would* do that bothers me,' she said, and left.

'I would too,' the uniform said when she'd left. 'I can think of lots of dirty things I'd like to do to her. I bet she wears black knickers.'

I didn't bother to reply, and he looked rather hurt

that we weren't going to discuss the policewoman's choice of underwear.

'I think you want a statement, don't you?' I said instead, and he took out his notebook and I told him everything that had happened since Day's phone call.

As we sat together, and I talked, and he wrote what I said down, I smoked and picked pieces of road out of the palms of my hands, and flicked them into the sink with the broken glass.

Half an hour passed, and Harper came out of the living room alone. If anything he seemed to be in a worse mood than when he'd gone in. He looked into the kitchen, said nothing, then went out of the flat. He was gone for another fifteen minutes before there was a ring on the front doorbell. The uniformed officer answered it, and Harper came back and joined us. Day still hadn't emerged. Whilst Harper had been gone, the uniform had made us both a cup of tea. He offered one to Harper who refused.

'So?' I said to him, without expecting much of a reply.

'His name was Steve, or so he said,' said Harper. 'He told the rest of the press contingent he was a photo stringer for a group of free newspapers in the area. He'd been out there, off and on, since Friday. He seemed to know what he was doing. Everyone took him at face value.'

I nodded.

'You're a prat, Sharman,' Harper went on. 'If you suspected something, why didn't you wait? We could have come down mob handed and pulled him easily. Who do you think you are? Enlisting the aid of some wet behind the ears woodentop.'

The uniformed officer didn't seem too pleased at

the description of his colleague.

'I'm sorry,' I said.

'Sorry? You will be.'

'What can I say?' I said.

'Not much.'

'What's going to happen to Peter Day?'

'We'll think of something.'

Harper roamed round the kitchen, picking things up and putting them down.

'Listen,' I said, 'I don't feel too great. Can I go home?'

'Go? I'll say you can go,' said Harper. 'Has he made a complete statement?' he asked the uniform.

'Yes, Sarge,' came the reply.

'Then get out of my sight, Sharman. And don't let me see you anywhere round me again until I want you. Understand?'

I understood.

36

I was back home by four. I took off my ruined trousers, jacket and shirt and threw them in the corner. My knee was cut and grazed, and two lines of dried blood ran down to the top of my sock. I took the socks off too, and tossed them on top of the rest.

I went into the bathroom and cleaned the wound and my leg and the cuts on my hands. They weren't serious. Then I applied disinfectant, found fresh socks, a clean shirt and a pair of old, soft jeans to put on.

I went into the bathroom to look at my face. The policewoman had been right. My eyes were puffed and swollen and two perfect black rings surrounded them. Luckily the tape hid most of the damage to my forehead. But I still looked like I'd gone a couple of rounds with Bruno and come off second best. I shrugged at my reflection and went back into the living room.

I looked at the kettle, and then at the depleted bottle of vodka, and decided to take a walk to the off licence. I couldn't be bothered with a pub. I didn't need the company.

I walked down the road and into Thresher's. The geezer behind the counter said, 'What's the other bloke look like, then?'

Like you in twenty seconds if I come over the
jump, I thought, but said nothing. It was my local
offie after all, and it wouldn't do to commit ABH
on the owner, even if he was asking for it. Besides,
he stocked a good line in exotic beers that I like to
try from time to time.

So I just smiled a smile I didn't feel and asked for
a bottle of Jack Daniel's, paid for it and left.

I went back home and did serious damage to the
bottle. It didn't help much, but at least it didn't talk
to me. I fell asleep in front of the TV about one in
the morning and dreamt about Sophia.

Not pleasant dreams.

37

The phone woke me again. It was always doing that lately. The curtains were drawn, but not properly, and I could see that it was full daylight outside.

I found the thing under a cushion and answered it.

'What?' I said, through the most vicious hangover I could remember for, oh, at least a fortnight.

'Nick?'

'*Yes.*'

'It's Piers.'

'Who?'

'Piers. The photographer. Friend of Chas's.'

'Sure. Sorry, Piers. You woke me up.'

'It's ten o'clock.'

'Did I order an early morning call?'

He sounded confused, like he'd got the wrong number. 'Is this Nick Sharman?' he asked.

'Yeah. Whoa! Wait a minute.'

I put down the receiver, went over to the sink, put on the cold tap and stuck my mouth, then my whole head into the flow. Too late I remembered the bandage on my face, but by then it was soaked.

Shit, I thought, grabbed a tea towel, dried what I could and went back to the call.

'Piers,' I said, when I picked up the phone again. 'What can I do for you?'

'I know him.'

'Who?'

'The bloke the police are looking for.'

I squeezed my eyes shut which hurt even more than having them open. 'Are you sure?' I asked.

'Course I am.'

'How?'

'My girlfriend. She's a photographer too. The year before last, things were getting a bit tight money-wise. She taught a course for Lambeth Council. Night school, you know.'

I knew. 'What kind of course?' I asked.

Bit by bit I was coming awake. I saw the nine-tenths empty bottle of JD standing on the carpet and shuddered.

'Darkroom work mostly. Processing and printing. I used to meet her for a drink sometimes afterwards. That's when I saw him.'

'Where did the course take place?'

'South Bank Poly.'

'And you're sure it's the same bloke?'

'Course I am. He didn't recognise me, but it's the same bloke right enough.'

'Did you speak to him?'

'When?'

'When you were all hanging around outside Sunset? Or Day's flat? Or wherever?'

'No.'

'Why not?'

'Because he's an amateur. I heard he was stringing for some stupid little free sheet. You mix with people like that, you become one. Besides, I never liked the look of him. He was a creep, you know? I'm not surprised it turns out he's a serial killer. I only heard about what happened this morning. I was off yesterday.'

'Have you got a name for him?' I asked.

I held my breath as I waited for him to answer, and squeezed the phone tightly until I was frightened it might fly apart in my hand.

'Yeah. Steve. Steve Paulus.'

'Spell that,' I said.

He did.

'Unusual,' I said.

'Isn't it? That's how my girlfriend remembered.'

'You haven't got an address.'

'No. She threw the files away long ago. I suppose someone at the Poly might. But it was only a night school class. No big deal. Anyway, on those types of courses, people come and go. They just sit in sometimes, to get out of the cold.'

'Who else have you told?' I interrupted.

'No one.'

'Not the police?'

'No.'

'Why not?'

'I don't like the police.'

Who does? I thought. 'So why are you telling me?'

'Because I don't want him running round killing more people. I don't want it on my conscience.'

'So phone Brixton Police Station. Ask for Inspector Lambert or Sergeant Harper.'

'I don't want to do that.'

'Why not?'

'Because I thought that if Chas and I . . .'

'You want an exclusive, is that it? And maybe comfortable jobs for the pair of you in Wapping or Battersea Bridge?'

'Something like that. But Chas is off today. At least until later. He's meeting someone for lunch at his office at one.'

'Phone him at home.'

'I've tried. His machine's on, and his bleeper's turned off or broken or something. And besides, it's just a name. Nothing else. There's not a lot we can do with it.'

'But you thought if you told me, and I told the police, you'd be in on the kill. Me being friendly with Chas and all.'

He didn't answer.

Nice guy, I thought.

'OK, Piers, you've got a deal,' I said. 'You find Chas and put him in the picture and I'll tell the police. It'll take time to check that name out on the files. I'll make sure you get your exclusive.'

'Great, Nick, thanks,' said Piers. 'Can I give you my number?'

I took it, but didn't bother to write it down, then terminated the call.

I sat on the sofa in yesterday's clothes and thought about what Piers had said, and everything else I knew about John or Steve or whatever his real name was.

Then I got up and put on the kettle.

The gauze on my forehead was waterlogged, so I gently peeled it off and went into the bathroom. The butterfly plasters were still holding the edges of the cut together, although they were dark with old blood. But at least the damn' thing wasn't bleeding.

I went back and made some tea, then picked up the phone again and dialled.

I got the number I wanted and listened to the ringing tone of the extension I'd asked for at the switchboard.

'Community Charge,' said a voice I recognised.

'Andy?'

'Speaking.'

'Nick Sharman.'

'Oh, no. Not you again. You never sent that cheque you promised.'

'Sorry,' I said. 'It slipped my mind.'

'Oh, did it. You and about fifty thousand others.'

'Sorry, mate. But I thought that the poll tax was all finished with this year.'

'This *year*. The way things are going we'll still be taking people to court fifty years from now. So what do you want? No, don't tell me. You want another favour. Right?'

'Yes.'

'Well, you can carry on wanting.'

'Come on, Andy.'

'No, Nick. I told you before, this stuff is confidential.'

'This is really important.'

'Tell me about it.'

'A matter of life and death.'

'Excuse me if I don't quite believe that statement.'

'It's true, Andy. I swear. I don't even know if this name will show up. The bloke could live anywhere. It's just a flyer. A hunch. Try it for me, please, and I'll come down and pay you my civic taxes in new fivers, and buy you the best dinner of your life.'

If I'm still around, I thought.

He thought for a moment.

'Come on then,' he said eventually. 'What name have you got?'

I told him. Spelling the surname.

There was a short pause and I heard him tapping away at the keyboard of his computer, then he said, 'Stephen Anthony, with an "H", Paulus. Is that him?'

Bingo, I thought.

'Is there just one?'

'The one and only Stephen Paulus on our records.'

'Brilliant,' I said. 'And the address?'

'I shouldn't.'

But he did. The address that he gave me, and I copied down on a clean piece of paper, was in Dulwich.

'Thanks, Andy,' I said. 'That's another one I owe you.'

'Just pay your debt to society and I'll be happy.'

Debt to society. That was a good one. I had so many.

'I promise,' I said, told him I'd see him soon, and hung up.

I looked at my watch. Eleven o'clock. Chas would be in his office at one. I knew he'd insist on Piers contacting the police straight away. He wasn't about to mess with the forces of law and order, no matter how important the story was.

That gave me a couple of hours' head start.

It was all the time I needed.

38

I was in the car, last night's clothes and a stinking hangover and all, within two minutes. As I drove in the direction of Dulwich, my stomach was jumping and I was chewing on the inside of my mouth like a madman.

By the time I found the street I was looking for, then parked the car in a pretty little turning off the next street along, I almost had to prise my fingers off the steering wheel.

I walked to where I was going. John/Steve must know me, and if he knew me, he knew my car. I was more anonymous on foot, even with the plasters and black eyes. And I didn't want him to see me coming.

It was a big, wide boulevard, lined with old, tall trees, beginning to lose their leaves now but still clinging on to enough foliage to cast dark shadows on the wide pavements. The houses were big, worth a packet in any part of town. Round there, a packet plus. They were almost mansion size, some of them, and set well back behind high, neatly tended hedges and evergreen-filled front gardens.

Perfect for the kind of business that John/Steve was doing. And he had to be worth money to live there. I wondered how he'd spend it where he was going.

When I found the house whose number corresponded to the one that Andy had given me, it wasn't the biggest in the street, nor the smallest, and if I'd been expecting a horror film set, all cobwebs, shuttered windows, overgrown garden and sway-backed roof, I was disappointed.

The hedge was as neatly clipped as the best of the others I'd passed. The fence and gates were painted a gleaming white. The front lawn, flower beds, and the two big shiny-leaved trees whose branches stroked the ground in the faint breeze from the west were beautifully tended.

The house itself looked pristine. Paintwork fresh, brickwork clean and neatly pointed. Windows sparkling, and what looked like a new roof gleaming dully in the autumn sunlight.

But most interestingly of all there was no sign of a burglar alarm. Most of the other houses I'd passed sported all sorts of electronic boxes on their fronts, fitted with bells and sirens and flashing lights. And no doubt, in many cases, direct lines to the local police station.

But not this one. I suppose that the last thing John/Steve wanted was the local Old Bill on the scene if a squirrel or any other small rodent set off an alarm.

Behind the gate that led up to the garage was parked a white Bedford panelled truck with the back windows covered in reflective foil. All the better to abduct you with, my dear, I thought. There was no sign of a motor cycle.

I went in by the gate at the end of a path that led to the front door, and walked slowly towards it.

I climbed the three steps that led to the door and rang the bell beside it. I heard its plaintive buzz echo down the hall. There was no one in. No one

living anyway. I knew from ringing a thousand door-
bells on a thousand doors when the house is
deserted.

Just to be sure, I rang again. Then banged on the
knocker and finally fisted the glass in the door until
it almost shattered under the blows.

But no one in that long, quiet street paid me the
slightest bit of attention.

After a minute, I went to the side gate and tried
it. It was fastened by a cheap lock and one good
shove opened it. I walked down the side passage to
the back of the house.

The garden at the rear was long and wide too.
And well looked after. It was not overlooked from
the sides, and the back fence was hidden by half a
dozen more trees as old and large as the ones in the
street.

There was a back door that led into the kitchen.
The top half was glass. A dozen small, translucent
panes puttied neatly into squares of white-painted
wood.

I went in like the one bad mouse in the Beatrix
Potter stories I used to read to my daughter to get
her to sleep.

I was going to the worst place in the world, but I
didn't know it yet.

It was a doddle getting in. Too easy, if anything.

I slipped off the leather jacket I was wearing.
Balled it round my fist and punched one of the panes
in the back door. The noise of the glass hitting the
floor inside seemed as loud as two milk floats in a
head-on collision. But still no one cared.

I put my hand through the hole and slipped the
catch on the lock. He hadn't even bolted up. I
imagine you get complacent if you get away with
too much for too long. I walked in and stood on the

black and white vinyl-covered floor, patterned like a chess board and so clean and polished you could eat your lunch off it, and the first thing that hit me was the heat inside. Literally.

It must have been ninety degrees in there. Someone had turned up the central heating. Then some. I felt sweat break out on my face and sting the cuts on my forehead. The boiler was mounted in one corner of the room and I went over to it. The thermostat was turned to the maximum setting. I turned it right down. I might at least be comfortable.

I turned on one heel and slowly looked round the kitchen. There wasn't a thing out of place. Everything in sight was neatly squared off, like soldiers on a parade ground. Along one wall, carefully graded by size, was a row of knives and cleavers. They were slotted into wooden racks and gleamed faintly in the light. I shuddered at the thought of what they might have been used for. The place gave me the creeps. It was just too tidy, if you know what I mean. There wasn't a dirty spoon in the dry washing-up bowl in the sink, or a crumb on the draining board. And it smelled weird. Sour and stale. Like the drains were blocked. But then anywhere that hot, with all the windows closed, was going to smell. But not that bad.

I crept across the floor on the rubber soles of my shoes. I knew that the place was empty, but I didn't want to make any more unnecessary noise. God knows what I'd wake up if I did.

I opened the cabinets on the walls. They were piled with neatly stacked plates, cups, saucers, mugs, all in straight lines again. I had the feeling that the expression 'anal retentive' had been coined for the owner of this house.

Then I opened the cupboard under the sink. It

took me a second or two to register what I saw, and when I realised what it was, I jumped back as if I'd been stung and smacked my elbow painfully on the cabinet behind me.

The cupboard was seething with cockroaches. Hundreds – no, thousands – of them crawling blindly over each other, or just frozen still, like they'd been there for a thousand years.

I don't know if I screamed or not but I certainly made some primitive noise in my throat. Half fear, half surprise at what I'd found.

I stood there trembling, then kicked the cupboard door shut. But I was still aware of them behind it, in the darkness.

When I looked more closely round the kitchen, and up at the ceiling, I saw more roaches. They clustered in the shadows at the corner of the room, and there was another nest of them behind the cooker, and a third behind the fridge.

God, but they made my skin crawl, and I knew without a doubt that I was in the right place.

I decided to investigate further.

Although the house was completely silent, I seemed to be able to hear something, like tinnitus inside my head. I imagined it was the dying screams of John/Steve's victims that had bounced around inside the fabric of the house so strongly that they had been embedded in the very brickwork. Or maybe it was the sound of a million roaches rubbing together behind the walls in their slow dance. At the thought, I shivered, even though the temperature was still stifling.

There were two doors off the kitchen. One led into the hall and was open. The other, which I guessed led down to the basement or cellar, was closed and secured with two Chubb locks. I stood and looked at it and tried to imagine why it needed *two* locks. I didn't want to think, and certainly didn't want to find out. It could be knee deep in insects down there for all I knew. Knee deep in anything. And the smell seemed stronger the closer I got to the door.

I shook my head and went into the hall which was empty except for a coat stand sans coats and a small, highly polished table by the front door that contained a telephone placed exactly in the centre. There were three other doors off the hall. Two on the left hand side. One on the right. Also on the right were the stairs leading upwards.

I opened the first door that I came to. It led into the sitting room. Also too neat. Like it had never been lived in. There was a TV set in one corner. A big one. On top, side by side, were the current editions of the *TV* and *Radio Times* neatly slotted into plastic folders. There was a three-piece suite, still covered in the protective film that it had come in from the factory, a long sideboard, a set of shelves that held nothing and a low, wooden coffee table next to the armchair of the suite.

There were flies in there too, batting at the windows behind the net curtains. And more roaches. On the walls and hanging from the ceiling. One ran across the floor in front of me, and I kicked at it but missed, and it vanished under the sideboard. When I'd finished looking around I went out into the hall again.

Suddenly there was a clatter from the front door and I froze, fresh sweat breaking out under my armpits and down my back. I saw two letters tumble down to the mat on the carpet in front of the door, and heard footsteps receding down the path outside. I relaxed. It had only been the postman with the

lunch-time delivery. I went and picked up the
letters. Both were addressed to Stephen Paulus. I
propped them next to the phone and went into the
second room on the left of the hall. I was still aware
of the smell that permeated the house. The room
was done up like a small hospital ward. A metal-
framed bed with a floor pedal to raise and lower it.
A sink plumbed into one wall. A set of medical
scales. Bed pans and urine bottles lined up neatly
behind green plastic curtains that covered one of the
alcoves by the fire place. The full Monty. Christ
knows who had slept there.

Next I tried the room opposite. It was empty
except for a fitted carpet, a black coat and a
handbag.

My heart literally sank at the sight of them. Any
doubts I might have had about Sophia having been
brought here vanished, and the knife stabbed my
stomach yet again.

I knelt down by the bag, opened it, and emptied
the contents on the floor. It was hers all right. It
smelled of her, and I recognised some of the contents. I stood up, leant my arm against the wall and
put my head down. I could smell my own sweat,
sharp in the warm air. In a sudden fury I kicked at
what I'd emptied from the bag. Lipstick, address
book, purse, keys scattered and bounced off the
walls. I was suddenly terribly sorry that I'd done it
and collected the stuff together and put it back
where it had come from.

I took the bag with me and left the room. Outside,
I put my hand on the newel post at the foot of the
stairs and looked up. As I did so, I felt the hair on
the back of my neck rise. My instincts told me not
to investigate any further. That I wouldn't like what
I'd find.

I shook my head and cleared my throat. The sound echoed down the hall and I put my right foot on the first step and started to climb. There were ten stairs on the first flight. I counted them as I went. At the top was a short passage to the left. It contained two doors. The staircase itself made a quarter turn away from the passage, up a further three steps, then another in a longer flight. At the top of the three stairs were two more doors. One on the left, one facing me.

I entered the passage. The doors faced each other. One was a bathroom, as neat as the other rooms I'd been in. Closed tightly round the bath were shower curtains with a pattern of purple Forget-Me-Nots. I walked over and ripped the curtains off their rings. They dropped to the floor. The bath was empty except for a lone cockroach. I left it. The second door revealed a small toilet. Empty.

I went back down the passage and up the short flight of stairs. I opened the door on my left. The room was small and was completely empty. It didn't even have a carpet on the floor, just bare floorboards. I shut the door carefully and opened the one that faced the stairs. It was a bedroom. John/Steve's I imagined. It was as neat and tidy as a room in an army barracks or a monastery. It contained a single bed, made up, a small chest and a wardrobe. I opened the wardrobe door and looked inside. There was a suit, some shirts, a couple of pairs of trousers on hangers, and what looked like two sets of hospital whites. Whether or not John/Steve worked in one, or they simply went with the room downstairs, I couldn't begin to guess. I opened the drawers in the chest. Socks, underwear. Nothing else. Like the rest of the house nothing personal anywhere. I left the room as it was.

I climbed the next flight of stairs to another landing containing two doors. Once again, one on my left, one facing me. I tried them both. Both were empty. Bare as caves. I went back on to the landing and looked up the final flight of stairs that now faced me. They were narrower than the rest, and darker. At the top were two more doors. Above them was a ceiling. After that there could only be attics.

I began to climb.

I opened the first door I came to. Inside was nothing but junk. A higgledy piggledy mess of cardboard boxes, old furniture, piles of dusty curtains. All sorts of crap stacked as high as the ceiling. I left that too. I'd come back if needs be.

So finally I opened the last door, and entered hell.

Sitting in the corner of the room, facing the door, Sophia was waiting.

39

I stood in the doorway and looked at her. The room was dim, illuminated by only one, small dormer window, but I could see clearly. I could see everything I needed to see clearly. Too clearly.

Apart from her still form, the room was empty.

It smelled even worse in there. Violent death is not a clean or pretty thing. It knows no dignity or pity for its victims.

She was still dressed in the clothes I'd watched her put on the morning she'd left me for the last time.

Blue suit, black blouse, black tights. Only her shoes were missing.

Her left hand rested on her lap. Her right was palm down on the floor. It was swollen, and the skin was black, mottled with grey. Dark blood crusted the cruel wound where her three fingers had been brutally severed from it. I wondered how long she'd taken to die. For dead she was. But I had to make sure. I could hardly bring myself to touch her, but I did. I had to.

I walked over, squatted down on my heels and found the pulse point on her left wrist. There was nothing, and her skin was cold and stiff.

The fingernails on that hand were ripped and broken too, where she must have fought her killer.

I wondered what she had been thinking as she died, and whether she called on me for help. Or anybody. I didn't even know if she believed in God, and if she'd prayed for his help in the last seconds of her life.

A fat lot of help he'd been if she had.

Her head was tilted forward and to one side, and her long, thick hair covered her face. I couldn't bear to look at it. I didn't want to see her as she'd been at the moment of her death. I would rather remember her as I had last seen her. Happy. Or at least as happy as I could make her.

Although her tights were torn at the knee and badly laddered, it didn't look as if the rest of her clothes had been disturbed. That was something at least. But not much.

I looked down at her disfigured hand, and as I did, a cockroach crawled out from the sleeve of her jacket, over the back of her wrist, teetered, then dropped to the floor and scurried away in the direction of the door.

I couldn't bear it. I moaned a long animal noise of disgust, stood up and mashed the thing into the floor. Grinding it with the sole of my shoe until it was paste.

Then I leant against the wall and slid down into a sitting position next to Sophia's body.

This way madness lay. I knew that. Sitting there with her body. But I didn't care. I was well on the way to insanity anyway, there in that terrible house where all humanity had been denied.

Then, and only then, as I sat there, did tears come. I put my head down to my knees, covered it with my arms and let them flow unchecked.

How long I sat there sobbing, as the earth turned, I don't know. A few minutes? Hours? I couldn't say.

But eventually, as all things must pass, first the sobs, and then the tears ceased.

I felt in Sophia's handbag for tissues and wiped my face. The tissues smelt of her perfume, and for a moment I thought I was going to start crying again, but I didn't.

I stood up, and with just one final backward glance I left that grim room and went downstairs. I didn't touch her again. I couldn't. I knew that if I did, it would be the end for me.

I picked up the phone that stood on the table by the front door and dialled the number of Brixton Police Station from memory. When I got to the last digit I stopped, shook my head, and gently replaced the receiver. It was no good. I couldn't do it.

Instead I went back into the kitchen, took the largest, heaviest, sharpest-looking knife with the finest point from its rack, and went into the sitting room, sat in the armchair, facing the dead TV screen with the knife in my hand, and waited with the door to the hall open wide.

The noise in my ears was louder now. I was sure it was the cockroaches making it. Behind the walls and in the ceiling they scurried on God only knew what errand.

I saw one walking across the ceiling above me. It suddenly dropped and landed on the coffee table, and began a long, slow inexorable walk in my direction with its antennae feeling the air in front of it.

I hefted the knife in my fist as it got closer. It was long and black and horrible. One of the biggest I'd yet seen. A king of cockroaches. I'd read somewhere that they were the first living thing on the planet, and that they would probably be the last.

When it got within reach I slammed the knife down, through its hard black carapace, the yellow muck inside, and deep into the wood of the table, maybe three quarters of an inch, maybe more. The knife quivered there from the force of the blow and I watched as the life leaked out of the roach, its legs fluttering feebly as it died, and wondered who'd be the first to get to the house. Stephen Anthony Paulus or the police.

40

It wasn't very long before I heard keys in the locks of the front door. It wasn't Old Bill. They wouldn't be that polite. I wondered if Piers had got hold of Chas, and if he had phoned the police or was hanging about, waiting for the exclusive of the year.

I tugged the knife out of the table and stood up at the sound of the tumblers turning. The body of the cockroach was impaled on the end of the blade, and I shook it off and it bounced off one of the walls and landed on the carpet. I knew that Paulus would see the letters I'd propped up against the phone, and wondered if he'd run. And whether or not I'd be able to catch him.

But he didn't.

Instead he said in a soft voice, 'Is anybody there?'

'In here, Stephen,' I replied. 'In the living room.'

He came silently down the hall and stood in the doorway. It was the geezer who'd been outside Day's flat and had got away on his motorbike. He was dressed the same and he held a black crash helmet in his right hand.

'Hello again,' I said. 'How's your bad luck?'

He put the helmet on the table. Right in the centre. 'What are you doing here? This is private property,' he asked, but his voice didn't carry much conviction.

'Sue me,' I said.

He looked at the knife in my hand, but didn't mention it.

'So what *are* you doing here?' he asked again.

'What do you think?'

'I don't know. But I do know you're trespassing.'

'Don't fuck about, Stephen,' I said. 'I've been upstairs. I know who's there. I haven't been in the cellar yet, but I can guess what I'd find if I did.'

'What?'

'I said don't fuck me about.' I was holding the handle of the knife so hard I thought it might permanently graft itself to the skin of my hand.

I got the feeling that he was almost glad to see me. Relieved. As if keeping the secret had been too much for him. Like having a present in November, and not being able to open it till Christmas Day.

'Do you want to see?' he asked.

'It can wait.'

'Shall I tell you what's down there, then?'

I hated him for saying that.

'I told you,' I said. 'I can guess.'

He paused, and as I looked at him, he reminded me of nothing so much as a naughty schoolboy being pulled up in front of the headmaster for smoking at the back of the toilets. 'So you found me,' he said, like he wanted to be found.

'Looks like it,' I said.

'How?' he asked.

'It's my job,' I replied.

'Where are the police?' he asked.

'Coming.'

'When?'

'Soon.'

He nodded.

'You don't seem too bothered,' I said. I wanted

him to be bothered. I wanted him to beg, or fight, or run, or anything. Anything rather than just stand there as if he was waiting for a hamburger to be cooked at the counter of Burger King.

He shrugged. 'I knew you'd catch me sooner or later,' he said.

'So why do it?'

'I had to.'

'Is that it?'

He nodded.

'And you expect me to leave it there?'

'What's it to you?' he asked.

'The woman upstairs. Your last victim. She meant a lot to me.'

'I'm sorry,' he said.

Sorry. And he expected me to be satisfied with that.

'Not good enough,' I said.

He shrugged again.

I could feel my insides churning and sweat was running down my sides under my shirt and jacket, and my knees were shaking. And I was suddenly very cold.

'Not good enough,' I repeated. Just slightly louder.

He looked at me pityingly. 'It'll have to be,' he said.

'No.'

'Look,' he explained patiently, as if to a small child, 'I did it. I killed all those people. Now I've been caught, I'll go on trial. Plead guilty, because I am. Then I'll be sent to a maximum security mental facility like Broadmoor. I don't mind. It's what I expected. I've had a good run for my money. It's OK in there. TV, books. I may even write one myself.'

You little cunt, I thought. You've got it all planned out.

'Not necessarily,' I said.

'What then?' he asked.

'I could kill you myself, before the police arrive.'

'No, you won't.'

He was so sure. That's what pissed me off.

I changed the subject.

'What do you do, Stephen?' I asked.

'I work in a hospital. In the pharmacy.'

'Lots of interesting drugs,' I said.

He smiled a knowing smile.

'That's right,' he said.

'And access to all those toys you've got in the other room.'

He smiled again and nodded.

'And I suppose you bring a few samples of your work home?'

He nodded again.

'Show me,' I said.

He turned and walked back down the hall to the room that was like a hospital ward. I followed him. When we got inside he went over and drew back the plastic curtain that covered the alcove, and opened a cupboard in the wall that was so cleverly concealed I hadn't even noticed it when I'd looked before.

I went over and looked in it. Timothy White and Taylor's, remember them? A chain of chemists. Big time. That's what the inside of that cupboard reminded me of. It was full of boxes of prescription drugs. All sorts.

'Got any sleeping pills?' I asked.

'That's what you like, is it?' he said.

It was my turn to shrug. 'Not particularly,' I said. 'I think I just might have some trouble sleeping for a while.'

He didn't ask why, but reached in and pulled out a white cardboard packet.

'Mandrax,' he said. 'Illegal over here now.'

I took the pack and put it in my jacket pocket.

'Got any pain killers?' I asked.

His smile turned into a beam.

'My speciality,' he said. 'Why do you want pain killers?'

'I might need them later,' I replied.

He pulled a face and took a large plastic pill box from the top shelf of the cupboard. The printed label read 'Ketalar'.

'Ketamine,' he said. 'Ketalar's the brand name. I can shift a lot of these. Stupid junkies love them. They call them Special-K or Kit-Kat. They're good pain killers, but take too many and they do funny things to your head.'

'Thanks,' I said, and took the box and put it in my pocket too.

I had an idea that I was going to need as much pain killer as I could use before I was much older.

'The police are a long time coming,' said Paulus, almost wistfully.

'You can't wait, can you?' I said. 'You've got it all worked out.'

Once again a fleeting smile crossed his lips. But he said not a word.

'Stephen,' I went on, 'I can't let it happen like that.'

His eyes flickered to the knife that I was still holding in my right hand.

'You'd never get away with it,' he said.

'Don't be so sure. I find you here. You grab a knife. We fight. I kill you in self-defence.'

'You wouldn't.'

'Wouldn't I?'

I could see he still didn't believe me. I had to make him. I had to do that before I could do anything else.

I took the knife and inserted the needle sharp point into the leather of my jacket, just under my left shoulder. Sharp side down.

It slid through it easily, and the shirt beneath. Then into the meat of the muscle at the front of my arm. I dragged the knife down and it slit my jacket and shirt, and the skin and flesh too, as neatly as a scalpel. I pulled the knife down nearly to the crook of my elbow, and as I did, I watched Paulus's face.

I felt hot blood bubble from the wound and soak my shirt and run down my arm, and I felt momentarily dizzy. For a split second it occurred to me how funny it would be if I passed out. But I didn't. Then I pulled the knife out.

Half of the blade was tinged bright red.

I kept my eyes fixed on Paulus's as I held the knife up for him to see.

'Fingerprints,' he said.

'I'll wipe them off with your blood,' I replied.

And then he knew I'd do it. I saw it in his eyes. He knew, just like Sophia must have known, and all his other victims, when he was about to kill them. He knew I'd do it.

I felt a surge of triumph run through me as it finally sunk in that I'd do it.

So I did it.

I stuck him like a pig. Or like the cockroach I'd stuck earlier. Because that's what he was. A cockroach.

I stabbed the knife in just beneath his breastbone. His face showed surprise but no pain, and he clamped both his hands on to my wrist. It was no good. I twisted the knife, and pulled it upwards, and heard bone and cartilage pop, then I dragged it further up through his ribs until I could drag it no further.

I let go of the handle and shook his hands off mine.

He staggered back and fell into the hallway.

I watched as he lay there, the dreadful chest wound I'd inflicted sucking and spraying blood all over him and the floor around him as he tried to breathe.

I watched as he lay there, as the flow of blood diminished as he died.

I looked at my arm. Blood had soaked the edge of the cut in my leather jacket and all at once it began to hurt. Badly.

I took the box of pain killers out of my pocket, levered the top off with my teeth and swallowed one. Then I went and phoned the police to find out what the fuck was keeping them.

A selection of bestsellers
from Headline

SEE JANE RUN	Joy Fielding	£4.99 □
STUD POKER	John Francome	£4.99 □
REASONABLE DOUBT	Philip Friedman	£5.99 □
QUILLER BAMBOO	Adam Hall	£4.99 □
SIRO	David Ignatius	£4.99 □
DAY OF ATONEMENT	Faye Kellerman	£4.99 □
THE EYE OF DARKNESS	Dean Koontz	£4.99 □
LIE TO ME	David Martin	£4.99 □
THE LEAGUE OF NIGHT AND FOG	David Morrell	£4.99 □
GAMES OF THE HANGMAN	Victor O'Reilly	£5.99 □
HEARTS OF STONE	Mark Timlin	£4.50 □
JUDGEMENT CALL	Suzy Wetlaufer	£5.99 □

All Headline books are available at your local bookshop or newsagent, or can be ordered direct from the publisher. Just tick the titles you want and fill in the form below. Prices and availability subject to change without notice.

Headline Book Publishing PLC, Cash Sales Department, Bookpoint, 39 Milton Park, Abingdon, OXON, OX14 4TD, UK. If you have a credit card you may order by telephone — 0235 831700.

Please enclose a cheque or postal order to the value of the cover price and allow the following for postage and packing:
UK & BFPO: £1.00 for the first book, 50p for the second book and 30p for each additional book ordered up to a maximum charge of £3.00.
OVERSEAS & EIRE: £2.00 for the first book, £1.00 for the second book and 50p for each additional book.

Name ....

Address ....

....

....

If you would prefer to pay by credit card, please complete:
Please debit my Visa/Access/Diner's Card/American Express (delete as applicable) card no:

Signature ....Expiry Date ....